# The One

Sweet Pickle Books
47 Orchard Street
New York, NY 10002

a Chloe Gamble novel

# By Ed Decter
### and Laura J. Burns

## Simon Pulse
New York London Toronto Sydney

SIMON PULSE

An imprint of Simon & Schuster Children's Publishing Division

1230 Avenue of the Americas, New York, NY 10020

Copyright © 2009 by Frontier Pictures, Inc. and Ed Decter

All rights reserved, including the right of reproduction
in whole or in part in any form.

SIMON PULSE and colophon are registered
trademarks of Simon & Schuster, Inc.

Designed by Mike Rosamilia

The text of this book was set in Adobe Caslon Pro.

Manufactured in the United States of America

First Simon Pulse paperback edition March 2009

2 4 6 8 10 9 7 5 3 1

Library of Congress Control Number 2008943234

ISBN-13: 978-1-4169-5435-4

ISBN-10: 1-4169-5435-X

*To Cheryl and Abby—"The Ones" in my life*

—Ed Decter

*To Peter, my constant support*

—Laura J. Burns

# Acknowledgments

Thanks to John J. Strauss, the best screenwriting and producing partner anyone could dream of. Together we have discovered that the highs are higher and the lows not as low, just as long as you have someone along for the journey.

—Ed Decter

As always, my thanks to the best writing group in Los Angeles for keeping me sane.

—Laura J. Burns

*chapter one*

## Nika Mays's Manuscript Notes: Prologue

When the police came to see me about the "incident," I told them a lot of things about Chloe Gamble, but I didn't tell them about this manuscript. I tried to convince myself that the reason I didn't turn it over was because I was protecting Chloe. But deep down, I knew that the real reason was that Chloe's story was valuable and someday I was going to profit from it.

I didn't set out to be the person I've become. There was a time, not that long ago, when I would have handed my manuscript over to the homicide detectives. But somewhere along the line, maybe when things started really clicking for Chloe, I seem to have lost my bearings and drifted away from what was right toward what was right for me. Looking back, I wonder if that's a lesson I learned from Chloe herself.

If the Hollywood PD guys ever do fork over the twenty bucks for this book, I think they'll understand why I kept it from them. It's because Chloe's story was too important to end up in some filing cabinet at the homicide division. I never once wrote down my private thoughts until the day I met Chloe Gamble. That sounds bizarre, doesn't it? It's as if I didn't even exist until Chloe Gamble walked into my life. Some people around town might tell you that the reverse is true—that she wouldn't have existed without me. But only I know the real story. Nothing on earth could have prevented Chloe Gamble from becoming a star. She wouldn't have let it.

Here's the thing I figured out about Chloe. Sure, she's beautiful, but there are models in any magazine that are more perfect. Still, if all those models in *Vogue* or *Elle* were in a room dressed in lingerie and stilettos and Chloe walked in the door in jeans and a Gap T-shirt, the only girl in the room would be Chloe. And I'm not just talking about men looking at her—I mean the women, too. I knew this about Chloe from the second that I met her, but I didn't know why until I was up late one night and *Ocean's Eleven* came on (not the original Rat Pack *Ocean's Eleven*, but the one with Clooney). I was just sitting there in my apartment, alone (as usual), eating some Pinkberry and staring at George, and then it all became clear. In that scene where Clooney is sitting in the casino restaurant talking with Julia Roberts, something in his eyes and the way he cocks his head to the side says, "This is going to be naughty and it's going to be fun—and it's only between us, no one else." That's how it is when someone meets Chloe, whether it's a girl or a guy—that's exactly how she makes them feel, like they are going on some type of private adventure, and you may end up in bed or you may not, but either way, it is going to be a blast.

Rereading this, it seems as if I have some type of girl-crush on my former client. Well, maybe. That's the thing about Chloe: She takes you places you never dreamed you would go.

The only part of Chloe's story I don't know much about is her life before she came to Hollywood. She never talked about it—said it was sixteen years she wanted to forget. Some people call Los Angeles "La-La Land" or "Hollyweird," but Chloe always said, "Hollywood is the land of forgetting."

## Sweet Sixteen

I spent my last birthday in Texas in the window booth of a Luby's in Abilene. I remember it clear as day, not because it was my sixteenth birthday but because it was the day I changed my life forever and you tend to remember days like that.

I have nothing against Luby's. Their food is decent and their air-conditioning is always good, which is crucial in Texas, especially in the summer. But there's no getting around the fact that Luby's is a cafeteria and little girls don't grow up with the dream of spending their sweet sixteen standing in line pushing a plastic tray.

The rich girls in Dallas and Austin get Porsches or new boobs for their sweet sixteen. If you don't believe me, look it up—the number-one sweet-sixteen gift in the state of Texas is a set of bra-popping tits. I know this for a plain fact because I have to compete against those massive racks nearly every weekend. I may be the only girl in the history of Texas to win twelve straight beauty pageants with her own God-given boobs.

Here's what you need to know about pageants: They suck because they are rigged. Most times girls know the judges. I mean, who do you think runs the pageants? It's all the Jaycees and Rotarians. It's not about how pretty you are or how well you play the damned guitar; it's about who your daddy plays golf with and how much business he gives the local State Farm agent whose plus-size wife just happens to be the chairwoman of the event.

So if you're thinking of entering a pageant, don't. You'll be up against every local girl who won the Miss Midland Blue-bonnet contest or the Odessa 4-H Livestock Queen title. Then you might find yourself sharing the stage at a cheesy Holiday Inn banquet hall with some rich daddy's girl from River Oaks who travels with a pageant coach, her dance instructor, and a seamstress who custom-designs all her beaded gowns. Or, if you are particularly unlucky, you will come up against me.

I never lose a pageant. That's not boastful—it is a plain fact. I sing pretty near better than anyone. Spurlock High School (that's where I'm from—Spurlock, Texas) lost its music program a few years back because of some budget cuts. So I never got any formal coaching on how to sing. During long drives to the junior pageants my mama—her name's Earlene Gamble but everyone calls her Early—would play whatever AM station came in clear and I'd sing along with every song. After a while, I discovered I could imitate almost anyone; it didn't matter if it was country, pop, or rock—I could sound like Martina McBride or Gwen Stefani or even Alicia Keys.

Travis—he's my twin brother—started to turn off the radio and request songs for me to sing. So, as we crisscrossed the great state of Texas on Route 87 from Amarillo to Lubbock or on Interstate 20 from Fort Worth to Pecos, I sang songs that made other people famous and learned which ones worked for me and which ones didn't.

Some of the wealthy pageant contestants have professional musicians make up digital instrumental CDs so that when they get up to sing, they are accompanied by what sounds like a whole orchestra. I couldn't afford anything as fancy as that, so I just got up on stage and sang all by my lonesome. You've got to be good to sing that way because there is no place to hide if you miss a note. I never miss a note.

But singing (or tap dancing or baton twirling) doesn't win you pageants. Most girls on the circuit think that Beauty (yes, with a capital *B*) is what gets you the sash and tiara. These are the contestants with the sweet-sixteen fake boobs, the backless, low-cut ball gowns, and the Vaseline coating their teeth (for more glistening smiles). And if you think a few of these girls don't try rolling around with some big fat car dealer who happens to be a judge, then you're just plain naive. These are the girls who take the words "beauty queen" to mean that if you are born with a mane of blond hair and sky-blue eyes, you are truly royalty. These girls are the easiest to beat because most of them are lazy. They think skipping a few biscuits at breakfast is all they have to do to keep their figures and that mascara and hair spray will do the rest. The queen bees are all so focused on how they appear that they overlook the one component of the pageant that can mean the difference between being a loser and winning it all—the interview.

At the end of every pageant, the emcee (usually a sleazy disc jockey from a local radio station or a chamber of congress member who took a theater class at SMU back in the day) asks each contestant a few questions. If you've seen the Miss America pageant (the Super Bowl of all pageants), you probably remember some of the lame questions that the emcee asks about world peace or global warming. Trust me on this: Girls who smear Preparation H on their cottage-cheese thighs have nothing important to say about greenhouse gases. Most contestant professionals, the girls with coaches and involved parents, are taught how to reply to the interview questions with noncontroversial answers and a smooth delivery. And that is why I win.

My brother's soccer coach (Travis is an all-state midfielder) always tells Trav's team to "attack the enemy where they are weakest." That's what I do with the interview questions. If I'm in a cow town, like Waco, I play the "role" of a farm-fresh 4-H girl who is dazzled by all the lights and is so "darn grateful" to be on stage with KTFW 92.1's morning rock jock. But if I'm up in Dallas, I make sure to show a lot of leg and talk up my aspirations of being a fashion model (total lie) and my desire to attend SMU (even bigger lie).

If you are shocked that I would lie in front of a banquet hall full of people, then you need to grow up. Where does the truth get you? Nowhere is where. You can tell the truth and spend your life taking tickets at the Palace Theater box office in Spurlock—been there, done that. Never again, thank you very much. The reason why I win every pageant is because I hook into the fantasies of the judges. I can't explain to you why the other contestants don't do the same thing, except maybe that they're stupid.

And if you're wondering why I'm wasting your time going on and on about my tips and tricks for winning beauty pageants, it is because I thought you needed to know why I was the only person sitting in the Abilene Luby's with a check for ten thousand dollars in my purse.

"You give it here, Clo," my mama said.

"What about all those other checks? You've been putting them in the account, right?" I asked.

Instead of answering me, my mama spoke to my brother. "Trav, can you go up and get me some of that butterscotch pudding? I just love it."

"Answer her, Mama," my brother said. He's no fool—never has been.

"Answer what, darlin'?"

"What did you do with the money?" Travis said.

"There was *expenses*," was all my mama could say.

"I guess wine don't buy itself," Travis said.

I can honestly say that I only love one person on the face of this earth and that is my brother, Travis. He's got my back and I have his—and that's how we've both made it this far with the bad hand we've been dealt when it comes to parents.

"Some of that money was spent on *you*! You needed them new soccer shoes!" My mama was getting all out of breath and dramatic, which is the first thing she does when she's cornered.

"*I* bought Trav those cleats. And the new tires for the car and the gas and my makeup and the new sewing machine. So what 'expenses' are we talking about?" I said.

"You're just children! You don't know the first thing about what it takes to run a household! You don't know the sacrifices I've made for you two!" Tears formed at the corner of my mother's eyes.

Travis looked at me with a slight upward roll of his eyes. Tears and the list of "sacrifices" she has made are always the second act of my mama's dramatic performances. My brother and I had become so used to ignoring her sloppy theatrics that it surprised me that the rest of the customers at Luby's couldn't take their eyes off her.

I have to admit, my mother has a talent for making a scene. She's almost as good at that as making boxes of wine disappear. In my whole life she has only taught me two valuable things. The first was how to sew. If you are foolish enough to enter the world of pageants without a lot of money, the one and only way you can survive is if you can operate a Singer and make your own ball gowns. The second, and most important, thing my mother taught me was to make sure I never grew up to become like her.

A Luby's assistant manager came over to check up on us. "Anything I can get y'all?"

"We'd like a new mother, please," Travis said, which caused me to double over with laughter and my mother's face to redden.

My mother turned to the manager and said, "Sometimes my son don't have no more manners than a lizard."

The assistant manager nodded compassionately. "I got me three lizards of my own," he said. "You mind your mama now," he told Travis.

I should mention that my mother is painfully beautiful, so men, like the assistant manager, take her side at all times.

Travis didn't respond to the assistant manager because he was staring out the plate-glass window at something across the street. My brother's face had gone slack, as if he'd seen a car crash or something.

My mama and I turned to look out the window at the same time. Across the street a man wearing jeans and a shiny rodeo-champion belt helped a slender girl a few years older than me into his pickup, pausing only to give her a sloppy, wet kiss.

The assistant manager was curious as to what we were looking at. "Y'all know that gentleman?"

"That 'gentleman' is my daddy," I said.

This was far too much information for the Luby's assistant manager. He shot a sympathetic glance at my mama and scuttled away like a crab.

"He said he was checking out a job site near Paradise." I saw my mama's fingers closing around a steak knife so I grabbed her wrist.

My daddy repaired air-conditioning systems, so he was always "checking out job sites" when in fact he was tomcatting around with every young thing he could amuse with his old rodeo stories and easy smile.

My father's pickup drove away and my mother released her grip on the knife.

"Mama, how's this any different from what we already knew?" I asked.

"Now we seen him!" My mother's tears were real now.

I couldn't help it—I found myself feeling sorry for her. That's a miracle considering most of the time I wish she'd dissolve into thin air.

My mother's green eyes narrowed. "Wait till he gets home—he'll get the surprise of his miserable life."

"That's right. Because we won't be there," I said.

That stopped her. I didn't know what her big revenge plan was, but I sure knew mine.

"Where we gonna be?" my mama said.

"Los Angeles," I said as I stood up.

*"What?"* Travis looked as if he'd been smacked in the face with a mop.

I opened the front door of Luby's and a gust of oven-hot panhandle air hit me, and I said, "Stick a fork in me—I'm done with Texas."

## E-mail from Travis Gamble

Cooper, sorry I didn't show up at the Waffle House. Big earthquake in the Gamble family—earth split open, I fell in. Tell Coach I may not be back for spring soccer season. I know, dude, I suck, but it's not my fault. Chloe got it into her head to take off for LA! We didn't even stop at home; we just hit Interstate 10 and bailed! I wanted to pick up all my gear and Chloe said, "Everything that's left behind is what we're leaving behind." What's that even mean? Before you go all ballistic on my ass—tell me, what I was supposed to do? You know the women in my family; somebody has got to watch over them. . . . Can you do me two favors? Don't hate my guts, and drive by my house late one night and slash my father's tires. I'll make contact as soon as we land someplace—this earthquake isn't ending anytime soon.

*chapter two*

## Nika Mays's Manuscript Notes:
## Greenlight Chapter

Every wannabe actor from Pascagoula, Mississippi;
Sandusky, Ohio; or Valentine, Nebraska, thinks
they know what it means to be a movie star. Movie
stars get their pictures on the cover of *People*
magazine, they fly on Gulfstream jets, and they're
given Harry Winston jewelry and Armani gowns to
wear on the red carpet. Almost without fail, when
a young actress comes to Hollywood, it is the cover
shots, private jets, and haute couture she dreams
of. But not Chloe Gamble. Here's what "movie star"

meant to Chloe: It meant that her name came first on the call sheet.

Every night, just before wrap, the second assistant director hands each member of a film crew a legal-size sheet of paper. This document tells everyone in every department—from the costume assistant to the studio chairman—what scenes are filming the next day, where those scenes are shooting, what equipment is needed, and who is needed to film them. It's the single most important piece of paper there is on a movie set, more important even than the script. This piece of paper is known as the call sheet.

Sure, the call sheet has headings for the transportation department and the catering people. It's got listings for grips, cameras, wardrobe, and stunts. But the most important section is the one labeled "Cast." Cast members are listed by role. But their placement on the call sheet is not random. In fact, the cast list on the call sheet reveals the single most important fact about the production. Only one cast member may be listed first on the call sheet and that person is the star. The star is who makes the movie go, the one who gets it "greenlit." That is the person who makes the most money and therefore has the most power.

Chloe Gamble didn't know what a call sheet was when she arrived in Los Angeles. But whether she knew the lingo or not, she was planning for the moment when she saw her name at the top. Of course Chloe wanted to make money (everyone does), but she wanted money only as a means to accumulate power. Because power, especially greenlight power, meant that not one person on earth could tell Chloe Gamble what to do. But no one getting off the proverbial bus starts at the top. Most wannabe stars begin way, way at the bottom, in a beige stucco rental unit at the Oakwood Apartments in Burbank.

That's right—Burbank, California (or, as it is known on any one of the three hundred smoggy days a year, "Blurblank"). It's in the San Fernando Valley. Home to more major studios than anyplace else on earth. That's right—Disney, Universal, and Warner Brothers, not to mention the networks. ABC, CBS, and NBC are there, and lots of the smaller cable nets, too. Forget Hollywood—that's just where the tourists go. The San Fernando Valley (just call it "The Valley"—it might as well be the only valley in California) is where the real work of showbiz gets done.

So if you want to be a star, Burbank is where

you'd better be, at least during pilot season. Everybody says there are no seasons in Los Angeles, but they're wrong. There's summer, and there's pilot season.

It starts around December and runs through April. That's when the television networks create all their new offerings—a bunch of shows written, shot, and produced every year, most of which never make it onto a single TV in the country. Maybe 5 percent of them get picked up and put on the TV schedule, and the people involved in those fledgling shows stand a tiny chance of getting noticed, of getting famous. But that's enough incentive to bring thousands of actors to town every year, each one of them hoping and praying to land a pilot. It's like a massive migration of birds, only instead of flying south for the winter, the actors fly west, to Burbank. And they descend on the Oakwood Apartments. The studios and one-bedrooms fill up with twenty-somethings desperate for a speaking part on the newest *CSI* spin-off. But the two-bedrooms are usually taken up by families. Child actors are required by law to come with a parent or legal chaperone in tow. They settle into the Oakwood and pretend that the full kitchen (complete with microwave) in their unit means that their lives will still be normal there.

Not true. Because the second they step out the door, they find them—the parasites. That's what Chloe used to call them, anyway. The acting coaches, the stylists, the photographers. The wannabe managers. All the people who want to make it in the Business and who plan to do it by attaching themselves like remoras to the Next Big Thing. They know the actors will all be at the Oakwood, so they make sure they're at the Oakwood, too. Talk to some stage mother from Dubuque while you're sucking back a Red Bull by the pool, and the next thing you know, you're managing her son who wants to be the next Shia LaBeouf. Offer to shoot some artsy photos for the eighteen-year-old high school musical star from Charleston, and soon enough you can seduce her into starring in your next porno. (Did I mention that the Valley is the porn capital of the world? Yeah, those people know about the Oakwood, too.)

But why pilot season? Don't these actors want to be movie stars? Who cares about TV? I'll tell you who—anybody with half a brain. Take a sixteen-year-old from Spurlock, Texas, like Chloe Gamble. She arrives in town with nothing, and she needs to pay the rent. Sure, it would be nice to get a minor role in an indie film. Or a tiny part in a studio picture. She might even get noticed. But she won't get paid nearly enough money to live on in Los Angeles. This is a pricey town. What she needs is a job with steady pay, and not one that involves refilling Heinz ketchup bottles. If an actor lands a part in a successful TV show, she gets a paycheck every week. It's almost like having a real nine-to-five job, only the pay is exponentially better. The seventh guy on the call sheet (if he's a series regular) makes about twelve thousand dollars per episode. If he is lucky enough to be in a show that gets picked up for twenty-two weeks, that's two hundred and sixty-four thousand dollars for nine months' work.

For lots of actors, that would be enough—more than enough. They'd get their faces onto *Access Hollywood*, they'd make a little fuck-you money, and they'd be able to move out of the Oakwood and into a pretty sweet house in the Hollywood Hills. But it wasn't enough for Chloe Gamble. She never planned to stop until she became part of the smallest minority in show business—the group of A-list actresses who, when they accept the starring role in a movie, trigger the studio to fully

fund the production and greenlight the film. At any
given time, there are only two or three actresses
who have that kind of power. Chloe wanted to be a
greenlight girl.

## Home Sweet Oakwood

The drive from Abilene to Los Angeles was plenty long enough
for me to make the list. My mama and Travis were annoyed
that I wouldn't take a turn or two at the wheel, but I had my
weekly stack of celebrity mags to read through and I didn't
want to get distracted.

"It'll be a while before you get your face in those rags," my
mama said, leaning over from the backseat. Travis was driving
and I had permanent shotgun. I hate being in back. You can't
see a thing, not that there was much to see. The desert in California seemed to stretch out to forever.

"I don't see why we gotta spend good money on a bunch of
trashy magazines every week," my mama went on.

"You're just mad because we didn't let you buy a six-pack
of Zima at the last pit stop," Travis said.

"Besides, these magazines are *research*," I said.

My mama just snorted, but Travis looked at me in surprise. "You looking for hair and makeup tips?"

"Nope. I'm finding out everything there is to know about
teen actresses."

Travis frowned. "What's there to know? They're all in rehab or pregnant."

"Exactly. Lindsay, Miley, Britney, Britney's little sister—all got rich and famous and they all screwed it up."

"Those Spears girls treat their mama like dirt," a voice said from the backseat.

"There's nothing you can learn from those losers," Trav said.

"Except what *not* to do," I said. "These girls' lives are like a road map of every mistake you can possibly make. That's why I'm making my list."

"What list is that?"

"My Not-to-Do list. I'm going to get famous like those other girls, but I'm not going to do anything to flush it down the toilet like they did."

The thing about Trav is, he gets it. Right away he shot back with "Number one: Don't get a tattoo of your boyfriend's name on your ass and show it off to all the paparazzi."

I grinned. "Number two: Don't smoke crack in front of a surveillance camera."

"That ain't funny," my mama said from the back. "That crack ruins your teeth."

I shot Travis a sideways look. "Number three: Don't let your crazy mama manage your career."

While my brother laughed, I slipped on my earbuds to drown out Mama's squawking. Thank God I had them in the car when we took off from Luby's. My iPod is old and doesn't have much memory, but I couldn't live without it. Pageants are all about waiting—waiting for your turn to get in front of the makeup mirror, waiting for your turn to go onstage, and waiting for the judges to "build up the drama" and announce the winner. When I plug into my music, it's like I'm transported to a world all my own and I can think.

Recently, I'd been listening to a lot of J.Lo for inspiration. There's a bunch of singers I could name that have better voices, but there's one thing you've got to give to J.Lo—she's a chick who made herself famous by sheer force of will. I bet she didn't care if her mama complained all the way from Abilene to Los Angeles. I bet she didn't listen to her mama at all.

## Not-to-Do List

1. Don't get sloppy drunk.
2. Don't drive drunk.
3. Don't get caught driving drunk.
4. Don't abandon your Mercedes after driving drunk.
5. Don't go out without makeup.
6. Don't go out without panties.
7. Don't make out with a girl.
8. Don't get ugly tattoos.
9. Don't get ugly piercings.
10. Don't show your ugly tattoos or piercings.
11. Don't go to airports with weaponry.

12. Don't lip-synch, ever.

13. Don't barf in public.

14. Don't sunbathe naked.

15. Don't have a fistfight with your boyfriend. Or his ex.

16. Don't shave your head.

17. Don't shop for feminine products in front
    of the paparazzi.

18. Don't date DJs.

19. Don't date out-of-work musicians.

20. Don't date musicians with drug addictions.

21. Don't date anyone who sells drugs.

22. Don't do Lenny Kravitz.

23. Don't check into the hospital for "exhaustion."

24. Don't check into rehab for anything.

25. Don't claim a sex addiction.

26. Don't take nude photos with your boyfriend.

27. Don't make a sex tape with your boyfriend.

28. Don't forget to destroy all nude photos and sex tapes
    when you break up with your boyfriend.

29. Don't get pregnant, ever.

30. Don't shoplift.

31. Don't steal from a department store and claim
    it was research.

32. Don't shoot anyone.

33. Don't go on trial for shooting anyone.

34. Don't go to jail, ever.

* * *

The Oakwood Apartments were totally booked.

My mama pleaded with the girl (who had multiple nose piercings) at the desk. "Not even just a room?"

I could tell Miss Nose Ring wanted to roll her eyes, but she didn't. "It's, um, *pilot season.*"

"What's that mean?" my mama asked, turning to me.

"A pilot is the first episode of a TV show. But—"

"I wanna see the manager," my mama cut me off, turning back to the desk girl.

Travis leaned in to talk into my ear. "She's hoping it's a guy."

"So am I," I said back. Mama might be a loser, but she's no idiot. She knows it's easier to get men to do what you want, long as you got a nice ass.

When the manager showed up, I breathed a sigh of relief. He was a middle-aged balding guy who spoke with an accent; it could've been Middle Eastern or maybe Italian. I couldn't tell. We never saw many foreigners in Spurlock. He had a little nametag on his breast pocket that read "Omar." My mama gave him her best smile and took that moment to adjust the strap on her bra. That's an international language.

"I surely hope you can help me," Mama said. "My Chloe here tells me this is the *only* place to stay in LA. She read about y'all in *Us* magazine or something."

Actually, I'd found the Oakwood in a Google search at the

library back home, but whatever. Their website said they were the closest place to all kinds of studios, but then again, their website advertised a whole slew of available apartments and now they were booked. Don't believe everything you read online.

"Well, we are very crowded right now." The manager stared at Mama's bra strap and what was beneath it. He didn't even try to hide it. "All of the bigger apartments are occupied."

Mama leaned forward. "All we need is a room."

"A studio," I put in.

The guy's eyes flicked to me, then back to my mama.

"I have a one-bedroom," he said. "It's more expensive than the studios, but it's the only vacancy I have. It's been closed for renovations on the kitchen—"

"Done deal," I said.

"How much more than a studio is it?" Travis asked. He glanced at me. God bless those with practical minds.

"Three thousand a month. Two-month deposit," the manager said quickly. He didn't bother to look at Trav.

"That's too rich for our blood," my brother said.

"Omar, these children have just been through a frightful experience with their good-for-nothing daddy." Mama put her arms comfortingly on Trav's and my shoulders. "You think you can find it in your heart to take just the first month's rent?" She then pulled Trav and me slightly behind her so that she was all the manager could look at. "Soon as I find work, I'll get you the rest. I promise, Omar."

I thought Mama might have overdone it by mentioning the poor manager's name twice. Omar just stared at her, thinking it over. Mama slowly pushed her long hair back over her shoulder, letting her hand linger for a while. It was a classic move; almost every contestant in a pageant has one. For some reason men find slow movements sexy—don't ask me why. The hair/shoulder move was my mama's secret weapon, sure to work on cops who pulled her over for DUI and on stubborn landlord types.

"Okay, one month," he said. "Just don't tell any of your neighbors." I noticed that beads of sweat had formed on Omar's forehead.

When we got to the apartment, I threw myself down onto the bed and let Travis deal with the kitchen. The landlord had said the dishwasher wasn't working, but I figured my brother could fix it in about ten minutes. Hard to believe that a broken dishwasher meant they couldn't rent the place out.

"Don't get too comfortable," my mama said from the doorway of the bedroom. "Mama gets the bed."

"You do not." I rolled over onto my stomach and stared her down. "The one who pays the rent gets the bed."

Mama laughed. "Don't get a swelled head, Clo. You ain't no star yet."

"You just wait."

Travis stuck his head into the room. "It's a queen-size bed. You two should share it," he said. "I'll take the couch."

I sighed. Travis always knew how to snip the little red wire and diffuse the dynamite. And besides, as soon as I got an acting job I'd be moving out of the Oakwood and into a place with a queen-size—no, make that king-size—bed of my own. Maybe I wouldn't even give my mama the address.

Mama was snoring when I woke up the next day. At some point in the night, she must have dug out a bottle of wine she'd squirreled away in the trunk of our beaten-up Ford, because I smelled it on her breath. I left her there, tangled up in the polyester sheets, and headed out to the kitchen. Travis was busy rummaging through a cupboard, wearing only his boxers.

"There's not a single thing in this place that isn't beige," he said. "Even the coffee mugs are beige."

"The painting over the couch has a purple flower in it," I said. "Besides, it's nicer than our place back home. It's got a balcony."

"Overlooking the parking lot." Travis glanced over at me. "You think Dad noticed we're gone yet?"

"Don't know, don't care," I said. "He's just some of the baggage we left behind. From now on we live here, in the land of forgetting."

"Act much?" Travis said. He handed me a steaming mug. "They left us a couple free tea bags in the drawer."

"Nice." I took a sip of the Lipton. I refuse to drink coffee: It ruins your skin.

"Whoever had this place last forgot to cancel their newspaper subscription. I found this outside. Also these." Travis dropped a *USA Today* and a stack of business cards onto the tiny kitchen table.

I ignored the headlines and checked out the cards. "Photographer—head shots," I read out loud.

"Head shots? Sounds like hunting more than photography," Trav said as he took a sip of tea and grimaced. Trav was hooked on iced coffee or any cold drink Starbucks served.

I kept looking through the business cards. "Stylist. Manager. Another photographer. Acting coach. Acting coach. Acting coach. Homeschool tutor."

"What's that all about?" Travis asked, grabbing the sports section.

"I'm not sure," I said. "Back home, the exterminators always leave their cards under the door, looking to get hired. Maybe that's what these people are doing."

"Seems kind of pathetic. Is that how you get jobs in Hollywood?" Travis said.

"I don't know how to get jobs here."

Travis frowned. "Then what are we gonna do? Ten thousand is a lot of money, but it won't last long in this city. We're out three thousand already for this apartment. We still have to buy food and clothes. I've been wearing the same jeans for four days."

"Mama's gonna have to find a job," I said.

Travis snorted. "We are shit out of luck if we're counting on Mama."

"I HEARD that, darlin'," my mama yelled from the bedroom.

"Don't worry, Trav. I won all those pageants. I'll win here," I said.

"I don't know much, but this place ain't Abilene."

"We've got seven thousand dollars and a beige apartment with a balcony. We're gonna be just fine," I said, without much behind it.

"Well, don't go hiring any acting coaches or stylists. We can't afford it," Travis said.

"I don't need coaching or styling," I told him. I flipped through the cards again. "But we are going to visit this photographer. Get dressed."

Her name was Jude Morgan. Tell the truth, I didn't know if she was going to be a guy or a girl until she opened the door. Jude Law was the only person I knew with that name.

"Chloe?" she asked. "Come on in."

"This is my brother, Travis," I told her.

"Twins?"

"Good eye," Travis said with his best lady-killer smile.

"Comes with the job," Jude said, smiling back.

I smirked at my brother. Jude was just his type—tall, lanky, brunette. Like every cheerleader he'd ever dated back in Texas.

He didn't go for blondes. I don't know why, but with Jude, I got the sense that poor Travis was fighting way out of his weight class.

"Have you been interviewing photographers for a while?" Jude asked me as we sat on her beige sofa.

"You're the first."

"To what do I owe the honor?" she asked.

"You were the only business card that had an address at the Oakwood," I said. "We don't know our way around town yet."

Jude laughed. "Buy a Thomas Brothers map. You'll need it. I've been here for six months and I still get lost."

"Where are you from, Jude?" Travis asked. My brother is cute, but he's not too complicated. Jude didn't seem to mind the flirting.

"I went to art school in New Mexico," she said. "But I want to do fashion photography, and believe me, there's no fashion in Albuquerque. So I came here. You?" Jude looked back at me, her eyes traveling up and down my body. Now I knew why Travis was getting no play.

"We just rolled in from Texas," I said.

"You'll do great," she said, still staring at me. "You've got it."

"That's a fact," I said.

"And she's modest," Travis felt the need to add.

"Modest girls don't end up stars," Jude said with a shrug.

I held up Jude's business card. "All actresses need head shots?"

She gave me a little half smile. "Only if they are interested in a little thing we like to call 'work.'"

"Near as I can figure, I need to get my first check by the end of next month."

Jude laughed and said, "Please don't lose that."

"Lose what?" I said.

"The honesty. It's the first thing to go," Jude said. "I take it you are low on money?"

"If by 'low' you mean almost none," Travis piped in.

"And I suppose you don't know a soul out here in the business?"

"Just you," I said with a smile.

Jude got quiet for a minute and looked straight at me as if deciding on something. She was probably studying my crooked nose. It sounds ugly, but it's actually cute. People like imperfections, one more thing most pageant girls never understood. My crooked nose makes me seem approachable. I wasn't uncomfortable with the silence or her direct gaze. I was sure she wasn't coming on to me. I'd seen a lot of that at the pageants and this was different. I felt like I was back at the closing-interview portion of a beauty contest, when the judges were deciding about me.

"I'll make you a deal," she finally said. "I'll tell you everything I know about Burbank, or Hollywood, whatever, and in return, I want you to pose for me."

"Pose?" I asked.

"Head shots," Jude said.

"How much?" my brother, Mr. Practical, asked.

"No charge."

I was stumped. That doesn't happen often.

"Hold on, that don't seem right," Travis said, voicing my thoughts. "You give Chloe the lay of the land *and* take her picture? For free? What's in it for you?"

"An investment," Jude said. "Chloe is gorgeous, don't you think, Travis?

"For a sister." Which is the answer Trav always gives when asked about my looks.

"So if she makes it big, and I have this feeling she will, I can say I helped her get her start. It'll land me better clients, and maybe someday I'll get where it is I want to go."

"Where's that?" I said.

"Anywhere out of the Oakwood," Jude said with a smile.

"Before I say yes, can I see your portfolio?" I said.

Trav kicked me under the table. "Clo . . ."

"It's okay, Travis. Free head shots that suck aren't going to help your sister." Jude opened up a large black leather portfolio filled with the most beautiful photographs I'd ever seen—as good as the ones in *Vogue* or *Elle*. There were almost no pictures of men, only women.

"See, Chloe, I'm you but with a camera," Jude said.

"And modest," I said.

"Modest girls don't end up stars," Jude said with a smile.

And right there, in that very moment, I knew she was going to be my first friend in Hollywood.

"Okay, done deal. So what else do I need?" I asked. "Head shots—what else?"

Jude flipped the plastic-coated pages of her portfolio to find a head shot of a pert-looking blonde. She pulled it out of the plastic sleeve and flipped it over. On the back of the photograph, there was the actress's name and a list of the productions she'd been in.

"A résumé, for starters," Jude said.

"Résumé? We just got here," Travis said. "What's Chloe supposed to put on it?"

"I won beauty pageants," I said. "A lot of them. Should I stick that on a résumé, or would I get laughed at?"

"Do you have anything else to put on there?" Jude asked, although I could tell she already knew the answer.

"Not a damn thing."

"Then play it up, beauty queen," she said. "All actors need to be a certain type. Casting agents like to put people into categories—it makes their job easier. So when some show needs a fresh-faced cheerleader or beauty-queen type to be the hero's girlfriend, you're the one they'll call. Get it?"

"Can you shoot my head shots so I'll look like that type?" I asked.

Jude grinned. "You catch on fast. We'll do full-on pageant shots, and then I'll do some other more edgy shots just to give you a range. You around this afternoon? We can catch the late sunlight and do some outdoor shots."

"And maybe hang at Starbucks afterward," Travis said. "You know, as a way to say thanks."

I had to bite my lip to keep from teasing him. Trav was used to having girls throw themselves at him—Jude was knocking him off his game.

"Thanks, Travis, but I think I'm a little too old for you and a little too gay," Jude said.

"Seriously?" Travis said.

"Seriously," Jude said.

I swear, if Jude could've taken my brother's picture in that instant, she would've had a huge Internet sensation on her hands: "Texas hick meets his first lesbian." It was hilarious.

Jude glanced at me. "But if *you* ever decide to swing the other way, you let me know."

"We're twins, remember?" I said. "That means you're too old for me, too."

"Girls mature faster." Jude smiled. "See you this afternoon? Wear a shirt without a pattern. Oh, and more makeup than usual. The camera washes people out."

"I'll paint on my pageant makeup—that'll get her done," I said. "Let's go, Trav."

Travis followed me to the door, his face red as a tomato. He turned to Jude just as we were about to leave. "Sorry. I just . . . I've never met anybody gay before," he said.

"Yes you have. You just didn't know it," Jude said. "Or they didn't know it."

Travis thought about that. "I always wondered about my friend Bobby, y'know? He was always *looking* at me. . . ."

"I'll bet he was." Jude chuckled. "You're as hot as your sister. Maybe you should be an actor, too."

"No way," Travis said. "I'm just the brother. Chloe is the star."

We found my mama out by the huge rectangular pool in the middle of the apartment complex. She was sprawled out on one of the beige chaise lounges with her shirt unbuttoned; trying to pass off her bra like it was a bikini top.

"At least she's got her pants on," Travis said.

I could have thought of a thousand funny responses to that, but I got distracted by the people Mama was talking to. Well, *one* of the people she was talking to. A girl about my age, with long, straight hair—blond, with a nice set of honey brown lowlights—a perfect body, and a nose by a seriously talented plastic surgeon. In Texas we would have called her a pageant panther.

She locked on to me the second I stepped through the gate surrounding the pool area, and I could feel her defenses go right up as sure as if she'd just pulled a gun on me. I wasn't offended. I felt the same way about her.

"Clo, hon, come meet Kimber and her mom," my mama called. "They're here for that pilot season thing, too!"

"Shocker," I whispered. Travis laughed.

"This here's my girl, Chloe," Mama told Kimber and her thin, pale mother. "And her twin brother, Travis."

"Kimber Reeve," my competition said with a fake smile, reaching out to shake my hand. "My mom is Anne."

"Anne Williams," the mother put in. "Kimber uses her middle name for professional purposes."

"It's a SAG thing," Kimber said, making sure to look past me to show she was already bored with this conversation.

"Well, there's just nothin' at all *saggin'* on you!" I said with my utmost Texas twang. "I think it'll be *years* 'fore you start to *sag*."

Travis and my mama stared at me, but I ignored them.

"Um, SAG? The Screen Actors Guild? When you join it, if you ever do, you'll have to find a name no one else has," Kimber said through clenched teeth. "They won't let you use your own name if somebody else got there first. When I got my card, there was already a Kimber Williams."

I knew exactly what SAG was and what the rules were, but for the moment it was more important I rattle Kimber's cage.

"Kimber is also an Equity member back in New York," her mother said. "But that's for stage work. SAG is for film."

"New York?" I gasped. "Y'all aren't really from *Manhattan*?"

"We live in Connecticut—*Darien*," Kimber's mom said, as if it meant something.

"But I've done theater in the city," Kimber added. "Off Broadway, at the Public."

I don't know much about Broadway, except that every pageant judge in the state of Texas thought I should be on it after hearing me sing. But I found it important that Kimber mentioned it right away—it must carry some currency here in Los Angeles. Noted.

I gazed at Kimber as if she were Angelina Jolie and said, "Y'all are just soooo experienced! I bet little old you has just got about a million auditions set up!"

"Five this coming week," Kimber said, warming up now that she'd established her superiority over me. "My agent says I'm on the short list for all five shows. Hopefully I'll get offers on two or three and then we can leverage that into a bidding war."

I made sure to gasp again with awe. "You haven't met any honest-to-goodness *stars*, have you?"

Even though Kimber was from some fancy place like Darien, Connecticut (or at least it sounded fancy), I could see she liked the idea of having a groupie to impress. It proved something I'd always thought—scratch a socialite and underneath you'll find a beauty queen.

"Tomorrow I'm testing for the network for *Virgin*." She paused, and I could tell she expected me to faint with envy.

"What's that?" my mama asked.

I needed to play the part just a little bit longer, so I said,

"Well, it's just the most important new TV show in the world, Mama! I saw an itty-bitty story about it on that *Access Hollywood*."

Kimber's mother seemed like she would have preferred to be anywhere else at the moment instead of chatting with a bunch of trailer trash who had just rolled into town from Nosepick, USA. "It's the Todd Linson pilot for NBC. It's his first foray into television," Kimber's mother said. "It stars Anders Lee and—"

"Me. After three thirty tomorrow," Kimber said, making sure to put her hands on her hips for emphasis.

"Aren't you nervous?" I said, as if Kimber were going into battle in Iraq.

"My father says nerves are for losers." Kimber smiled as she said this but never let her eyes stray from mine.

I saw my brother's jaw tighten.

"That sounds harsh, dear," Kimber's mom said. "Your dad is a bond trader, so what does he know about auditioning?"

I didn't know what a bond trader did, but it was clear Kimber had deep financial backing to pursue what she wanted. That made her particularly dangerous. My own father's form of support was to keep a pageant schedule on the visor in his truck so he would know when Mama, Travis, and I would be out of town so he could stop by Spurlock Pharmacy, pick up a box of condoms, and go call on his "lady friends."

"Y'all didn't get to meet Anders Lee, did ya?" Mama asked.

"Now, that is my kind of man. Didn't he win one of those Academy things?"

"No, Mama, he lost to Russell Crowe," I said. "But I'd sure as heck be nervous just about meetin' him—I can't imagine actually *actin'* with him! You didn't really, did you?"

Kimber gave me a superior smile. "Once. And he'll read with me again at the network test tomorrow."

Kimber's mom gathered up her purse, BlackBerry, and keys. "Now, if you'll excuse us, Kimber is meeting with her acting coach in ten minutes. It was so nice meeting all of you."

"Break a leg, Kimber," I said with as much syrupy sweetness as possible.

"Tell us all about that hunky Anders Lee if we bump into you again," my mama said.

"Oh, I'm sure we'll see each other again," Kimber said, looking only at me.

"Oh, count on it!" I said.

As soon as Kimber and her mother left the pool area, my brother turned to me and said, "Okay, what the hell was *that*? Why were you talking that way?"

My mother ignored Travis and said, "You get what you need?"

There are moments, maybe once a month or so, when my mother is not half stupid. "Just enough," I said to her.

Travis was frustrated. "What are you two talking about?"

"Girl stuff," was all I said.

# E-mail from Travis Gamble

Coop! How's Spurlock? Feels like I've been gone for a year, even though it's less than a week. We live in LA now, in some apartment complex my sister found. It's no big deal, except for the pool.

Remember that time we were checking out *Maxim* magazine and you said, "Where the fuck do these chicks live?" Well, now I can tell you—they live right here in the Oakwood! There's one of them in the swimming pool right now and five others lying around in the smallest bikinis I've ever seen. I miss home and all, but I have to say I am enjoying the view here!

Chloe's on a mission to become famous. Apparently step one is to get a bunch of pictures taken of your face and send them all over the place. They call them head shots. Like, who wants to see an actress's head? There are lots of other more interesting body parts!

Anyway, it's stupid. But the photographer we found is scorching. And she's a lesbian! Hottest. Thing. Ever. Chloe had her first photo shoot today. You know her—she's a natural. I think she just pretended the camera was a beauty-pageant judge. And I got Jude—she's the hot photographer—to take some head-shot pictures of me, too. I'm not sure why—just in case, right? I'll e-mail one when I get them. Coach can throw darts at it when he hears I'm not coming back. Later, dude.

P.S. If you see my dad, DO NOT TELL HIM WHERE WE ARE.

# chapter three

## Studio School

"I thought you said we were going to check out the high school," Travis said. He frowned at the door labeled WORKOUT ROOM in the clubhouse at the Oakwood.

"We are." I pushed open the door next to the gym, which had a hand-painted Day-Glo sign reading QUIET PLEASE— FUTURE STARS AT WORK tacked onto it. Inside was a big beige conference room with a bunch of empty desks. A short guy with curly hair was writing algebra equations on a whiteboard. He turned around, looked us over, and went back to writing. "You guys are new," he said over his shoulder. "Here for pilot season?"

"My sister is," Travis said.

"What about you?" the curly-haired man said as he put down the whiteboard marker.

"I'm . . . kind of . . . along for the ride," my brother said.

"Ahh, the nonpro sibling. Don't worry, half the kids here are in the same boat."

Travis gestured to the desks and the whiteboard. "Clo, what's all this?"

"The Oakwood Studio School." I grinned. "I told you this place has everything."

"*This* is the *high school?*"

"And the grade school and the middle school," the curly-haired guy said. "I'm Ryan, by the way."

"I'm Chloe Gamble and this is my brother, Travis," I said. "You guys have more teachers and classrooms, right?"

"Nope. This is it. All we do is help you follow your regular school's curriculum during the time you're looking for work, or we'll come tutor you on set while you're shooting," Ryan said as he checked his watch. "Before the hordes arrive, let me see your school's course work and any paperwork from your teachers."

Travis looked to me and I said, "We don't have any of that."

Ryan looked deeply confused.

"We kinda didn't tell our school we were leaving," Travis said.

"Oh," Ryan said, as if wondering whether or not to call in the proper authorities. "Where are your parents? Are they intending to oversee your curriculum?"

"Our mama wouldn't even recognize the word 'curriculum,'" I said.

Ryan tugged at one of his brown curls. He really didn't look happy, and I wasn't feeling too great, either. This place wasn't exactly the "school away from school" promised on the flyer I'd found near the Oakwood office. Clearly, it wasn't a real school at all.

"Maybe we can call some of our teachers back in Texas and get them to send assignments," Travis suggested.

"That'll work. And I'm going to need a parental consent form and the first month's student fees."

"Fees?" I said just as the door opened and a set of eight-year-old redheaded twins walked in. "You mean this costs *extra?*"

"First rule of the Oakwood—everything costs extra," Ryan said.

I checked the clock on my BlackBerry. It wasn't even eight a.m. yet. "Never mind," I said. "We're not doing this."

"We're not?" Trav asked.

I pulled Travis past the Doublemint twins and toward the door. "Look, I ripped you away from Spurlock and all your friends. I'm not going to be responsible for trashing your entire life. We're going to go to a normal school and one we don't have to pay for."

"How exactly are we going to do that?"

"Damned if I know."

When I opened the door, I got a nasty surprise. Kimber

Reeve stood on the other side, just stamping out a cigarette. She was with a cute-but-bland guy who could've been the fourth Jonas brother if he didn't have his mouse brown hair done in dreadlocks. He probably thought it made him interesting, but he was wrong.

When Kimber saw me, she rolled her eyes. Then she walked right past me as if we hadn't met yesterday, leaving me holding the door like a servant or something. I let her get almost all the way into the classroom before I pounced.

"Kimberly, hey!" I gushed in my most southern of southern drawls. I turned to her friend. "Hi. I'm Chloe, and this here's my twin brother, Travis. Y'all must be an actor, too—you're so cute."

"Uh, I'm more of a musician, actually. I'm Max." His eyes drifted down to my halter top. "Kimber was just telling me about you."

I shot a glance at Kimber, who was fuming. Perfect. "I shoulda guessed you were a musician, with that crazy hairdo! It makes you look *dangerous*," I gushed, leaning in to touch Max on the arm.

"We're late," Kimber said, grabbing his hand.

"Y'know, I am just *so* surprised to see you here," I told her. "Why, I thought y'all'd be gettin' ready for your fancy audition this afternoon."

Kimber forced a smile. "My mother thought going to class would take my mind off of it."

"Wow, I'd be a mess if I was you. I wouldn't be able to

concentrate on readin' or writin' or nothin'!" I gave my best dumb-blonde giggle. "But you're such a pro-fessional, I'm sure you'll do just fine—you prob'ly don't have a thing to worry about!"

Kimber just shrugged, looking a little rattled. She sashayed over to one of the desks, pulled out a binder, and pretended to be absorbed in some math homework. Max followed like a good boyfriend, but his eyes were still on me.

"Scuse me, Max? There must be a public high school round here, right?" I said.

"Well, yeah, Hollywood High," Max said. "But—"

"You should definitely check it out," Kimber cut him off. "The studio school is expensive, and you're *not working* so there's no reason you can't go to public school."

I ignored that little dig. Hollywood High. That would work. "Let's go wake up Mama," I told Travis. "We're going to Hollywood."

## E-mail from Travis Gamble

Hey, Coop, what's up? Don't stress—I'm glad you told me you saw my dad. I guess he's not missing Chloe, Mama, and me too much if he's sitting at the DQ with some girl who works at the hair salon. You know he hasn't even tried to call Mama. Not once. I don't miss that asshole, not one bit. But it's weird. I miss everything else—you guys, the good barbecue, even Coach Ebell and his air horn. It doesn't feel like home here. Chloe wants us to start school—she says that'll help things get back to normal. But I think normal is a long ways behind me now.

All the kids at this Oakwood place are actors. They're busy working or talking about work or going to auditions. I don't know anything about all this Hollywood stuff. I'm just like my sister's entourage or something. Nobody even looks at me.

I need to get a plan, like Chloe. She's too busy looking forward to ever look back. When I was home in Spurlock, I didn't need a plan. But now I do. Maybe I needed one the whole time and just didn't know it. See what Hollywood has done to me? I've lost my damn mind. Later.

P.S. Tell Coach Ebell to move you to midfielder. I don't think I'm coming home anytime soon.

## Hollyweird

"Might as well just skip school until next September," my mama muttered as she drove us down the 101 freeway toward Hollywood.

My mama kept acting like we'd be heading back to Spurlock once I got this crazy acting dream out of my head. No way. I was *never* going back, and neither was my brother.

Mama yawned and pulled a strand of hair away from her eyes. "Y'all are sixteen now—you don't even have to go to school no more."

"That there's a golden bit of advice, Mama," I said. "Let's put that on a T-shirt and sell it at trailer parks!"

"That's disrespectful," Mama said.

"More disrespectful than encouraging your kids to drop out of high school?"

"Could you two stop it? We're here," Travis said.

As we pulled into the parking lot at Hollywood High, the first thing I saw was the giant mural along the top of the building. A bunch of huge painted faces stared down at us, movie-star glamorous.

"Who are all those people?" Mama asked, squinting up at the mural.

"Famous alumni," I guessed.

"I don't recognize any of them," Travis said.

I took a closer look. "That might be Laurence Fishburne," I finally said. The rest of them were all old-time movie stars, and I didn't know their names.

"That one there's Dorothy from *The Wizard of Oz!*" Mama was totally happy just to see famous faces, even if they were in some tacky mural on the side of a high school. She didn't even notice the broken glass in the parking lot, the plaster walls that had been tagged with graffiti, or the serious group of gangsta types staring at us from the doorway.

"Are there bangers here?" Travis asked quietly, looking at the guys near the door.

One thing I can say about Spurlock—there weren't any gangs, so I didn't know much about them. But one thing I did know—the guys on the stairs in front of Hollywood High weren't posing. They were nasty—I could see it in their eyes—and they kept staring straight at us. We didn't belong, and they wanted us to know it.

Mama was still gawking at the mural, so I swatted her on the arm. "Drive out of here, Mama. Let's go get breakfast somewhere."

"We're not going inside?"

"No, not ever." I pulled the shift lever into drive and we shot out of the parking lot.

"Chloe, it's no big deal to skip a few months," Travis said. "Maybe by next semester, we'll have money for the studio school."

"Don't you start now. Just hush a minute and let me think," I said.

Mama pulled into an IHOP down Sunset Boulevard. Travis got busy with some steak and eggs and I got busy Googling on my BlackBerry.

"I hope you don't think your daddy is gonna keep paying for that phone of yours," my mama said, flicking her long red nail against my cell.

"*I* pay the bill, Mama. Daddy just provided the mailbox." I made a mental note to change the billing address of my cell service.

"What are you searching for?" Travis said, peering over my shoulder at the tiny screen.

"Another way." I grabbed a piece of toast from my plate and took a bite. "C'mon, we gotta go."

"I need more coffee," Mama complained.

"We're on a tight schedule here, Mama," I said. "I didn't expect to have to look for schools all day."

"See, it's not so easy to look after a family," Mama said, as if she knew the first thing about it.

I ignored her. "Go, Trav." I gave my brother a shove. "You drive. We're going back to the Valley, fast."

Turns out, nothing is fast in Los Angeles. There was so much traffic on the 101 freeway that it took forty minutes just to get back to the Oakwood, even though it was only four miles away. I looked at my watch. Ten o'clock. We had to get this done quickly or I'd be in trouble.

"Okay, turn left up there and go for two more miles," I said, checking the big book full of Thomas Brothers maps that I'd bought. Jude was right—maps were key here. It was just too damned easy to get lost.

"Can't y'all just drop me off at home?" Mama said from the backseat.

"No, Mama. Schools tend to like parents around to sign forms and all that," I said.

"Be fair, Chloe. Mama never signed forms at Spurlock High," Travis said. "You just forged her signature instead."

"True." I ignored Mama's outraged gasp. "But that won't work where we're going. Here! Turn now."

Trav swung the car into a parking lot nestled behind a tall

hedge. Immediately, the noise and ugliness of the crowded street were left behind. In front of us stood a large Spanish-style building covered in ivy. Travis pulled into one of the spots marked GUEST, then turned to me. "Okay, spill. What is this place?"

"St. Paul's Academy. According to three different parenting and education websites, this is the best prep school in the Valley," I said. I climbed out of the car, pulled my sunglasses on, and headed for the doors. Mama and Travis followed.

"Prep school is for snotty, rich kids," my mama said. "You're mighty proud of your big check, Clo, but ten grand ain't gonna get you in here."

I said, "Don't worry, I've got this."

Inside, the door to the admissions office was closed. I didn't bother to knock—I just went right in. An older woman in a too-young-for-her headband sat at the desk.

"Hi!" I said cheerfully. "I'm Chloe Gamble and this is my brother, Travis. We're here to enroll."

The lady blinked at me. "I'm sorry?"

"We just moved here, and I heard this was the best school in Los Angeles," I said.

"Well, yes. But you can't just . . . enroll." The headband lady didn't seem to know if she should mock me or pity me. So instead she turned to my mama. "We have a very selective admissions process—it takes months. There are very few spaces available, and we receive many more applications than we can accept."

"Well, hand over an application, then. I'll fill it out," Mama said.

The poor woman just stared at her.

"Can we see the person in charge?" I asked. "We're kind of in a rush."

The headband lady got a sour look on her face, but she stood up and disappeared through another door. When she came back, she had a tall, frowning man with her.

"I'm Dr. Cardillo, dean of admissions," he said to Mama. "I'm afraid we have no openings at the moment. It is the middle of the school year, after all. If you'd like to apply for next year—"

"No, we need to start right away," I said. "And we'll need some financial aid, too."

Dr. Cardillo glanced at me, then kept on talking to Mama. "It really isn't possible. Our school enrolls a very high caliber of student, and the application process is rigorous to ensure that we stay that way. We simply can't skip over it."

"What if we could offer you something?" I said. "How about sports? You must need good athletes."

"We already field excellent teams in almost every major sport," he said.

"So that's important to you, then," I said. "Maybe you'd make an exception for a great player?"

He hesitated for a few seconds. "No, I'm afraid not," he finally said. "Not in the middle of the year, and not without the proper application process."

"Oh, isn't that a shame." Mama tried a long, slow hair flip.

Dr. Cardillo didn't even respond. I was going to have to handle this by myself.

"But we just moved here. There's no way we could've gone through the whole process," I said. "We didn't even know we were coming to LA until . . . we had to pick up and leave our home in Texas."

The headband lady looked horrified, as if she had been thrown into the audience of a *Jerry Springer* episode. But Dr. Cardillo's expression softened slightly.

I held his eye and spoke in my best serious voice. "Please, we can't wait until September. My brother and I would hate to fall behind in our studies. Our only other option is the public high school, and . . . have you been there?"

"I have," he said slowly.

*Got him,* I thought. He was wavering.

"We'll need a *full* scholarship. Free ride," my mama said. I could've kicked her.

Dr. Cardillo's attention went back to Mama. He cleared his throat. "I'm sorry. I do sympathize with your situation, but it really isn't possible. Best of luck to you."

He scuttled back into his office without another word. The headband lady pretended to be busy on her computer.

"Guess that's that," Mama said. "Let's go."

But when we got back out into the hallway, I didn't head for the car. Instead, I walked deeper into the school.

"Chloe, where are you going?" Travis asked, sounding resigned. "Let's just forget it."

"No," I said. "Listen, I'm the one responsible for yanking you out of school, so that means I'm the one who has to get you back in, so we'll be square."

"Don't be stupid," Travis said. "I could've stayed in Spurlock if I'd wanted."

He was wrong. He is biologically incapable of letting me do something he thinks is risky unless he comes along to keep me in line. But I had no time to argue.

"Just let me take care of this," I said. "Then I can stop worrying about you and get on with what I need to do."

"Well, I don't want you two going to this stick-up-the-butt school," Mama said.

"Then it's a good thing this isn't up to you," I said. I started down the hallway again.

"That's disrespectful," Mama said.

"And the truth," I said back.

Mama gave a loud sigh. But she followed after me, just like I knew she would. The school was pretty quiet—I figured classes were in session. There had to be a study hall somewhere, though. I scanned the halls as I walked, until finally I found it—the library. The double doors were open, and there was a group of about ten or fifteen kids hanging out at the tables, no teacher in sight. The kids paid no attention to us. I studied them for a second, choosing just the right boy. He was thin, a little nerdy, and actually reading a book instead of shooting the shit with the other guys.

I left Travis and my mama and went and sat down across the table from him. "I need your help," I said.

His eyes got wide, and he glanced around the room as if he couldn't believe I was talking to him. I had a feeling that the three jocks at the table behind me were pretty shocked about that, too. But I knew what I was doing.

"Uh, sure," the boy said.

"I'm Chloe Gamble, by the way." I made sure to lightly touch his forearm.

"I'm, uh, Tom Janger," he said, his voice cracking at the edges.

"Who's the soccer coach, Tommy?" I asked.

"Mr. Ibanez," he said.

"Where is he? Right now?" I said.

"He, um, he teaches history," my new friend replied. "He's probably in his classroom."

"I'm new here. I don't know my way around." I raised my eyebrows.

Tom stood up so fast that he almost knocked his chair over. "I can show you."

"Don't you need a hall pass or something?" I asked.

"Yeah, but it's okay. I don't mind. It's okay." He had a spot of bright red on each cheek.

I treated him to my most wholesome beauty-queen smile. "You are so sweet!"

He ducked his head and raced for the door, but he stopped short when he spotted Travis. "Don't worry, he's her brother," my mama said, smirking.

Poor Tommy turned even redder, then hurried out into the hallway. We followed him past a few trophy cases and around a corner, till he stopped at a doorway.

"In there," he said. "But he's—"

"He won't mind," I cut him off. I knocked on the door, then pushed it open and went right in. The room was big, with wooden desks and real chairs, totally different from the thirty-year-old metal one-pieces back at Spurlock High. The huge windows looked out over green athletic fields and the cloudless California sky. Yeah, we definitely needed to go to this school.

"Can I help you?" Coach Ibanez asked. There were maybe twenty people in the class, and they all watched curiously as I walked over to the teacher.

"I'm Chloe Gamble, and that's my brother, Travis," I said. "You need him on your soccer team."

Coach Ibanez looked from me to Trav, and then his gaze stopped on Mama. He swallowed hard, as if he was thirsty.

"But you'll have to convince the admissions office to give him a scholarship," I added.

Somebody in the front row laughed. Coach Ibanez spoke to Mama. "Ma'am, we're in the middle of class here."

Mama shrugged. I could tell she'd just given up—this

school was way out of her league, and she didn't want us to get in. It'd make her feel unworthy. There are mothers out there whose biggest wish is for their children to have better lives than their own—but those mothers are not my mother. She pretty much thinks that if life handed her lemons, then no one should make lemonade.

"This is more important than history," I said to the teacher. "Admissions doesn't want to let us in here unless we jump through a lot of hoops, so you have to help us."

"Miss . . ."

"Gamble," I said.

"Miss Gamble. I don't *have* to do anything," Coach Ibanez said. "And barging into my class isn't likely to make me want to help you."

"He was an all-state midfielder back in Texas," I said. "And he's got a secret weapon. Let him show you."

"Yeah, let him show us, Coach," a girl in the middle row called. "It'll be more interesting than the Peloponnesian War!"

Everybody laughed. Coach Ibanez clenched his jaw. He was a few seconds away from calling security, I could tell. He wasn't the kind of guy who liked to lose control of his class.

"Never mind," I said. "Sorry for interrupting."

When we got back out into the hall, my mama exploded. "What in the hell was that all about? This is a waste of our time!"

"Your time isn't worth much, Mama. I'm the one who earns in this family." I spotted a double door to the outside and pushed through it.

As we entered into the glare of the sunshine, we found the running track in front of us. Inside the oval of the track was the football field. The grass on the field was so intensely green, it almost looked as if it had been painted. Then I realized that it was artificial turf, like you would see at the University of Texas stadium.

In the middle of the field a bunch of girls were doing drills with soccer balls and looking bored. A handful of guys raced around the track while keeping an eye on the girls. Two gym teachers chatted in the shade of a palm tree, not even pretending to watch their classes.

"Get out there," I said to Travis.

Travis stared at me for a moment before he understood. "This could backfire big-time." Then he ran his hand through his wavy hair. That's his tell. He does the same thing when he plays poker. It means he is about to push in all his chips.

"Remember what Kimber's father always says," I told him. "Nerves are for losers."

He laughed, relaxing a little. I veered off the walkway and into the short bushes that lined the building. A glance into the window showed me a fat middle-aged lady teaching math. Wrong room. But the next set of windows revealed Coach Ibanez and his class full of students. I knocked loudly on the glass.

The kids in the closest row of desks turned and gaped at me. I pointed toward the field, gave them a grin, then left without a backward glance. They'd be watching. The whole class would, and so would Coach Ibanez.

Travis was already over by the girls with the soccer balls. One of the gym teachers got to him around the same time I did.

"We just need to borrow a ball for a few minutes," I told her. "My brother's gonna show off."

"You can have my ball," a cute redhead said, holding it out to Travis with a raised eyebrow.

"Can you set it up for me?" he asked.

"For you? Definitely." She walked out to midfield, making sure Travis had a nice view of her butt. Then she dropped the ball and lazily kicked it toward him. Trav was fifty yards from the goal, but he fired the ball downfield and into the upper left corner of the net. I know, there were no defenders, but how many people can shoot that far or that accurately? Not many. The girls all clapped, and the other gym teacher came over to watch.

"I bet you can't do that twice," the redhead said.

"Don't bet if you can't afford to pay up," Travis said with a smile. Red set up a ball again, and Travis shot it right in from half a field away. This time even the teachers clapped. There were some whistles from the guys running track.

"Who wants to race him?" I called to them. "He's fast, too!"

A super-skinny dude with a huge nose yelled, "I'll take Beckham."

Travis shot me a look. "I'm wearing Chucks."

"You saying you can't beat him?" I asked.

There were a few "ooh"s from the girls, and the rest of the joggers had stopped to watch. Travis shook his head, half pissed at me, half amused. "Nah, I'm saying my feet will hurt *while* I beat him."

"Let's go," Track Boy called. "Four-forty."

Travis jogged over to him. They set, took off, and ran. They were neck and neck for a long time. People yelled and laughed, watching them run. Trav dropped back a little at the far end of the track, and they went down the other side a few paces apart.

"It ain't gonna look so good if he loses," my mama said.

"We never lose," I told her.

They came thundering toward us, taking the curve fast. About twenty yards away from the finish line, Travis put on a kick of speed, running like a thoroughbred in the Derby. He passed Track Boy and finished about four yards ahead.

Everybody whooped and cheered, even the gym teachers. I glanced over at Coach Ibanez's classroom windows. A line of faces looked back at me. They were all watching, just like I knew they would be.

"Secret-weapon time, Trav." I called to the redhead, "My brother needs another ball."

The redhead gave Travis a suggestive little smile and picked up a soccer ball. "What're you gonna do with this one?" she asked.

"Throw it in," Travis said.

She made a face. "*Bor*-ing."

"Well, I can do a flip-throw and make it exciting," Trav said. "But that's not the secret weapon."

"What's the secret weapon?" one of the gym teachers asked.

Trav went over to the sidelines near our goal. He held the ball behind his head, took a few running steps, and casually threw the ball across the entire field. It landed about fifteen feet from the other goal and bounced in.

For a few seconds, nobody spoke.

"Again," the teacher said, her voice serious. She tossed him a ball. This time he did do a flip-throw, somersaulting during his run-up and throwing the ball across the field one more time.

Now both gym teachers were focused on Trav. "Throw it to Jen here," the first one said. "I'll defend."

The two teachers ran out to the far end of the field and turned to Travis. Jen waited, watching Trav, and the other teacher blocked. Travis studied them for a bit, then hurled the ball the entire distance—and right to Jen's feet. She jumped toward it, surprised, but she thought fast and kicked it away from the other teacher, sending it into the goal.

Just for good measure, Travis grabbed another ball, jogged to midfield, and threw it in again. Not as much distance, but straight to Jen one more time.

By now everybody from gym class was hooting and hollering, and I didn't even have to look at Coach Ibanez's room to know he'd be on my side.

"Nobody can throw like Trav," I said.

"The one thing his asshole father ever did for him," Mama said.

See, back when we were little, Daddy thought soccer was for wusses. He wanted Trav to play football, the way you're supposed to when you're from Texas. He said the only way he'd let Travis do soccer instead was if he could throw the ball at least forty yards. And then he handed Trav a medicine ball filled with sand. Well, my brother was so furious that he hurled that heavy ball across the whole backyard and nailed Daddy right in the chest. Daddy gave in on the soccer thing after that, but Trav kept the medicine ball. And he kept throwing it, all the time, building up his strength. When our yard got too small, he went out into the street and threw it. Then he went to the fields at the school and threw it. By the time we got to high school, Trav could do a longer throw-in than anybody else in the state. Every time the Spurlock Cowboys needed a throw-in, they waited for Travis to do it even if he had to come from the far end of the field. He was their secret weapon.

Today, he was my secret weapon.

"Rowan's ankle is still bandaged. He's out for the rest of the season," Coach Ibanez said to Dr. Cardillo ten minutes later. "Travis Gamble is an all-state midfielder. He's fast, he's accurate, and he's a hell of a thrower. He'll replace Rowan and do a better job. We need him."

"You don't get a star player dumped in your lap like this every day," Jen the gym teacher added.

The admissions dean sat at his desk, hands steepled in front of him. He was listening to them, but he was looking at me.

"Travis is worth it," I told him. "Nobody will mind if you bring a championship player in without all the proper applications."

Dr. Cardillo didn't answer. He knew I was right.

"It would be irresponsible of us to let this boy's talents languish just because he had to move midseason," Coach said. "He needs to play."

"Why *did* you decide to move in the middle of a school year, Mrs. Gamble?" Dr. Cardillo asked Mama. "Surely Travis's team was counting on him."

"We had a family situation," Mama said. "You see, his no-good daddy couldn't keep it—"

"We had no choice," I interrupted her.

Everybody looked uncomfortable, and I could see that they didn't know what to do with my mama. It had obviously been a mistake to bring her along.

"Travis would never let his teammates down if it was up to him," I said before Mama could chime in again.

"That's the kind of spirit we need," Coach Ibanez said.

Dr. Cardillo sighed. "Fine. He's in."

"And the scholarship?" I asked.

"That's asking a lot," the dean said.

"Only for this year. By next year we'll have enough money," I said. "I'll be working."

Dr. Cardillo frowned at my mama. She didn't seem to notice—she was too busy pouting because I'd cut her off. "Okay, okay," he said. "Tuition is waived for this year. It's only one semester, anyway."

"What about Chloe? She's in, too, right?" Travis asked. "With flexible hours so she can go to auditions?"

"I hardly think I can say no to her," Dr. Cardillo said drily. "Just don't let work come before education, Ms. Gamble. Actors who quit school are still just high school dropouts in the long run."

"I have no intention of being a high school dropout," I said, looking at my mother.

My heart was pounding as we got back into our crappy old Ford. I thought we'd never get out of there.

"Well, that ate up a day," Mama said with just a trace of a smile. Even she understood that we had just won our first huge victory in a new town.

Travis put his hand on my shoulder. "That was a good day's work, Clo."

"Are you kidding me?" I said. "My day's work hasn't even started yet."

"What are you talking about?" Trav asked.

"I've got to get back to Burbank ASAP," I told him. "Floor it."

# Nika Mays's Manuscript Notes: The Legend of Chloe Gamble, Part One

Some actors work their way up. Others burst onto the scene blazing like a comet. But only a select few come with their own legend. Lana Turner gets discovered at Schwab's Drug Store. Brad Pitt appears seminude in *Thelma and Louise*.

And then there's the legend of Chloe Gamble's first audition at NBC.

Here's the thing a lot of people don't know about Hollywood: Studios are as heavily guarded as the Pentagon. There's a lot of money behind the walls of a studio—the standing sets of TV shows, the millions of dollars' worth of equipment, soundstages holding expensive movie sets, entire office buildings filled with high-priced employees, not to mention the top-secret scripts and daily reels from not-yet-released movies and not-yet-aired shows. There are tons of things at a studio that people would love to steal. And then there are the stars—TV and movie stars who are hounded 24/7 by the paparazzi. They need protection. And when they're at work, at the studio, they've got it. Inside a studio lot, they're safe, isolated from the entire world outside. The studio has its own fire department, its own power and water departments—and its own security force.

Take NBC, the scene of Chloe Gamble's first audition. If somebody wants to get into the NBC Studios lot, well, they need an appointment. The front gate of the studio lot will have a computerized record of the appointment. And even then, the visitor will have to provide her ID to the guard at the gate, who will call to double-check that she's expected inside, no matter what the computer says. The trunk of her car might be checked for bombs (or stowaways). She'll have to wear a visitor ID badge, usually labeled with what building, floor, and room number she's going to. She'll have to check in again with the guard at the door, and then an assistant will be sent down to take her to a waiting room, where there's a receptionist to watch her, and maybe even another guard for good measure. When it's time to go into the room, an assistant will escort her. When it's time to leave, the assistant will escort her again. And every guard along the way will wave good-bye and watch until everyone is sure the visitor has gone in the right direction. Out.

Nobody gets into NBC without an appointment. Ever.

But Chloe Gamble did.

## Studio Break

"You done with that chalupa?" the kid with the greasy hair asked.

"No," I said for the second time. His only job seemed to be cleaning the tables at Taco Bell, and he was tweaking about my half-eaten food still sitting on the table. Just to prove I wasn't loitering, I took another bite. It was nobody's business but mine if I took an hour to eat a stupid chalupa.

I'd made Mama and Travis just drop me off here. Mama was eager to get back to her busy schedule of lying around and I figured Travis could find something to keep him occupied. When they left me at the Taco Bell, I said I'd take a cab home. Whatever. I'd figure it out later.

My table faced the window, so I had a perfect view of the busy street and of the studio on the other side of it. NBC. Right there. With the big logo and everything. It was weird to think about all the shows I'd watched on TV and realize that they had been made right there. Or maybe they hadn't been.

I wasn't sure what really happened inside. Maybe it was just offices and stuff. But at least one show got made there, *The Tonight Show*. I could tell because there was a line of people on the sidewalk waiting to get in the gates and a guy with a megaphone who kept yelling, "This is the line for *The Tonight Show* starring Jay Leno only! Please make sure you have your tickets before you get in line!"

I'd gone over and asked the megaphone guy, and he'd said they would bring the audience in at four o'clock. That would be too late. And besides, he'd said *bring* them in. Not *let* them in. I had a feeling this group of Leno lovers were watched pretty intensely once they got inside. After all, you never hear about Jay Leno being mauled by obsessive fans during tapings.

I'd gone back to the Taco Bell, ordered more food, and sat down at the same table. The only one who even seemed to notice was the greasy guy. But he didn't matter. I focused on NBC. A guardhouse stood in the middle of the main driveway, separating it into entrance and exit lanes. The arm of the gate was in constant motion, up and down. Every time I glanced over there, another car or truck was going in. But they all stopped and talked to the guard at the gate. The Leno security people were watching a separate sidewalk gate, which I guessed was for pedestrians.

A FedEx truck pulled up to the gate, then went in. A junky-looking van followed it. Then some kind of refrigerated truck.

Something beeped behind me, one of those cell-phone walkies. "Klink, you coming?" a voice asked. "What are you, in traffic?"

I snuck a look over my shoulder at the guy in the booth behind me. He grabbed his cell and replied, "I'm just grabbing a taco. Chill."

"Well, hurry up. They're breathing down my neck here," said the other voice.

Klink rolled his eyes, stuck his phone into the pocket of his jeans, and kept eating. I pushed the chalupa away and turned to face him.

"What's that on your shirt?" I asked, narrowing my eyes like I was studying the cartoon beaver on his tee.

"Beaver Building Supplies," he said. "Can you believe my boss picked that name?"

"It's cute," I lied. Klink stared at me, enjoying the view. I let him, just for a minute. Once I had his full attention, I kept talking. "What are you building?"

"Nothing. We're just the 'supplies.' I deliver lumber." He shrugged. "Pays the bills while my band gets started up."

"Cool." I didn't ask about the band. Rule #19 on the list. "I need to get a day job, too, I guess. I'm an actor."

"Yeah?"

"I just got here from Texas," I said. "I bet you meet a lot of actors in LA, huh?"

"Well, *I* do," Klink said. "But that's just because I go to the studios a lot. That's our biggest customer right there." He nodded toward NBC across the street.

"NBC? Really?" I gasped.

"They build sets. They need wood."

"So you get to go in there? You are so lucky!" I let a little hero worship slide into my voice. Klink squirmed a bit.

"It's no big deal. They just take my cargo and ignore me."

"Still, you get to see the real thing, where famous people are and everything." I got up and slid into his booth across from him. "Could you take me in there? I would kill to see what it's like behind the scenes."

He thought about it for a few seconds, sucking his teeth. "The boss doesn't allow ride-alongs," he said.

"But your boss isn't here," I said. "It's just driving me across the street. I'll duck down so nobody sees me. How would your boss even find out?"

Suddenly he laughed. "You're a piece of work, aren't you?"

"Haven't you met a Texas girl before?" I laughed, too.

"Okay, but don't tell anyone. I need this job." Klink grabbed his tray and stood up. "Let's go. I'm already late."

The stupid beaver logo was emblazoned on both sides of his truck, which took up two spaces in the Taco Bell parking lot. I climbed into the cab and bounced up and down with excitement while Klink started the truck. I was only half faking, too. I was pretty psyched to be getting into the studio so easily.

"You have to give the guard your license to get into the lot," Klink said as he waited for the light to turn.

"I don't have a license," I lied.

He frowned. "Then you better hide now."

I squeezed myself down under the big dashboard and giggled up at him. "Can you see me?"

"Yes. Pull that jacket over you."

I grabbed a jean jacket that was flung on the seat and tugged it down over my head just as we pulled up to the NBC gate.

"Hey, man," Klink said.

"What's up," the guard's voice came. "You just in and out today?"

"Yeah, just dropping off," Klink said.

"Okay."

I heard the gate squeak as it rose, and then we drove right onto the studio lot. I threw the jacket off me and climbed back up onto the seat. "I can't believe we just did that! We're like spies!"

Klink laughed. "You better not go spying around here. If they catch us, I'll lose my job."

I kept the smile on my face, but I felt bad. Klink had totally helped me out and I was going to get him in trouble. "Thanks for taking me in. You're really sweet," I said. I meant it.

"When you're a famous actress, don't forget me," he joked.

"I won't."

"Sure, they all say that." Klink shot me a serious look. "You gotta be good to the below-the-line people, Texas girl. No matter how big you get, remember the grunts who carry the cameras and do your makeup or lighting or whatever—they're the ones who make you look good. Too many actors treat the crew like dirt."

"Beauty-pageant girls are like that," I said. "I used to compete against these rich girls who had makeup artists and pageant coaches who traveled with them. A lot of them treated their yappy poodles better than they treated those people."

He winked at me. "You're a beauty queen? I should've known."

"Not anymore," I said. "That's all past tense now."

Klink pulled the truck up next to a garage door and stopped. "I gotta unload here. You better hide again."

"'Kay." I ducked down under the dash and waved as he got out. But as soon as I heard him open the back of the truck, I made my move. I opened the passenger door as quietly as I could, slipped out, and took off in the opposite direction. I didn't look back.

If Klink noticed I was gone, I hoped he wouldn't rat me out. It would only get him in trouble if he did.

I jogged to the end of the building and quickly turned the corner. Then I stopped to get my bearings. There were lots of other garage doors with trucks outside, and from inside

I heard the sounds of drills and hammering. This must have been some kind of workshop area, which was useless to me. I walked quickly past the open doors, holding my head high. If you look like you know where you're going, people tend to think that you actually do. I saw a few guys glance up as I walked past, but nobody stopped me.

When I reached the end of the next building, I found a small courtyard that led into a large parking lot. A fast look around showed me that I was on the far side of the lot from where we'd driven in. To my left was a big office building.

"Perfect," I whispered. I headed straight up to the glass doors that led inside, but when I got into the lobby, my heart stopped for a second. Directly in front of me was a huge security desk, with a guard staring straight at me.

"Name, please?" she said.

I gave a little jump and grabbed my BlackBerry, pretending I'd just got a call. "One sec—my idiot agent!" I said to the guard, and then I beelined right back out the door, holding the cell to my ear.

Outside, I walked quickly back the way I'd come. I couldn't get in the front; that much was clear.

I followed the walls of the building around to the back, scanning for doors. I passed one or two before I found what I wanted—an ashtray. One of those freestanding things with sand on the top and lots of butts scattered about. Now I just had to wait.

It took about five minutes, but finally a couple of people came for a smoke. There was a guy and a girl, both probably in their twenties, and both wearing little plastic badges strapped to their belts. The girl swiped her badge against the inside of the door, and it opened with a click to let them out.

I grabbed the door as it swung shut and gave the guy a panicked look. "Thank God! I forgot my badge and I'm locked out!"

Before the smoker girl could register how young I looked, I breezed past her. "I'm so late! You guys are lifesavers!" Once again, I didn't look back. You should never look back. It makes you seem insecure, and that's just an invitation for trouble.

It was quiet in the building. The hallways were carpeted, and people seemed to stay mostly in their offices. There were names on the doors, but that was it. I glanced at my watch and fought a little burst of panic. Somehow I had to figure out where to go, and fast.

An elevator bank appeared, and I hit the up button without pausing to think. Sometimes elevators have labels inside to tell you what stuff is on what floor. It was worth a try. While I was waiting, two beautiful girls came up to wait with me. They both had long blond hair, big blue eyes, and halter tops. They were both super thin. And they both wore stickers on their shirts that said VISITOR and their names in huge letters.

When the elevator came, I followed them on and let them press the button. They both got off on the third floor, but I stayed on and rode it back down to the ground. I had to find a sticker or I'd stand out too much.

I walked around until I came to the lobby at the front of the building. I was behind the security desk now, but I couldn't risk that guard seeing me. I hurried past and ducked into a door marked LADIES.

The bathroom was empty. I went straight to the trash can. "Come on, garbage, help me out," I murmured. This was the closest restroom to the exit. Nobody wants to walk around in public with a big name sticker on her chest. Somebody had to have thrown hers out before getting in her car, right?

I had just about started to panic when I found it—something sticky on the side of a crumpled paper towel. I peeled it off, opened it up, and said a little prayer of thanks to the gods of success: It was a visitor ID for somebody named Ingrid van der Goode. Well, I could pull that off if someone asked me.

I stuck Ingrid's sticker onto my blouse, checked my makeup in the mirror, and headed back to the elevators. A cute Asian guy was waiting, wearing his own visitor sticker.

"Hey," I said.

"Hi." He had a killer smile.

"Are you here for an audition?" I asked.

He nodded. "I'm testing for *Bob's Your Uncle*. You?"

"Um, I'm testing for *Virgin*," I said.

"*Virgin* is going to be huge! If you book the job, tell the producers to write an Asian guy into the script!"

"No problem! You don't happen to know what floor they do the tests on, do you?

"Didn't they tell you where to go at the desk?"

"Probably. I don't remember. I'm really nervous," I said. He seemed to think the *Virgin* pilot was a big deal, so it made sense that I'd be jittery.

"Well, they usually do all the network tests in the big rooms on three," he told me.

"Thanks." When the elevator came, we got on and rode up in silence. He was checking me out, but I pretended not to notice. He got off at the second floor.

"Break a leg," he said.

"You too," I said.

The doors closed, leaving me alone. I took a deep breath and centered myself. My performance wasn't going to start in the room with the network people. It was going to start right now.

The doors opened, and I stepped out onto another carpeted hallway. But this time there was a sign, a little black one with lettering that said CASTING VIRGIN on it with an arrow pointing to the right.

About twenty feet away, I came to a waiting area with four couches and a couple of chairs. There were several people sitting around, all of them so hot that they had to be actors and all of them staring intently at the pages of a script. I watched one of the blondes from the elevator, her lips moving as she read the lines to herself. I needed to get my hands on those pages or my whole plan would come to nothing.

*Two bathroom stakeouts in one day,* I decided. It was a no-brainer that every one of the actresses here had visited the ladies' room before coming to the waiting area. You don't go into battle without one last primp—every beauty queen knows that.

I found the restroom right past the waiting area. There was one girl at the mirror and another one in a stall. I stopped at the mirror and did a quick scan of the sinks while pretending to fix my hair. There was a script lying half-on, half-off the counter. It was far enough from the girl out here that it couldn't be hers. It had to belong to the girl in the stall. I had to think fast.

I dropped my bag on top of the script, pulled out my makeup kit, and dug through for my lip gloss. I quickly slathered some on, then shoved everything all back into my bag, along with the script pages. I gave the other girl a smile and left her applying mascara without having noticed anything weird about me.

But the stall girl would definitely ask about the script once she noticed it was gone. I couldn't get away with just taking it.

My heart was racing as I walked down the hall, checking open doors until I found an office with a guy at the desk. I jerked my Ingrid van der Goode visitor sticker off, then rushed inside. "Oh my God, my boss needs me to copy these for the actresses!" I cried. "Can you help me? I'm so sorry, but it's my first day and I have no idea where to go."

He got up, amused, and took the papers from me. "Okay, okay, breathe," he said. "The copy room's just down here." He led me three doors down the hallway and into a room with a bunch of Xerox machines. "Do you know how to use the copier?"

"Yeah, thanks so, so much," I said. "I'm sorry to bother you."

"No worries. We're all the newbies at some point." His eyes lingered on me for a few seconds, and then he turned to go. "Hopefully I'll see you around."

"Definitely." When he was gone, I quickly copied all the script pages. I stuck my Ingrid van der Goode visitor badge back on, took a moment to calm down, then went back down the hall to the waiting area. A short Latino girl was frantically searching the floor, her eyes teary. Everybody else was pretending not to notice.

"'Scuse me, are these yours?" I asked her, holding out the script pages I'd taken from the bathroom.

"Oh my God, you found my sides!" she cried. For a brief second, I thought she might hug me.

I guess these script pages were called "sides." I'd have to remember that.

"They were in the ladies'. I thought somebody must've lost them," I said, graciously handing them over.

Then I took a deep breath. I was done, I was there, and I had everything that I needed. It was time to relax and start my career.

I turned, walked over to a couch near the window, and sat down next to Kimber Reeve.

"Well, howdy, Kimmy!" I said.

She looked up from studying the sides and her eyes widened in shock.

"You ready for your network test?" I asked. "Because I know I am."

# chapter four

## E-mail from Travis Gamble

You mocked me for getting those head shots, Coop, but check this: I just went over to that hot photographer's place to look at the contact sheet (a page with tons of thumbnails of my face—freaky). And there were these two girls there, actresses—clients of Jude's, I think. (I know what you're hoping, but NO, they weren't there for a lesbian three-way.)

Anyway, they decided to help me pick out the best pictures. Jude says head shots are supposed to look good, but also look like you. So you can't just pick the best ones—you have to pick the ones you can actually live up to. Like, don't pick one where you have a surfer vibe if you can only act like a cowboy. Or something. What the hell do I know? But these actresses—Amber and Livia—they were all "you don't have to act—you should be a model." I'm serious, man. They were totally coming on to me. Livia even gave me her digits without me asking. Plus, she's eighteen so she's staying at the Oakwood alone—NO PARENTS!

Weirdest thing, though. After we picked out my shots, Jude showed me Chloe's contact sheet. Killer photos, I thought, but Livia and Amber hated them! You know my sister is gorgeous (for a sister), but these girls were like "her nose is crooked" and "her hair looks stringy" and all kinds of shit. Then after they left, Jude laughed and said she could tell by their reaction that those pictures must be the best ones she's ever taken.

I'm telling you, man, reality is upside down here.

But I've got Livia's number, so who cares?

# Virgin

Kimber Reeve sat there gaping at me, her mouth hanging open just like a fish. So I shrugged and began to study the script pages—*the sides,* I reminded myself. Didn't know why they were called that, didn't care. I scanned the pages quickly to get a sense of what was going on.

It was a scene about a girl fighting with her daddy and then slamming out of the room. Well, that would be no stretch for me. The first line even sounded like something I might say. This "Virgin" girl says, "I'm not me anymore. I'm someone else."

I kept reading, trying to memorize every word of the scene.

I've got a kick-ass memory. If I listen to a song on my iPod twice, I can nail it; every chorus and verse. After a few more reads, I'd have these side things memorized cold. I had no idea whether we were supposed to learn all the lines, but it couldn't hurt.

"What the *hell* are you doing?" Kimber finally spoke up in a harsh whisper.

"Network testing," I said. "I hear this is the best pilot there is. Todd Linson's first foray into TV—"

"Are you out of your fucking mind?" Kimber cut me off. She'd turned a really unattractive shade of purple, and I hoped she stayed that way for her audition. Not that anyone would really be paying attention to her once they saw me. Still, I like to have my competition a little off balance.

"You know I just got to LA," I said. "And I get the feeling I'm late for pilot season. So I have to jump-start things. You understand."

Kimber's face was truly interesting to watch. She'd obviously noticed that I didn't have the extreme Texas twang I'd had before. She'd probably figured out that I wasn't really the goober I'd been acting like. And she was shocked to see me here at NBC. I could tell she was trying to decide which scathing thing to say to me first.

She leaned in closer to me and dropped her voice. "Don't," she said. "Chloe, I mean it. Whatever you're planning, just . . . don't."

A few of the other actors were listening now. Everyone's

eyes were on their script pages, but they were paying attention to us. It didn't bother me. I like being watched.

I have to admit, I was impressed by how serious Kimber sounded, like she was looking out for my best interests. Maybe she could act, after all.

"Scared?" I teased her.

"No. Yes." She stared right at me. "Scared for you. You have no idea what you're doing."

The door next to us opened up and another short Latina girl was ushered out by a guy with a clipboard.

"I know exactly what I'm doing," I told Kimber. "I'm taking this job away from you."

Before she could react, I was up and moving, toward the door, past the clipboard, and into the room.

## Nika Mays's Manuscript Notes: Casting Section

Let's just start with the facts: It is virtually impossible for an unknown actress to land a starring role on a TV show. And no matter what, no matter how many community-theater roles she's had, or how many car-dealership commercials she's shot back home, or how many music videos she's shaken her ass in—or how many beauty pageants she's won—she had to get an agent before she even got in the door. No actor gets near a network test unless she has an agent.

Here's why: Without an agent, there is no way the unknown actress could get submitted to the casting director of a TV show to get an audition. Even if somehow the unknown actress's head shot and résumé did make it to a casting director, the chances that it would get plucked out of a pile of two thousand other head shots of actresses submitted for the same role are very small indeed. Then, even if somehow her head shot was exactly the right look for a specific role and she was actually called in for an audition, she would read for a casting assistant, not the actual casting director. The casting assistant's job is to weed out the actresses that would "waste the time" of the casting director. If casting assistants want to keep their job, they have to make sure not to send the time wasters in to see their boss or it will make them look bad—and nobody in Hollywood ever wants to look bad.

But if a casting assistant actually believes that an unknown actress won't waste his boss's time, he schedules a second audition for the casting director. Then the difficulty level ratchets up a notch.

The casting director sees very few unknown

actresses. His job is to see known actors who have worked extensively and have the TV credits to prove it. Why? Because casting directors have to submit their choices for every role to the executive producers (often the writer/creators) of the television show—and not waste *their* time. So if the casting director sends a known actress to the producers of the show and the actress tanks in the room, the casting director can say, "But she was wonderful in *Grey's Anatomy*!" But if a casting director sends an unknown to the producers and she tanks in the room, it makes the casting director look bad. And no one in Hollywood ever wants to look bad.

Still, every once in a while an actress with no credits is so talented and poised in her audition that the casting director will take a chance and send her to the executive producers. That's when the nightmare really begins.

The unknown actress is now at the level where she is competing against not only known actresses with credits, but against actual TV stars. Famous women. Women who are recognized on the street and photographed by the paparazzi. Women whose names and faces are known throughout the world. These women do not even have to visit the casting director—they go directly to the executive producers. Often they don't even audition; they simply meet with producers and discuss the role to determine if they would like to participate in the project. The executive producers are inclined to work only with actual TV stars simply because they know that eventually they will have to submit their choices for each role to the television network, and the people who run networks love nothing more than actual television stars to help attract viewers and, more important, *advertising sponsors* to the show. So executive producers don't want to risk sending an unknown actress into a network test for a show because they do not want to waste the network's time.

Are you seeing the pattern? If you waste the network's time, it makes you look bad. And nobody in Hollywood ever wants to look bad.

That's the secret of it all. Looking bad in this business is like having a disease, a contagious and fatal one. The instant you look bad, everyone who's ever said a good thing about you will also look bad. So people run—away from you, as fast as they can. When you look bad, you are alone. Untouchable. That sounds dramatic, but there is simply no way to overstate it. One misstep—one actress who fucks up her audition on the wrong day for the wrong person—can mean a huge setback in your career. And that's enough to make every casting assistant, every casting director, and every television producer live in constant fear.

So about that unknown actress? Well, let's say she's defied the odds and made it through the audition process to reach the executive-producer level. At that point, she still has to audition for the studio that's making the show. Then, once all those people are on board—agents, directors, producers, studio executives—then, and only then, will the actress test for the network. The network (ABC, NBC, CBS, or Fox) is the entity that pays the bills and calls the shots. An actress can be loved by every single person every step of the way, but if the network honchos don't like her, she's toast. They don't even have to give a reason. If the network says no, the answer is no.

Nobody wants to be the unfortunate person in the room with a network president—or, God forbid, a network chairman—who doesn't like the actress testing for the role. Because there's so much blame flying around, you never know who's going to get hit with it. I've known executive producers who have lost jobs on their own shows just because they dared to fight the network over a casting choice.

That room? It's a terrifying place. Everyone there has worked her ass off just to get to the point of network testing. This is not a time for error or improvisation. The writers and producers, the directors and the executives, they're all simply praying that the actors they've picked don't fumble their lines or reek of cologne or have a bad hair day or do anything—anything at all—to make the network honchos unhappy.

The last thing anybody wants at a network test is for the unexpected to happen.

Chloe Gamble was unexpected.

## The Test

The room got quiet as soon as I walked in the door.

There were maybe fifteen people sitting there, all of them facing me. Two women sat at a table near the front, a bunch of papers and head shots scattered around before them. They had to be the casting people. Both of them frowned at me.

The guy with the clipboard came running in behind me, but he froze when he saw those frowns.

"She, um, she just . . ." He didn't seem to know how to form the words "she just barged in."

One of the women went pale. The other one shot a

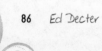

panicked look over her shoulder at a guy wearing a baseball cap. I followed her gaze to his face and felt a little jolt when I realized who he was—Todd Linson, the famous director Kimber's mom had mentioned. I'd looked him up on Google. He didn't say a word, but I got the feeling that it was only because he was too astonished to speak.

Next to him sat Anders Lee. He looked older in person than he did in his movies, and his hair was grayer. His eyes darted from me to the casting women and back to Todd Linson. The guy was a big movie star, but I could swear he was nervous.

My heart began to pound. This was weird. The room had a strange, intense vibe that I hadn't been expecting, and these people weren't looking at me the way a panel of pageant judges would have. These people were looking at me as if I were some kind of ugly, poisonous insect.

The pale casting lady cleared her throat. "You must have the wrong room," she said. "Who are you?"

*Who am I?* The tension in the room had thrown me for a second. But this was just like any beauty pageant—I simply had to find my role, the persona that these people wanted to see. I grabbed the Ingrid van der Goode visitor sticker and yanked it off. "I'm Chloe Gamble," I said. "And I'm here to test for *Virgin*."

Silence. Heavy, oppressive silence was all I got. Nobody was smiling or nodding or even checking out my tits. All of them were just staring at me, and that's when I realized what that weird vibe was. It was fear.

They were afraid. All of them. Scared, freaked, petrified. No one seemed to know what to do. And it was all aimed at me. They were scared of me. "Scared *for* you"—Kimber's words came back to me.

This was a mistake.

My throat grew tight as the truth hit me. This was a huge, huge mistake. I shouldn't have come here; I shouldn't have just run into this room with no warning. There was something going on here that I didn't understand.

An older guy in a suit sitting at the back of the room suddenly shifted in his chair, blowing out an impatient sigh. I fixed my gaze on him and smiled my best beauty-queen smile. He didn't look away, but his eyes seemed to stare right through me. I couldn't read a thing in his expression. There were three more men in suits, and they leaned in to whisper to one another. So that was the executive section, people from the network, I guessed. The older guy must be the big cheese.

*Casting people down front, creative guy wearing ratty jeans and a T even though his last movie grossed three hundred million, and executives in suits. Got it,* I thought. So now I knew who to impress. I turned my gaze to Todd Linson. His show—he was the one who mattered.

"Who's going to read the scene with me?" I asked him, letting my gaze wander over to Anders Lee and back.

Linson didn't answer me. Instead, the casting lady spoke again, and now her voice was dripping with venom. "Leave immediately, or I'll call security."

"But . . ." I was surprised to hear how thin my voice sounded. I forced myself to take a breath and looked around at the people watching me. At every pageant I'd ever been in, I stood in front of the judges and let them drink me in while I figured out what they wanted. That's the trick. Figure out what they want and give it to them.

Their faces were unreadable. I could barely see Todd Linson's eyes underneath his cap.

*What do they want me to be?*

I fought the panic that was beginning to bubble up from my stomach.

*What do they want? They want Kimber Reeve.*

I opened my mouth, but I didn't know what to say. I didn't know how to be Kimber, because Kimber would never be here, in this room, without an appointment.

"Matt, call security," the casting lady said. The guy with the clipboard nodded and headed for the door.

"No, wait! Please," I said without thinking. I turned back to Todd Linson. I had maybe five seconds to get him or some-one else to listen to me before I was kicked out on my ass. No time to find a role. No time to think of a good lie.

"I just got here from Texas, and I don't know the ropes yet," I said.

In the back, the big guy's eye twitched with something like annoyance. Linson leaned over to say something to Anders Lee. The casting lady began to stand up.

I hurtled on, not sure what I was going to say until the words left my mouth. "Have you ever been to Texas? Spurlock, Texas? That's my town, and it's not like a quaint little hick town in the movies. It's a dead-end backwater where people's lives are so small that they only see the world through the bottom of a Lone Star bottle. They spend their lives working at the Tastee Freez and they die in the house they grew up in and all they care about is football and Jesus and who's banging who. My worthless daddy is a *hero* there because he won a freakin' rodeo in Midland twenty years ago. One rodeo—that's all it takes to make you a stud in Spurlock. He fucks everything in a skirt, just 'cause at one time his hand was steady enough to rope a damn cow."

Linson was listening now. Out of the corner of my eye I saw Matt go over to a video camera in the corner. I took a shaky breath—at least he wasn't going for security.

"You know how that feels?" I rushed on. "Your daddy screwing girls just a year or two older than you, and everyone in town knowing about it? And my mama was the prettiest girl in Spurlock. But now she hates him, almost as much as I do, at least when she's sober enough to care."

Todd Linson's eyebrows rose. Good sign.

"But you know the crazy part?" I went on. "It didn't even

occur to my mama to leave. She knows he fools around all the time, and she finally caught him right in the act, and even then she didn't think to leave. Nobody in Spurlock ever leaves. It was all I could do to get her to drive me to my beauty pageants in other towns. I won them all, by the way. My mama has no imagination, but I do. I knew right from the start that the pageants were my ticket out. Maybe they weren't as glamorous as your lives, but they paid me money and they got me exposure to the world. I'm the one who said, 'We're going.' My mama would've stayed right there and kept on whining about Daddy's affairs, and he would've kept right on ignoring all of us, and my brother and I would've been stuck forever, and they all would've thought it was normal. But screw that—I'm better than that."

They were all paying attention now, but Todd Linson couldn't take his eyes off me. It really looked like he was on my side. But when I looked toward the back of the room, the big guy's eyes were still completely cold. And I could sense that the fear in the room had gotten stronger, or maybe it was just that it had seeped into my own body and made me scared, too. The red light on the video camera felt like a laser aimed at my head. I blinked, forcing myself to ignore it.

"I don't belong in that place," I said, keeping my eyes on the director. "It must just be some hideous joke that God put me there to begin with. Every day I wake up and expect to find myself living my real life, the one where everybody realizes that I am a million-watt star, and I don't need to jump through hoops trying to outmaneuver rich girls with cushy lives just to get my tiny crumb of approval, the one where I have enough money to buy every single house in Spurlock, Texas, and burn them to the ground. I am not going back there, not ever. I dragged my brother to California with just the clothes he was wearing because I was so sure I could support him, and I will. I can't fail at this; I can't be the one who made a mess of our lives. I'm the one who's supposed to save us."

I locked my gaze onto Todd Linson, making him the center of my world.

"Mr. Linson, I'm asking you to let me test for your show. You won't regret it, I promise. You'll say you knew me when, 'cause I'm not stopping until I'm the biggest star you've ever worked with."

Linson let a small smile curl onto his face. He turned to the casting lady. "C'mon, Geraldine, let's just let her read. If she's got balls like these, it might be interesting."

Got him. I'd done it.

But the woman was shaking her head. "She could be an escaped mental patient for all we know."

"Maybe it's supposed to be a joke," one of the executives said. "Maybe we're all on *Punk'd.*"

"We don't know her, and on top of that, *we don't have a deal with her,*" the casting lady said. She made it sound like that was the worst thing in the world, and maybe it was, because it shut everyone else up.

I tried to think of something to say, some way to spin it, but I was out of ideas. I brushed my hair back over my shoulder slowly, letting my hand linger. Anders Lee's eyes gleamed, but Linson did something I didn't expect—he turned around and looked at the big guy in the suit, reading his face. Waiting for *his* answer.

My breath caught in my throat. The big guy. He was the one. Everybody in the whole room was perfectly still, staring at that man in his pin-striped suit. Even Todd Linson, the famous director. It was *his* show, but I guess it wasn't really his after all.

I'd been playing to the wrong judge.

Linson didn't call the shots—this network executive did. And by making my plea to Linson, I had ignored the most powerful person in the room. A mistake—a huge one. I raised my eyes to look toward the big guy, waiting for his response just like the rest of them.

He didn't move. He didn't even lift an eyebrow. But that was his answer and I knew it.

"Call security," the casting lady said. "She's a psycho."

I wanted to fight, but I didn't know how. I'd never seen people like this before, so cold and tense and serious. They didn't give me anything to work with, and they didn't care how pretty I was. All I could do was run away.

I only made it to the door of the room before the security guards arrived. They weren't fat high-school-dropout security guards like at the Wal-Mart back home in Spurlock. These guys were young and strong and totally serious. I think they maybe even had guns, or at least they acted like it.

Two of them grabbed my arms, one on each side. A third guard walked in front, and still another one followed behind. They acted as if they were dragging me out even though I didn't squirm or resist or anything. I couldn't. I felt sort of stunned. Nobody had ever hated me this much before. No one in my life had ever kicked me out of a room. My head was spinning, but I was clear on one thing at least—I would never, ever tell the truth about myself again. Because in the land of forgetting, the truth is for shit.

"Clear the way!" one of the guards yelled, and then they took me back through the waiting area past all those other actors. The Latina girl from the bathroom met my eyes. She shook her head sadly as if I was the most pathetic human being on earth. The rest of them just watched, fascinated. I swear I saw somebody holding up a cell-phone camera. It was probably the most exciting thing that had ever happened to them at an audition before, seeing somebody get completely humiliated.

I couldn't help myself. My eyes went to Kimber Reeve.

She wasn't looking, the only one in the whole room. Kimber just stared down at her sides, eyebrows scrunched up in concentration as she studied her lines.

*She doesn't want them to realize she knows me.*

The truth hit me like a slap in the face. Kimber was pretending not to see me, not to know me, not to even notice that I was being dragged through the room like a murderer or something. She didn't want to be tainted by me, as if simply acknowledging my presence might cost her the job on *Virgin*.

The rest was a blur. The guards were pulling me down the hallway, past the room with the Xeroxes, into some other elevator. The lead guard was barking a play-by-play into his radio the whole way, as if an entire squadron should be preparing to meet us downstairs. I didn't pay attention; I didn't care. All I could think about was Kimber. She'd told me not to do it. She'd known what a huge mistake I was making. And now she was trying to protect herself from the disaster that was me.

It was that bad. I had fucked up that much. People didn't even want to admit they knew me.

"In here and sit your ass down," the lead guard snapped. The two holding me threw me into a small room with a bunch of monitors along one wall. The female guard from the front desk was waiting there, and she immediately began patting me down, searching for God knows what.

I sat in the folding chair. Somebody popped up with a digital camera and snapped a picture of me with no warning.

"Name?" the leader asked, pulling out a clipboard with some kind of form on it.

"Ingrid," I said.

"Search her bag," he told the female guard. She grabbed my purse and started rifling through it.

"Fine. It's Chloe. Chloe Gamble," I said, just as she pulled out my Texas license.

The guy wrote that down.

"Want me to call the cops?" one of the other guards asked.

The leader was silent for a minute, sucking on his teeth. "Not yet," he finally said. "First we'll give Ms. Gamble a chance to cooperate."

"The cops? Seriously?" I said. I hadn't been expecting that.

"You're trespassing." The leader pulled up another folding chair and sat down across from me. "How'd you get into the lot?"

"I came in for the Leno show."

His eyes narrowed. "Your name's not on that list."

How did he know? He hadn't even checked it. But I just shrugged. He could check the *Tonight Show* list easily enough, and my name wasn't on it.

"Look, either you tell me the truth or I will call the police," he said. "How'd you get in?"

I thought about Klink and his job at the Beaver company and how he had told me to be good to the grunt workers, like him. He thought he'd lose his job just for driving me past the gate. If they found out he was responsible for me, not only would Klink get fired, his boss would probably lose the whole account. Well, I wasn't going to drag them down with me.

"You have one minute to answer me," the lead guard barked.

"I just snuck in," I said. "The security at this place is pathetic, and now you know it. You're welcome."

He kept looking at me, and I looked right back.

"You want me to call you in?" he asked.

"No," I said. "But if you want to, go ahead. I'd love to tell the cops how you felt me up searching for concealed weapons in my miniskirt."

"We had a female guard do a routine pat-down," he said.

I smiled. "Who do you think the cops would rather believe—you or me?" I crossed my legs, letting a lot of skin show just to make my point.

The leader shook his head in disgust. An ink-jet printer spit out my picture and he stuck it onto the form with a clip. He then stood up and tossed the clipboard to one of the other guards. "Put her on the watch list," he said. "And send her name to the other studios."

I felt like someone had hit me between the shoulder blades with a pickax. Every place in town was going to be on the lookout for me. There wasn't an audition in Hollywood I could crash now, even if I'd wanted to.

The lead guard didn't so much as glance at me as he headed for the door. "Get her out of here," he said, and then he was gone.

My two escorts walked me all the way out of the building,

across the parking lot, and through the gate before they let go of my arms. Nobody said another word to me.

The sidewalk was empty, but the guards in the gatehouse were watching. Now that I was alone, I was starting to feel a little nauseated and there was a strange buzzing sensation in my head. I had to get out of there before I puked or started to cry, or both.

Blindly, I went back across the street. I would go back to my hiding spot and wait out these awful feelings. I'd figure out what to do. It couldn't be as bad as it seemed right now. I couldn't have really screwed up my entire Hollywood career before it started.

When I pulled open the door of the Taco Bell, the greasy guy was waiting.

"I knew you'd be back," he said, licking a strand of cheese from his lips.

And then I turned and ran before he could see the tears spill over onto my cheeks.

## Nika Mays's Manuscript Notes: The Legend of Chloe Gamble, Part Two

It's not quite the story of fresh-faced Lana Turner getting discovered while having a soda at Schwab's Drug Store. Chloe Gamble's legend is a little darker, but I've always thought that it was just a sign of how times have changed. Everybody knows Chloe's story because scandal is like catnip to people these days. Back when Lana Turner got discovered, nobody would even have thought of telling the real story. Truth is, she was cutting class and it wasn't Schwab's. But back then, Hollywood wanted to protect its stars. The industry put out glamorous stories, not sordid ones.

Now Hollywood wants dirt. The industry has no use for innocence—it thrives on scandal.

That's why Chloe Gamble's crashing the NBC audition is a legend. Because it was the absolute worst thing that any actress had ever done in the history of the profession of acting. And that made Chloe infamous. Right away, everyone knew what had happened. The story shot through the industry like an injection of adrenaline right to its heart.

Chloe Gamble crashed a network test and got thrown out on her ass.

Sometimes, being infamous is more valuable than being famous.

# chapter five

## Reboot

My feet were aching something fierce by the time I got back to the Oakwood. I could've called a cab, but somehow I found myself walking and walking and walking, as if I might be able to leave the humiliation behind me just by walking away from it. A few people honked at me, and I'm used to guys honking and hollering when they see me. But then one car pulled over and a lady stuck her head out and asked if I was okay. I guess people really don't walk here, 'cause she looked at me like I might be on meth when I said I had just felt like stretching my legs.

I unlocked the black iron gate of the Oakwood, stepped onto the cement-paved pathway, and stopped. Up the staircase on the right was our apartment. It was getting dark. Mama and Travis would be home, waiting on me for dinner. I'd have to tell them where I'd been. I ran through a couple lies in my mind, but I was too tired to pull it off. Travis can't always tell when I'm spinning something, but Mama sure can. She'd dig in and want the whole true story, and if I told it to her, she'd hoot and holler and lord it all over me. She loves it when I get knocked down a peg or two.

Without thinking, I walked on past the staircase and headed for the long, open walkway that ran between three of the buildings. My footsteps echoed off the cement, and the smell of smog-dusted birds of paradise from the courtyards reached my nose. I could dimly hear the sound tracks from old Disney Channel reruns drifting out of apartments as I walked to a cool, shaded area near the back fence of the Oakwood. For the first time since I left NBC, I took a really deep breath.

The day had been endless. I could hardly believe that tomorrow morning I had to get up and drag my butt to St. Paul's. How could I go back to being a regular high school kid after running clear across the country only to crash and burn in the most horrible way imaginable?

Jude opened her door on the second knock, looking kind of breathless.

"Chloe, hey." She frowned. "What happened to you?"

"I'm exhausted," I said. I hadn't even realized it until that very second, but now I felt like my knees might give out, and the hallway of the Oakwood seemed to spin around me.

Jude grabbed my arm and pulled me inside. A long-haired girl was sitting on the sofa with a Coke. I stopped short. "I'm interrupting."

"Nah, we're done," Jude said.

The other girl raised her eyebrows, but she got up and carried her can to the sink. "I guess we are," she said. She left without even introducing herself.

As soon as she was gone, Jude rolled her eyes. "Some people just can't face reality."

"What's reality?" I asked.

"Things end. People move on," Jude said, sounding impatient. I nodded. Some folks may have thought she was being cold, but I figured she was just being realistic. If only more people thought like Jude—and me—the world would have a lot less unnecessary drama.

I sank down onto the sofa and eased off my heels. I had about five blisters. "I walked all the way home from NBC."

"What are you, crazy? That must be five miles."

"One and three quarters according to Google maps," I said. "But it felt like five."

Jude sat down on the other end of the couch. "Want to tell me why?"

"I needed to think," I said. "I might've just ruined my Hollywood career."

"Oh, come on, you don't even have your head shots yet. You don't have a career to ruin," Jude said cheerfully.

"I crashed a network test for *Virgin*."

That wiped the smile off her face. I'd been kinda hoping that it wasn't as bad as I feared, but Jude's reaction told me that it might be even worse.

"Maybe if I dye my hair black and use a different name and stay away from NBC, I can still find work," I said.

"Wow." Jude chewed on her lip. "You didn't . . . did you actually get in there to read?"

"I got in, but they threw me out. Put my name on a list, frisked me, almost called the cops. Everything awful you can think of," I said.

"Wow."

"That's not helping," I said. "You said you'd tell me what to do. What do I do?"

Jude considered it, sizing me up. "You go back home to Bumfuck, Texas," she said.

"No. I'm not going back, ever."

"Good." Jude got up and went over to her desk. "Then you start over from scratch. Here's your contact sheet. Best head shots I've ever taken."

She handed me a sheet of photo paper with about twenty different thumbnails of my face.

"We'll pick two for starters," Jude said. "One sexy, one wholesome. Did you write up your résumé yet?"

"Yeah." I'd done it yesterday evening, the day she told me to.

"We'll get a couple hundred photos printed, put the résumé on the back, and do a mailing to all the agencies and management companies." Jude handed me a little glass cup. "It's a loop—a magnifying glass. Pick your favorite shots. I already picked mine. Then we'll compare."

I held the loop to the contact sheet, then hesitated. I felt a wave of tears coming, and I forced it back down. Crying was for the runners-up—not me. "Is it even worth the effort?" I said. "Can I recover from this?"

"I don't honestly know. I've never heard about anybody doing something so stupid," Jude said. "But here's what I do know—wherever you go, it's all about you. You've got some kind of . . . gravity or something, and it even shows in your pictures."

"Gravity gonna land me a job anytime soon?" I asked.

"Not by itself," Jude said. "You need chops."

"Chops? We headed for a barbecue?"

"Acting experience. We'll find you a coach. Someone to help you smooth the Texas edges." Jude grabbed her PDA and began scrolling through her contacts. "An acting coach, if they are any good, can give you the tools to be a real actress. Then you don't have to rely on crashing auditions to get noticed and get thrown out on your ass again."

"I can't afford a coach," I said.

Jude frowned. "You can figure out how to get into a major studio but you can't finesse a way to get some coaching?"

I shrugged. "After today, I'm not sure I can finesse anything."

"Look, it took balls to break into NBC and it will take balls to keep going even though you almost got arrested," Jude said. "You got to have faith in yourself because, sure as shit, nobody else will."

"It'll take even bigger balls to find a way in next time, now that they know who I am," I said, surprised to find myself laughing.

"Nope. It will take an agent. That's what gets you in the door." Jude gestured to the contact sheet again. "That's what our mailing is for."

I put the loop to the page and began studying my own face. "But who's gonna represent me once they know I'm *blacklisted*?" I asked.

Jude didn't answer. There was no one, and we both knew it.

## Nika Mays's Manuscript Notes: Hollywood Psych

Madonna. Sure, she's over the hill now, but let's use her as an example. She was pretty. She could sing okay. End of story. There were a million other girls out there who were prettier and had better pipes. So why did Madonna become a supernova? Because she Would. Not. Stop. That woman did not take no for an answer. She did anything, anyone, anywhere to become a star. That's what you need to make it huge. I'm not talking about Hilary Duff huge—I'm talking about Miley Cyrus huge. The big, big stars are driven, monomaniacal, eyes-on-the-prize lunatics. There are so many actors in Hollywood who are seriously talented but just haven't made it. Lots of them have nice lives working as perennial guest stars on *Law and Order*. Others play gangsters in every Mafia movie that gets made. Some of them make a fortune by landing a role in a commercial that hits a nerve. There are a few who turn to teaching acting instead of doing it. The musically inclined ones, they might spend their careers singing backup for Janet Jackson.

But the big ones, the really huge stars, they don't settle for a nice life. They've got a focus so sharp that it's almost frightening to behold, and they don't stop until they get what they want: first-name-on-the-call-sheet superstardom.

Psychologists have theories about what drives people like that. Here's my theory: What drives them is a need to escape. It seems to me that there are two things they all want to escape from: their dysfunctional families and their dysfunctional hometowns.

Have you ever wondered why so many people from New Jersey are successful in showbiz? I've never been to the Garden State myself, but look at the list. Bruce Springsteen, Bruce Willis, Whitney Houston, Frank Sinatra, Jon Bon Jovi, Queen Latifah, Ice-T, Jack Nicholson, and Meryl Streep—all are from New Jersey. At some point, each of them must have said, "I have got to get really famous just so I can leave Jersey." Seriously, New Jersey must be the worst place in the world to have spawned so many stars.

Chloe Gamble wasn't from New Jersey, but Spurlock, Texas, couldn't have been much better. And she had the bad family situation covered. But after meeting her, I realized that there was a third thing that drove people toward success: failure. It sounds strange, but if Marlon Brando's career hadn't been in the toilet before he did *The Godfather*, would his comeback have been so brilliant? If Drew Barrymore hadn't been an addict at the age of ten, would her adult success seem so incredible? Is Robert Downey Jr. truly the best actor of his generation, or is it just so astonishing that he's still at it after countless bouts in rehab?

After her NBC debacle, Chloe had her first brush

with cataclysmic failure. That failure, instead of defeating her, became her fuel.

## Stylin'

"Get up, Mama," I said. "Get your ass outta bed!"

My mama grunted and rolled away from me, flinging her arm up to shield her eyes. I knew that move, having seen it about a million times. Nobody wants light shining in her eyes when she still has alcohol coursing through her veins.

I checked the floor. Clean. So I knelt down and took a look under the bed. There it was, a bottle of Bacardi. My mama's drink of choice is wine because she thinks it makes her classy. But if she can't find wine, she'll have whatever's handy. That's how deep her class runs.

"Where'd you get this, Mama?" I asked. "Rum makes you sick."

"Only in the daytime," my mama mumbled.

I rolled my eyes and reached for the Bacardi. There was about an inch of liquid left in the bottle. "I'm dumping the rest," I said, then ran to the bathroom with my mama on my heels. The absolute best way to get her out of bed is to threaten to dump her booze. But she's slow when she has a hangover, so I can always get to the toilet before her. I was already pouring out the rum by the time she grabbed my hand.

"Goddamnit, Clo, what'd you go and do that for?" she said.

"You reek. Get in the shower," I told her.

"That's disrespectful," she muttered as she stepped into the tub.

"Your shirt's still on," I said.

My mama pulled her blouse off and tossed it onto the bathroom floor, and then, without bothering to take off her bra, she sank down into the basin moaning and cradling her aching head.

"We used up the last of the Excedrin," I said, turning the water on full blast. She cursed when the spray hit her, but she didn't have the energy to climb out.

"I don't know why I ever let you drag me out here where I don't know nobody," she blubbered. When it comes to my mama, teary self-pity always follows a bender. Her mascara was running in long black streaks down her face. I was amazed at how many times I had seen my mother in this same pose. I was also amazed at how much I didn't care.

"I'll make you some coffee," I said.

By the time I got back with the steaming mug, Mama was clean and getting dressed. We'd gone on a tactical mission to the Target in Van Nuys, and each one of us now had three different (and inexpensive) outfits to wear. Well, Travis and I both had to wear a sort of uniform to school, but I guess that counted as an outfit even if it was boring. I still got more eye traffic than any other girl at St. Paul's.

"Chloe, we're late," Trav called from the living room. "You coming?"

"I can't," I called back. "I got an audition."

My brother stuck his head in the room, ignoring Mama. "You do not," he said.

"Well, I got business to take care of," I said. "Can you tell the office I'm at a meeting? I turned all my homework in yesterday." We'd been in school for two weeks now, and I was bored already. A day off wouldn't hurt. I'd finished all my reading for the month and done my calculus homework through the end of the textbook. What was the point of sitting in class if I could figure out the work on my own?

"How are you going to get to a meeting if I take the car to school?" Travis asked.

"Mama and I have some business to attend to," I said.

"We do?" Mama ran a brush through her wet hair.

"Yeah, we do."

Travis raised his eyebrows, but he didn't say anything. He just grabbed the car keys off the dresser, gave me a wave, and left. I went over to the closet and pulled out the deep blue evening dress that I'd rescued from the trunk of the Ford. It was in the pageant bag that I'd left there after the Miss Abilene Princess win. I'd steamed it in the shower while Mama was out drinking and it looked good as new. I'm always real careful not to get makeup or sweat stains on my pageant gowns because the dry-cleaning bills are so high.

"You mind telling me what you're up to?" Mama said as I slipped the beaded gown over my head.

The dress was cut on a bias, low in the back with slits way up the sides. I referred to it as my "hooker at cotillion" gown and it worked really, really well with judges. They liked a little naughty mixed in with their nice. I'd sewn the gown myself, so it fit me like a second skin.

"Showing off," I said. "Let's go."

"It's eight in the morning," Mama said. "You look like you just came home after getting laid on prom night."

"You drink rum with that mouth?" I said as I ushered her out into the open-air hall. I dragged Mama to an adjacent building. I checked a business card in my hand and knocked on unit 3-C. It belonged to an anorexic-looking gal in her mid-twenties. She had black eyeliner on and short red hair. She looked me up and down. "Nice dress."

"Thanks. My mama made it," I lied. "I'm Chloe Gamble and this is my mother, Earlene."

"Call me Early," Mama said, shooting me a look as she reached out to shake hands. She hadn't made the dress, but she could have. She's the one who taught me to sew, and she used to make my gowns back when I first started the pageant circuit. She stopped doing that once she'd gotten me to where I could do it on my own, which was the whole reason she taught me in the first place. But Mama wasn't stupid enough to call me out on a lie in front of somebody else.

"I'm Meg," the anorexic girl said. "Come on in. You're an actress?"

"I will be," I said.

"Well, you look good but not appropriate," Meg said. "I can help you figure out what to wear and *when* to wear it."

Mama looked deeply confused. "Meg here's a *stylist*, Mama," I said.

"Huh," my mama said. "Sounds expensive."

Meg looked a little offended.

"Do you have a lot of clients?" I asked as we went into the studio apartment.

"I've got about five or six girls I dress. I only do private clients in between jobs," Meg said. "During the season I work on *Fast Boys*."

Mama gasped. "That biker show?"

"Yeah, I'm a wardrobe assistant," she said. "But the show's on hiatus now so I pick up whatever work I can."

"What about when you go back to your full-time gig?" I asked. "I guess you need some help then, keeping your private clients happy?"

"Sorry?" Meg looked confused.

"Well, if you're working full-time on a show, how do you have time to be a stylist for other people?"

"Oh. Um, I smoke a lot of cigarettes and drink a lot of coffee." Meg shoved a pile of handbags to the side of her couch and gestured for us to sit.

"If you had an assistant, maybe you could take it a little easier," I said. "My mama is looking for work."

I expected a squawk from Mama, but she just stared at me through narrowed eyes. Meg was the one who squawked.

"Are you kidding? I can barely pay the rent with what I make myself," she said. "I can't afford to pay somebody else."

"But if you had Mama to help you, you'd have more clients and more money," I said. "She can sew, and she can design really well, too. You said you like my dress—she made it."

Meg was on her way back to the door. "Yeah, it's great. But I'm looking for clients, not help. Sorry."

As I followed Mama back outside, Meg gave me a little half smile. "If you ever really do want a stylist, you call me."

"Sure." I didn't bother saying no, but why would I need somebody to tell me what to wear? I could do that in my sleep.

Mama was already stomping back toward our place. "We've got more appointments, Mama," I called.

"Maybe *you* do," she said. "I ain't looking for no piecework, Clo!"

"What else you gonna do? You can't type for shit and you don't even have a high school diploma. You want to be a waitress?"

"Your daddy never expected me to work," Mama snapped. "Maybe I'll just go back home."

"Might be a little crowded with all the twenty-year-old

sluts lying around the house, don't you think? Daddy hasn't even so much as called you! He's probably glad we're gone," I said. Mama's eyes welled up, but it didn't stop me. "You know how to sew, Mama. And Lord knows we need the cash."

"You didn't know me back in the day. . . ." Mama said.

"What day was that? When you were sixteen and got knocked up by Daddy?"

Mama's eyes narrowed. "I won sewing contests at the 4-H! Where you think that Singer came from? Nobody bought me that—it was first prize! I could do that skinny girl's job. I don't need to *assist* nobody." Mama pouted.

"Tell you what, you tell your glory days story to"—I looked at the second business card in my hand—"Amanda Pierce."

Mama sulked all the way upstairs and turned her back to me as I knocked on the next door. This time the woman who opened it was the opposite of anorexic—she was probably two bills and wearing a shirt cut low enough to reveal cleavage the size of Palo Duro Canyon back in Texas. Her hair was a mess of blond piled on top of her head, with a couple of purple streaks running from her temples all the way to the ends. She wore bright red lipstick, black nail polish, and a frown.

"Chloe Gamble?" she said.

"Mm-hmm, we spoke last night," I said. "This is my mama, Earlene."

Mama didn't offer to shake hands with this one. She just stared in horror. My mama has a thing about overweight people—she hates them. But I had to give Amanda credit—she looked just as appalled as Mama did. She looked my mama straight in the eye, and then she leaned in and *sniffed* her.

"Just what the hell do you think you're doin'?" Mama demanded.

"You're sweating rum," Amanda said.

"Am not!" Mama's voice was a full octave higher than usual, but I was impressed. Two seconds, and this lady had called it right.

Amanda shrugged. "It takes more'n a shower to lose the smell—it leaks out of your pores if you've had enough. I know from experience." She turned to me. "Honey, why are you wearing an evening gown?"

"I thought I'd show off what my mama can do," I said. "She made it."

Amanda looked it over, then circled her finger in the air, signaling for me to spin around. I did, but slowly, letting Amanda take in the full effect of the backless gown.

"Nice cut," she said. "Let me see the stitching."

I stepped closer and she grabbed the strap, lifted it off my shoulder, and checked the hem. Then she ran her chubby hands down the bodice and pinched at the fabric under my breasts.

"The bodice is the hardest part to get right," she said by way of explanation.

I knew that, but I just nodded. "That's what my mama says."

"This works." Amanda let go of me and shot an appraising glance at Mama.

"Well, of course. I know what I'm doin'." My mama had the nerve to sound offended, as if she'd really made my dress herself.

"You'd better sit down, Gamble girls," Amanda said. "Though I don't think you're here for a stylist, are you?"

"Chloe don't need to be dressed like *that*," Mama said, sneering at Amanda's ankle-length skirt and low-cut blouse.

"A stylist tailors the wardrobe to the person she's dressing. No reason a hot little thing like Chloe would want to dress like me," Amanda said. "She needs a younger look with just a hint of sex and a touch of schoolgirl. And *you* need to dress your age."

Before Mama could come back at Amanda, I jumped in. "You were right, Amanda. I don't want a stylist. I . . . we . . . can't afford one. My mama is trying to find work and I thought you might need someone to help with sewing."

Amanda wandered over to her fridge, pulled out a Diet Coke, and popped it open. She was thinking, I could tell. I looked around the place. It was a mess, with racks of clothes filling the living room and bolts of fabric heaped on the kitchen table.

"Are you on a show?" I asked.

She shook her head. "I do wardrobe for a few indie films here and there, but mostly I have private clients. I'll do personal shopping, closet management, anything the Beverly Hills wives want me to do. Occasionally I travel with a client, if they've got a premiere or a tour and they'll be in the public eye. Some girls want me to create a look for them, but they don't trust themselves to keep it up without me."

"I'm not like that," I said.

"No, I can see you're not." She grinned at me and grabbed a rice cake off the counter, washing it down with her diet soda.

"People really hire you to do all that crap?" my mama asked, still giving Amanda the stink-eye.

"Enough people that I could probably use some help," Amanda said.

I relaxed a little. She'd made her decision. "So you'll take on my mama?"

"Not so fast. I'll need to see some more sample dresses, maybe a blouse or two. An audition, let's call it."

Mama snorted. "You gonna pay me for that?"

"Sure." Amanda shrugged. "I'll pay you by the hour. If I like what I see, there'll be more work later on."

"Twenty bucks an hour," my mama said.

Amanda chuckled. "Minimum wage. I said I could use help, but I'm not minting money out of my ass."

"Done deal," I said before Mama could say something about Amanda's backside that she'd be sorry for. "You got anything to sew right now? Mama wants to start today."

"It's pilot season—I've got clients to dress for auditions

every day," Amanda said. "There's always something to sew."

"Great." I gave my mama a big smile. "Have fun, Mama!"

She was ready to throttle me, I could tell. "Where do you think you're goin'?" she asked.

"I go to high school, remember?" I backed out of the apartment before Mama could grab my arm. Last thing I saw was her face, puckered up like she'd been sucking lemons. Just being alone in a room with an overweight, purple-haired lady was about the worst thing my mama could imagine. Having to take orders from her on top of it might be more than Mama could handle.

Well, too bad. If I'd learned anything from my bad network test, it was this: I wasn't going to be getting work anytime soon. My mama would just have to step up and try something new—like being a mama.

## E-mail from Travis Gamble

What's up, Coop? Sorry I didn't answer you last night—I can only check e-mail when I'm in the school library. When Chloe's around, I use her BlackBerry, but she's been MIA a lot lately. Not sure what's up with her—she seems almost depressed. But I have to be imagining that, right? You know my sister—she thinks depression is only for rich girls from Dallas. Anyway, I don't know what could be making her sad here in La-La Land—the weather is always perfect, the girls are always smokin', and the soccer is freaking unbelievable. Get this—our coach used to play for Brazil back when they won the

World Cup. Dude actually has drinks with Ronaldo sometimes. I'm telling you, Coop, I was the shit back in Spurlock, but here I really have to work for it. My teammates are scary good. (But you know I'm still the best!) There are two guys up from Peru on student visas and they play year-round, so I'm thinking I'll do summer club soccer with them when school ends. This St. Paul's place is fancy (Clo says it's "preppy"), so they can afford to pay ass-kicking coaches and import talent on scholarship. You know, like me and my sister!

This is seriously the way to start at a new school: Have your sister make such a huge scene to get you in that you are instantly famous. My first day, everybody already knew who I was, my teammates had already Googled my stats from our games, and the two hottest girls in my chem class wanted to know why they couldn't find me on Facebook. Oh, yeah—the girls are fighting over me because I'm the new guy. Nice, right? Remember how Chloe was like the star of Spurlock High, everyone wanting to get with her? I'm getting a little taste of that here. And Clo was right—it's better to be in the spotlight than behind it.

But I don't have to settle for high school chicks anymore. I have a date tomorrow with that actress, Livia. Jealous yet?

Gotta book—I'm late for work. Yeah, that's right, *work*. More on that later.

## Coaching

I turned off my BlackBerry as soon as I had called a cab to pick me up outside the gates of the Oakwood. Mama would probably spend the whole day trying to call me just to bitch about her having to pull her own weight for once, and I wasn't in the mood to listen. When the taxi showed up, I gave the driver the address Jude had written down for me a few days ago. It turned out to be a strip mall in Studio City, a few miles away from the Oakwood. The driver naturally assumed I was headed for the Starbucks in the middle of the row of stores and pulled up in front. But the place I was looking for was up a set of stairs on the second floor above the coffee shop.

I climbed up the concrete steps and pulled open the door marked THE ALAN LEIBER STUDIO.

As soon as the glass door swung closed behind me, I felt a sort of calmness surround me. The lighting was soft in here, and the floors were covered in a spongy carpet. A few paintings hung on the cream-colored walls, and three big, soft couches were arranged into a sitting area in the corner.

Nine or ten people sat on the couches, a few of them talking, a few of them reading, and one sound asleep.

I went over there, picked out a blandly good-looking blond boy, and put on my sexiest smile. "Hi, I'm Chloe Gamble."

"Will Crayton," he said, instantly sitting up straighter.

"Can you help me, Will? I'm looking for an acting coach, and my friend said this was the best place to go."

Will nodded. "Yeah, Alan is a legendary teacher. But I don't know if he's taking anybody new."

"Our class starts in ten minutes," the stunning redhead next to him said. "He and Suzanne are probably in the office getting themselves organized." She pointed out a door on the other side of the lobby.

"Thanks." I gave her my best I'm-a-country-girl-just-off-the-turnip-truck smile. Never hurts to get girls on your side. Then I headed over and knocked on the door.

Alan Leiber opened it. I knew it was him right away, because he gave off an air of control. Not like he was a dictator, the way Daddy sometimes got when he'd had a few too many, but a sort of confidence that told me he was in charge.

"Hi, I'm Chloe Gamble," I said. "I need an acting coach, and I heard you were the best in Los Angeles."

Alan smiled, the tanned skin around his eyes crinkling up. "Well, my wife's pretty good, too. I'd say it's a tie."

"If that makes you feel better, say it," the woman at the desk behind him said with a grin. She was small and thin, maybe forty, maybe fifty.

"I'm Alan and that's Suzanne." Alan took my hand, not really shaking it, but holding it for a few seconds. He kept his eyes on mine, and I knew he was trying to read me. I let him, because I was doing the same to him. He looked kind of familiar. Jude had said he used to be an actor, but I couldn't remember seeing him in anything specific.

"I have to find work, fast," I told him. "So I need someone to teach me how to audition."

Suzanne took off her black-framed glasses and propped them in her short, spiky hair. "Not how to *act*, just how to audition?"

I nodded. "I messed up a big network test a couple weeks back, and that can't happen again. I can't pay you yet, but once I get a job I will."

"Slow down," Alan said. "We're booked solid for coaching, but you can take classes. But the rule here is everybody pays."

"I don't need a class," I said.

"Classes are step one. Coaching is step two," Suzanne put in. "Don't be so sure you can skip the steps. That may be why you messed up your audition."

"Come in and audit this class. That's free. We can talk more afterward." Alan got up and led the way across the lobby—with everyone from the couches following him like baby ducks—and into a long, narrow room. It was painted black, even the ceiling and the floor, and the only furniture was a bunch of folding chairs and some black wooden cubes that I guessed were some type of all-purpose scenery.

"Let's begin with Cristina," Alan said.

The gorgeous redhead I had spoken with sat on a cube on the small stage while everybody else watched her from the folding chairs in the audience. I slipped into an empty seat near the door.

"Remember, Cristina," Alan said from the front row. "It may be a monologue, but you're talking to *somebody*. Figure out who you're aiming this speech at, and make it feel like one side of a conversation. And, I don't have to remind you—"

"KEEP IT SIMPLE!" everyone in the room, except me, said in unison.

Cristina nodded, took a deep breath, and started reciting lines.

That's what it was, *reciting*. After a minute I realized that I wasn't even listening to the words. I had no idea who Cristina was supposed to be talking to, because she wasn't talking to anybody—she was just repeating lines she had memorized. She was beautiful; she had to be a model. Her skin and hair were flawless, but no one in the audience was even looking at her face. Cristina was so nervous, she kept bobbing her green high heels up and down, so everyone in the class, including Alan, could do nothing but stare at her perfect ankles.

When I heard a smattering of applause, I felt a jolt of surprise. I had no idea her monologue had ended.

Cristina and all the other students immediately turned to face their teacher.

"You lost us," Alan said. "You're mouthing the words, but you're not in any way connected to them. Why should we listen to you if you're not even listening to yourself?"

*Because she's stunning,* I thought, amused. *She thinks we'll sit still for anything as long as she looks seductive.*

"I listen to myself," Cristina said, tears collecting at the corners of her eyes.

"Cristina, can you tell me what you're feeling right this moment?" Alan said in a very gentle way.

"Frustrated."

Alan pointed at Cristina and smiled. "Right there. That was an honest and simple moment. You were really connected to what you were feeling. Next time, I want you to do the monologue again, but have the character feel the same frustration you feel right now."

Cristina's lovely face was confused as she went back to her seat. I bet it had never occurred to her that there was more to acting than being pretty.

"Let's hear from Del next," Alan said. He turned in his seat to look at me. "We run through everybody's monologues at the beginning, and then we'll break into smaller teams to work on some acting exercises. After that, we tackle scene work."

I nodded as if I knew what he was talking about.

Del was up in front now, an older gentleman with strange curly gray hair and a pointy nose. Not what I'd been expecting after Cristina the model. But when he started talking, I couldn't take my eyes off him. He was telling a story about a dog he'd once had when he was homeless and how the dog got sick. Three minutes in, I practically had to pull out a Kleenex to blow my nose. My eyes were teary and there was a lump in my throat, and when Del said, "Scene," it took me a minute to figure out that he hadn't been telling his own life story; he was acting out a scene from a play. Cristina was drop-dead gorgeous, but I was suddenly jealous of old guy Del.

"Excellent!" Alan said.

"Is Del a professional actor?" I asked the guy sitting next to me.

"He works all the time," the guy said. "Character stuff. He's one of Suzanne's coaching clients."

By the time everyone in class had gone through all of the monologues, I'd figured it out. The really pretty ones, like Cristina, were the same as the pageant princesses back home. They knew how attractive they were, they knew everybody wanted to get with them, and they assumed that their looks were dazzling enough to conceal the fact that they were lazy and uninteresting. The pageant princesses had been wrong about that, and these actors were wrong, too. Sure, everybody did want to get with them, but only *before* they went on stage.

Then there were the "character actors" like Del. "Character" seemed to be code for "Not Very Attractive." Those people were the best ones in the room. They didn't seem self-conscious getting up in front of an audience, not even the poor soul with the super-bad acne scars on her face. And they seemed to disappear into the part they were playing, so much so that you stopped thinking they were *actors*.

And finally there were people like the bland boy from the lobby, Will. Good-looking but not stunning, full of confidence the way a cheerleader or a class president or a golden retriever is, and just as boring. Those were the hardest monologues to sit through. At least with the stunners, you could watch them, see how they did their makeup and their hair, but the Wills in the room were just store brand.

I was only two hours into my first acting class and I had already decided what type of actress I wanted to be. And I also discovered I had a long, long way to go to get there.

"Chloe Gamble." Alan's voice broke into my thoughts. "Let's see what you've got."

I didn't have anything prepared and he knew it. I hadn't been expecting to take a class today. But I could tell from the way he and Suzanne were watching me that this was some kind of test.

Everyone's eyes swiveled toward me. I was the new girl, some lowly wannabe actress auditing their class; I shouldn't be taking up their precious stage time. I sensed that some of them, a few of the girls, wanted me to crash and burn. I took my time getting up to the front of the room so I could think. I wondered if I should whip out one of the Shakespeare soliloquies my English teacher back in Spurlock had had us memorize. But Lady Macbeth seemed a little out of place here, even though I thought my Lady Macbeth was kick-ass.

"This is from a pilot called *Virgin*," I said when I got to the front. "It's not long, but it's kind of a monologue." I had memorized the sides from my disastrous network test. The problem was, there was supposed to be the Anders Lee father character speaking in between some of my lines. But it didn't really matter. My character was a girl yelling at her dad, so I figured the dialogue would work well enough if I just strung it all together. Plus, like Alan had said, even though I was doing a monologue, I had to pretend that I was talking to somebody. That part was easy. I would be speaking directly to my worthless daddy.

I glanced at Alan. He had a little smile on his face, and I knew I'd passed the test just by having the stones to get up on stage.

"I'm not me anymore. I'm someone else. . . ." My voice sounded hollow in the black room.

If I had been singing a song, every note I had sung had been flat. My mouth felt dry. I tried not to panic.

"Can I start over?" I asked.

"Never," Alan said. "If you don't like where you're going, you have to find your way back."

*Whatever the hell that means*, I thought. In the audience I could see that Cristina and some of her model friends sensed blood in the water. I refused to give them the satisfaction of my failure. I had dealt with the same type of girls in every pageant in all those tobacco-stained Holiday Inns in Texas, and I'd learned to block them out. I took a deep breath and forced myself to picture my father flirting with that little tramp in Abilene.

"I'm not me anymore. I'm someone else. And this new

person, this other me, isn't connected to you anymore. I've cut myself free. You know those photos hanging in the hallway and framed on your desk? Next time you look at them, all you'll see is you standing alongside a stranger, someone you never got to know. Don't look so sad, Daddy. You haven't lost a thing. You never had a daughter. It was all just a bad dream. . . ."

I stopped. That was all of the sides I could remember. At some point during my performance I had closed my eyes, and as I slowly opened them, I became aware of the class staring at me in silence. The room, all the people, the fearful silence— it was just like the network test. I'd fucked up again. Blood rushed to my cheeks, and I sank down onto the black cube behind me.

"All right!" Will yelled. Suddenly everybody was clapping, and Del let out a long whistle. Even Cristina and her model friends reluctantly applauded.

"Ms. Gamble, very nice," Alan said. "Not bad for day one."

"Really?" I couldn't process the applause. "I'm not even sure what the rest of the story was about. I only saw two pages."

"Did that matter?" Suzanne said, addressing the other students.

"Not at all," Del said. "It really seemed like she connected with the scene."

"You have no idea," was all I could think to say.

"And, best of all, you kept it simple," Alan said, as if this was the ultimate compliment. "Nice work."

"Nice work" didn't seem like the most glowing review, but right at that moment, they were the two best words in the world.

We split into teams after that and did some weird exercise where you say something and your partner repeats it back, over and over again. I don't know what it was supposed to accomplish, but I do know my partner, Will, was psyched to be spending so much time with me. When the class was finally over, he followed me to the door. "You want to grab a coffee?" he said.

"Sorry, I have to go talk to Alan and Suzanne," I said.

"I could hang out," Will offered.

"I'm sixteen."

"Oh." Will looked like he'd been hit in the face with a wet mop.

"Still interested?"

"Um, maybe I'll catch you back in class sometime," Will said as he sidled away from me.

I hated to lower the boom on a basically nice guy, but what would be the point in hooking up with him? If he'd been a director or a producer or an agent—or anybody who could help me find work—maybe I would've suddenly been eighteen years old and flirted with him over coffee.

I know how it seems—like I'm a gold digger or a whore. Maybe I'm both, but as I see it, I'm practical. What am I supposed to be after? Love? Romance? Was that what my mama was looking for when she hooked up with my skirt-chasing, hard-drinking, air conditioner–repairing daddy? If so, then I'll take a pass, thank you very much.

Here's the God's honest truth—I've seen pictures of my mama when she was my age, and she was a darn sight prettier than me. She could have gone anywhere, done anything—she had all this power, and the saddest thing is, she didn't know it. So she hooked up with the first steer rider with a big, shiny belt buckle she could get her hands on and got herself knocked up with me and Trav by the time she was sixteen. So if I seem like a gold-digging whore, maybe it's because I have no intention of repeating my mama's mistakes.

Travis has a theory that when people say "love," what they mean is "hormones." I have to agree with him. About a year ago, I bought a box of condoms and decided to lose my virginity to a cute guy at school who I liked well enough. Guess I wanted to see what all the fuss was about. While this cute guy was grunting and groaning and ramming his pointy hips into me, he kept whispering, "I love you, Chloe. I love you." Wish I could tell you it was magical or life changing. It was neither. It wasn't half bad, but it absolutely wasn't "love."

So when I looked out the window and saw Will chatting up the redheaded Cristina, I realized he wasn't really looking for love when he asked me for coffee. I guess everybody out there is digging for some kind of gold.

I headed for the acting studio office. Alan and Suzanne were inside, heads together, talking quietly. I knocked on the open door.

"Chloe, we're just discussing you," Suzanne said.

*Nice work,* I thought. I felt something rising inside of me. I didn't recognize the feeling for a moment. It wasn't the way I felt when I won a pageant. That was always an unsatisfying feeling, like I had climbed to the top of a mountain and saw another even higher peak right behind the one I was on. This felt more like I had arrived at the top of Everest. Then I figured out what this strange feeling was—happiness.

"Thanks for letting me audit the class," I said. "It was a lot different than I imagined."

"How was it different?" Suzanne asked.

"Some of the people sucked and some of them were awesome. And I need to be awesome if I want to get work."

Alan laughed. "You do have a one-track mind," he said. "I wouldn't want to play poker with you."

"You'd lose," I said.

Now Suzanne laughed also. "You'll need that kind of thinking if you're going to work in Hollywood. But don't ever apply it to your friends or your coaches. You aren't competing with the whole world."

"My coaches?" I said.

"You said you can't afford classes. Maybe you'd be willing to make a trade," Suzanne said. "Our assistant just left to do an indie film in Charlotte, and we haven't replaced him yet. How about this: You work the front desk for us two days a week, and we let you take the intro class for free."

"What about private coaching?" I asked. "Can I trade for that, too?"

"Chloe, do you have any real acting experience?" Alan asked.

"No, just beauty pageants," I said. "But I certainly have been up on stage."

"Halle Berry started out as a beauty queen, too," he said. "But she didn't jump straight from that to winning an Oscar. She learned the craft first, and you have to do the same thing."

"I don't have time to take a million classes. I need to work," I said.

"You won't get work unless you can deliver," Alan said. "Today, when you were doing your monologue, was it the same as competing in a pageant?"

"No." I thought for a moment. "I had to use somebody else's words. I couldn't just pretend to be whoever I needed to be to win."

"But you brought something of yourself to that monologue as well, and that's what made it feel so true," Suzanne said.

"Now you have to learn to do that even when the monologue doesn't hit so close to home for you," Alan chimed in. "When you're portraying a character who's got a disability or one with a happy family or one who's older, richer, dumber, uglier than you are . . . It takes *craft* to pull that off. Don't you think?"

I didn't answer. Truth was, I'd only ever played versions of myself at beauty pageants.

"Being charismatic, making people watch you—that part you've got down," Alan went on. "But you need training to be a good actress."

"It will serve you better in the long run," Suzanne said, cutting me off before I could protest. "You want success and you want it right this minute. But if you want a *long* career, you'd better know how to act."

"Okay," I said. "But I want to trade for the acting classes *and* the coaching. Both."

They exchanged a look. "Tell you what—you let us know when you set up an audition and we'll discuss coaching then. In the meantime, take classes. Allow yourself to be an actor, not just a star waiting to happen," Alan said.

"I can't work here until after school," I said.

"That's fine," Suzanne said. "It's not too demanding. You'll be able to get some homework done."

"And I'm never playing poker with you," Alan said.

I smiled and said, "Thanks." When I got to the office door, I turned back. There was something comforting about the two of them, even if they did talk about a lot of stuff I didn't understand. This was the first place I'd been able to relax—other than Jude's apartment—since we got to Los Angeles. "Really. Thanks a lot."

During the cab ride back to the Oakwood, I closed my eyes and replayed the *Virgin* monologue in my head. It probably only took me two minutes to say the whole thing, but for those two minutes I hadn't been thinking about NBC or Todd Linson or that big guy in the suit. I hadn't been worrying about Travis or how to pay next month's rent. I hadn't been scheming or planning or trying to figure out my next move.

I hadn't been thinking at all. It was like some other person had taken over my body and somebody else had come up with the words to say. I just had to sit back and let it happen.

It was awesome, and I was going to learn how to do it better than anyone.

There was a grin on my face as I climbed up the stairs to our apartment. I went straight through the living room and out onto the balcony. If you looked down, you saw the parking lot, but if you looked up, you could see the sun shining through the hazy smog, making for some real moody and beautiful sunsets. I was just in time to catch today's. I leaned on the railing and watched the sky turn pink and orange, and I let myself bask in the gooey feeling that everything would be okay. I'd learn how to act while my mama would help pay the rent and Travis got a soccer scholarship to college. It would all work out fine.

The sound of yelling brought my eyes back down to earth.

A car was stopped in the parking lot below me—a shiny little convertible 3 Series BMW, so new that it still had temporary registration papers taped to the windshield. The top was down, so I could hear Kimber Reeve hollering at her boyfriend. Musician Max with the dreadlocks was trying to fight back, but Kimber wasn't having any. She had one hand on the wheel and the other pointing toward the passenger door. Max climbed out of the car and pulled his guitar out of the backseat.

I couldn't hear the exact words they were saying, but from the body language it looked as if poor Max had been kicked to the curb.

I could tell Kimber didn't care. She barely even waited for him to step back before she peeled out in her glistening new Beemer.

Forget the sunset and the stupid acting classes. Forget Mama supporting us. Forget every single happy thought I'd had. My whole body filled with rage. That girl—that rich, lucky girl with her bond-trader daddy and her snob of a mama—that girl had the life I wanted. The life I was going to get, no matter what.

I could tell by her new convertible 3 Series that Kimber Reeve had landed the role on *Virgin*. She was now a star.

# chapter six

## E-mail from Travis Gamble

Coop, man, you have got to get your ass out here. You can't even believe what's going on! Remember I told you about Livia, that actress? Well, she is one freaky chick. She's smoking hot, right, and she seems really into me. But I still haven't seen the inside of her Oakwood apartment. Maybe she's a tease. Whatever. Anyway, she wants us to go to some big party she got on the guest list for, but we need fake IDs to get in. I guess it's a party in a bar or something—who ever heard of being carded at a party? So Livia takes me to Chinatown to buy some fake driver's licenses. Dude, it's like another country. All the signs are in Chinese, and forget about finding someone who speaks English. I started to freak out a little, like, how am I supposed to know where to go? It's not as if we're doing something legal! But Livia got the name of this place from some makeup artist, and we go there and it's a cell-phone store. As soon as we walk in, the two guys who work there know right away why we're there and they whip out a camera and take license pictures and then just stick our faces into this computer program they've got. It's set up to randomly generate fake names and addresses. So we fork over some cash (remind me to tell you where I got the cash, BTW) and they hand us our fake IDs. Whole thing took maybe half an hour.

Then Livia wants to get dumplings. Dim sum, she calls it. So we go to this restaurant, which is like a gigantic cafeteria, and it's filled with people on lunch break. The waiters walk around with carts and you get all kinds of different dumplings, and you're supposed to eat them with chopsticks but I'm lame so I asked for a fork. I have no clue what I was eating but it was GOOD! Then, while I'm still eating, Livia climbs onto my lap! Can you believe that? In front of a hundred people, she's kissing my neck and chewing on my ear and shit. I'm telling you, freaky. She's fucking hot.

I can't wait for that party.

# Hope

Mama wasn't home when I got back to the Oakwood after my first day of work at the acting studio, so I headed out to the pool. I hadn't been out there since my crash and burn at NBC—I hadn't wanted to see Kimber and her smug smile. But

I was feeling okay again now that I proved to myself I could act. Two students had come up to me at the desk today to say they heard about my *Virgin* monologue. Nobody else got real applause for a monologue in that class, and I bet nobody else got to trade work for classes. I had kick-ass head shots and a class with the best teachers in town. I could deal with Kimber Reeve. Now that she had the job on *Virgin*, I was certain she would somehow come find me to rub it in. And I'd handle it, because knowing what to expect is halfway toward winning the battle.

Kimber wasn't there. But Travis was, and he had two hot girls with him.

"Trav, what the hell?" I said. "Don't you have soccer?"

"I decided to blow it off," he said, but before I could smack him, he laughed. "Chill, Clo. Coach had a teachers' meeting so there's no practice today."

My dense brother didn't seem to notice that his girlfriends were giving me the cold shoulder. I beamed at them. "Travis is so darn rude—he never remembers to introduce me," I said. "I'm his twin sister, Chloe."

"Sorry. This is Livia and Amber," Trav said. "They're actresses, too."

"Hey," said Livia, the dark-haired one. Amber just glanced up from her magazine, then looked back down. Neither of them even pretended to be happy to meet me. At least Kimber had been smart enough to fake politeness.

I pushed Travis's feet aside and sat on the end of his lounge chair. Livia frowned. So she was the one who'd claimed him.

"What are y'all up to?" I asked.

"Party tonight," Travis said. "Some big Hollywood thing, right, Liv?"

Livia nodded. "It's at Ibiza. Hayden Panettiere is going to be there."

"You should come with us, Clo," Travis said.

Livia's mouth dropped open. Amber put down her *Us Weekly* and shook her head. "No way."

I didn't bother arguing. Travis was offended enough for both of us. "Scuse me?" he said, his voice cold.

Livia shot Amber an annoyed look. "It was hard to get on the list," she told Travis. "It's not really cool to bring along extra people."

"Then we'll have to be uncool," Travis said. "I'm going. She's going."

Livia finally put on a fake smile for me. "It doesn't work like that. I'm sure *you* understand, don't you, Chloe?"

"Not really," I lied. What I understood was that these girls didn't want me at their precious party. But if it was a Hollywood party, I was going. "Aren't y'all friends with the hosts?"

Amber huffed and went back to reading, leaving Livia to deal with the situation. "It's not that kind of party. It's being hosted by Nike. We just got onto the guest list. . . ."

"Oh! Well, if you don't have the pull to get us both in, don't you worry about it," I said.

"I didn't say that," Livia snapped.

"Chloe could meet Hollywood people, folks who can help her get started," Travis said. "If you're only allowed to bring one guest, it should be Chloe. I can stay home."

My brother didn't know it, but right at that moment Livia had to decide just how into him she was. Enough to bring a hot girl to a party, even though she wanted to be the hottest girl there?

"No, it's okay," Livia said. "You can both come."

Huh. She must have liked Travis more than I'd figured, although she didn't bother trying to sound gracious. I didn't pay her no mind—I couldn't care less about Livia.

I had my first Hollywood party to think about.

## Nika Mays's Manuscript Notes: The Assistant Network

It takes about two weeks in Hollywood to figure out who's really important. A big movie producer is important, true. But the big movie producer's assistant is even more important. Ditto for the hotshot agent's assistant, for the TV show-runner's assistant, for the movie star's assistant . . . and on and on. These assistants aren't actually powerful on their own, but they are imbued with power by the people they work for. If you want access to said producer, agent, show-runner, or star, well, you'd better get his assistant on your side. Here's what people don't realize: When a player reaches a certain level in Hollywood, he ceases to be a functioning human being. An assistant enters the appointments into the player's BlackBerry, sets a reminder into the scheduling database, and programs the address into the GPS, so all the player has to do is obey what his smart phone tells him. Assistants also drop off the dry cleaning to the French laundry, supervise the housecleaning staff as they polish the Cristoffe silver, take the player's kids to the Crossroads School, and walk the player's maltipoo in Beverly Glen Park.

If the bigwig is truly big, she will have a whole army of assistants—one for work, one for home, one to go on location, one to man the office, one for whatever sexual fetish the bigwig can think of. Being a Hollywood assistant is a thankless job that usually involves enduring continuous abuse from your boss, insane tirades from other Hollywood players, and crazy work hours with no downtime or space for a personal life. But there are perks—the chance to meet and schmooze with famous people, free access to lots of great parties, and the opportunity to work your way up the ladder to bigwig-player status yourself.

Assistants in Hollywood take their jobs for one reason only—to become something else. Some of them want to produce, some to direct, some to write. Lots of them plan to become agents or executives, publicists or business managers. All of them share one big goal: survival until they reach the next level. Check back in five years, and lots of those assistants will be taking meetings and signing talent. Check back in ten, and several of them will be calling the shots and greenlighting the films. Assistants are the future of the industry, and they know it. That's why they start their networking early—with one another. Get to know enough people when they're on their way up, and one of those people will be running the town. Hopefully it will be you. In this town, it's all about who you know and who you know who will take your calls.

So there's a little thing known as the assistant network. Like any other professional network, it's a system of trades and favors. But the types of favors in Hollywood are not like anything going on among stockbrokers or software developers.

Here's how it works: Say your old-but-powerful boss wants tickets to a Springsteen concert. You can't just call up Ticketmaster and get him a couple of seats in the back. You need front-row seats and maybe a backstage pass, or else your boss will get himself a new assistant. That means you're going to have to call your friend Jennifer (note: for some reason, there are a *lot* of assistants named Jennifer), the assistant to a big music-industry agent. But Jennifer's not going to hand over kick-ass Springsteen tickets for free—you've got to have something to trade, something Jennifer wants.

So you call your other friend, Jennifer #2, who's an assistant at a PR firm. Jennifer #2 has tickets to the next Victoria's Secret fashion show, and you know Jennifer #1 would love those. Problem is, in order to get the tickets from Jennifer #2, you've got to call your friend Jennifer #3, an assistant at a product-placement company, and get her to send over a free iPhone. You give Jennifer #3's iPhone to Jennifer #2, who will "gift" it to her boss's big client, an actor who's thinking of jumping ship. In return, Jennifer #2 gives you the Victoria's Secret tickets. You trade those tickets with Jennifer #1 for the Springsteen tickets.

But you're not done yet. You still have to pay back Jennifer #3 for the iPhone. So now you have to ask your old-but-powerful boss for a couple of passes to the premiere of his next blockbuster so you can give them to Jennifer #3, whose boss wants to go to the opening and schmooze with the executives who refuse to buy any projects from him. Maybe he'll mend some fences, and then Jennifer #3 will look good, which means you'll look good, which means that Jennifers #1 and #2 will also look good.

If that sounds dizzying, think about this: A juggling act like that is just one of many that a typical assistant will do during a workday. In between all that, the assistant will be busy working the computer and doing the scanning, copying, collating, and scheduling for his boss. Oh, and he'll also be on the phone all day long, listening to every single call his boss makes, just lurking there to take notes and jump in to answer whatever questions or fulfill whatever needs his boss has while on the call.

It's true—there's always, *always* someone listening in Hollywood.

That's why assistants always, *always* know what's going on. Studio executives talk to casting agents, who talk to talent agents, who talk to business managers, and on and on. There are assistants on all of those calls, listening to all of that information and sharing it with one another over drinks later on. There are assistants arranging every meeting, reading every screenplay, sitting in every writers' room, and taking notes at every casting session. That's how information gets passed around the Hollywood grapevine—what script is hot, what actor is thinking of leaving his agent, what film is having serious budget issues . . . and what crazy unknown actress just tried to crash a network test for the hot new TV series.

Chloe Gamble's story spread like wildfire across the assistant network. There was a picture of her, surrounded by NBC security, bouncing from cell phone to cell phone all over town. By the end of the week, anybody who was somebody knew her name. Soon after, an NBC mug shot of Chloe was e-mailed to all the studios, and it was immediately uploaded and sent to the Blackberries of any assistant who liked gossip—which meant all of them. There were rumors of a videotape of the whole thing—the camera had been running in the room when she did her dog and pony show. Everybody was waiting for it to hit YouTube, but it's hard to leak NBC intellectual property without losing your job. Somewhere, sometime, that video will surface.

By midweek, the calls were flying; everybody was trying to find Chloe Gamble. Where was she? Who was her agent? She had to be repped by somebody, right?

Well, no. But nobody knew that. Nobody knew anything about Chloe Gamble except that she was good gossip. She was interesting, and she was beautiful, and she had a death wish. And according to the casting assistant who'd been in the room (and had people buying him drinks for days just to hear the story), she had charisma and star quality—that indefinable thing that every huge star has.

Chloe was famous. But she was also missing.

Nobody repped her. Nobody even knew how to find her.

And everybody wanted to.

## Business Party

Mama was good and plastered when Travis and I left the apartment a few hours later. She didn't even wake up enough to notice that I was wearing her platform heels. Travis drove us over the hill into Hollywood. He'd offered to drive Livia and Amber, but I don't think they wanted to be seen in our crappy Ford. It was just as well—I didn't feel like making small talk.

My brother was in a great mood, going on and on about how if St. Paul's soccer team won the sectional championships, they'd get a chance to play in a tournament in Las Vegas. Schoolwork here in LA was harder, but the soccer was better than down in Texas. And Livia wasn't even in school anymore—she was older and that was cool. I just let him talk. It was nice to hear him so happy for a change.

Hollywood was filled with neon glowing in the darkness. It took forever just to get from one traffic light to the next, what with the cars bumper to bumper in the street and the hordes of people crossing at every corner. We finally found a spot to parallel park on a narrow side street, and it took about five minutes for us to decode the NO PARKING sign enough to figure out if we were going to get towed.

"The line to get into this place goes around the block," Travis said as we walked up the hill toward the bar. "Bad enough we had to park twenty freakin' miles away...."

"We didn't have to," I said. "We coulda forked over fifteen bucks for the valet. If we had fifteen bucks."

Trav rolled his eyes. "Why are there people waiting in line for a party? Don't you have to get invited to a party? It's disrespectful to make your guests stand outside and wait."

"Okay, Mama," I teased him. "I don't think these people are invited."

"Then it's disrespectful for them to try to crash."

"Where are we meeting your little hottie?" I asked.

Trav shrugged. "She said she'd wait at the door."

"Good." I looped my arm through his and pulled him past the long line of hipsters waiting to get in. Up front, Livia and Amber stood there shivering in tiny miniskirts and baby-doll T-shirts. Two gigantic dudes sat on stools near the big, black double doors to the club.

I glanced down at my jeans and button-down shirt. It was my uniform shirt from school, but I'd left it undone practically down to my waist, and I had one of Jude's shimmery gold tanks on underneath. The jeans were skinny, which Amanda had okayed. And Mama's heels were sexy. But I still felt weird. All the other girls were in skirts. Maybe I should've worn mine. *I'm a girl who owns one skirt,* I thought.

"Hey, Trav," Livia said, slipping her arms around my brother's waist. She stuck her tongue down his throat before he could even say hi back. Travis didn't seem to mind. Amber rolled her eyes and so did the bouncers.

"Can we go in, please?" Amber said.

"We could just leave them out here," I suggested.

The bouncers laughed, which annoyed Amber even more. Livia finally let go of Travis and we all went in. The guys at the door didn't even check their precious list for my name, so I didn't think it was such a big deal that we had extra people after all. They asked Travis for an ID, and he came out with some fake license I'd never seen. But they didn't bother to card me, probably because I'd left so many buttons undone on my shirt.

Inside, the place was bigger than I had expected, more like a gigantic warehouse than a swanky club. The ceiling was high enough that there was a balcony-type thing suspended above the dance floor, which you could only get to by climbing a narrow metal staircase. I checked out the bottom of the steps. Two more bouncers.

"What's that?" I asked Livia.

"The VIP room," she said, as if it were obvious.

"Can we go up there, since we're on the list?" I asked.

Amber shook her head in disgust. "Being on the list just gets us in the door," she said. "God, you really just got off a hayride, didn't you?"

She stalked off into the crowd, pushing her way toward the dance floor.

"Sorry," Livia said, totally not sorry.

"We don't have clubs like this in Spurlock," I said. "We've got two bars, one that cards and one that doesn't. Speaking of which, Trav, where'd you get that fake ID?"

"Mmm, that's a fun story," Livia said, snaking her arms around my brother again. I didn't know if Travis realized it or not, but I had a hunch this chick was a psycho. I guess that doesn't bother guys—they seem to dig it.

While they made out, I took in the scene. Big club, with

an upstairs VIP room that I had to get into. Gigantic dance floor, pounding house music, and a bored-looking chick DJ in a booth on the far side. The bar was between us and the dance floor, a huge pink-neon-lined counter that had to be forty feet long. A bunch of cocktail tables dotted the floor around it, and lining the walls of the club on every side were big booths with pink leather benches. The place was packed, the bodies on the dance floor moving like one big pulsating organism.

I allowed myself five seconds to process that I had never in my life set foot in a place as overwhelming as this before. Even the party after the Junior Miss San Antonio pageant hadn't been so swank, maybe because they knew for a fact everyone there was underage.

Livia peeled herself off my brother and grabbed her cell phone. "Sorry, I'm vibrating," she told Trav, like that was the funniest thing in the world. She checked her cell, then began typing.

"Anything wrong?" Travis asked.

"No, it's just Amber. She's dancing with Billie Holloran's assistant." Livia stuck her phone back into her pocket and took Travis's hand. "Buy me a drink, babe."

We both stared at her.

"*Buy* you a drink?" Travis said. "I thought this was a party."

"Yeah." Livia looked blank.

"See, in Texas, a party has an open bar," I said. "That's just good manners."

Livia frowned. "You're not seriously telling me you don't have money for drinks," she said.

"Sure I do," Travis said. "What do you want?"

"An apple-tini." Livia pulled out her phone and started texting again. "And a cosmo for Amber."

"Did she just order a drink by text?" I asked.

Livia shrugged. "I'm gonna find a booth." She took off, leaving us alone.

Travis was already heading for the bar. "Hey, Trav, we better find out how much the drinks cost here," I said. "I get the feeling they're gonna butt-rape us."

"No worries, I've got money." He was grinning like a four-year-old on Christmas.

"What money?" I said. "Did you steal it?"

"Kinda. Ask me what I did this afternoon."

"You went to the pool with your little girlfriends," I said.

"Before that."

"You went to school."

Travis rolled his eyes. "I didn't have soccer, so I left early and went to a shoot for a catalog."

It was loud in there, so I wasn't sure I had heard him right. "A shoot?"

"Yeah. If you can get out of class for an audition, I can get out for a modeling gig." My brother stood there smiling, the pink light of the bar turning his blond hair into a fuzzy, sunny halo. He was pleased as shit with himself.

"What the hell are you talking about?" I demanded.

"Jude sent my head shots to a booker she knows, and they hired me for an ad in the Sears catalog. I'm an underwear model!" Now Travis was laughing outright. "I stood there for an hour in some tighty-whities and they handed me nine hundred bucks!"

The weird lighting, the loud music—the white-noise babble of voices, it all pressed in on me, making me feel dizzy. Reality seemed so far away that I wasn't sure anymore what was going on. Travis, a model? When did that happen? Here I'd been so freaked about finding work to support us, to support him, and he'd gone and gotten a job first. I hadn't even done it for him. He didn't need me to do it for him. But how could that be?

"Chloe." My twin grabbed my shoulders and squeezed. "Nine hundred dollars."

"Nine hundred dollars," I repeated. It was a lot, and we needed it. I never expected to be taking money from my brother, but we always shared whatever we had. What's ours is ours. Trav was waiting for me to smile, to laugh, to hug him. So I did.

"Don't ever tell Mama," I said when he let go of me. "Or that money won't be yours for very long."

"Just 'cause I'm a model doesn't mean I'm stupid," he replied.

By the time we got to the bar, I'd lost Travis in the crowd. Even with my mama's high heels, I couldn't see over the knot of people jockeying for drinks.

"You look lost," somebody said. I turned to see a cute guy checking me out. He had dark hair in a buzz cut with white tips, and I swear he was wearing some kind of mascara.

"I know where I am," I said.

"Good. Can I get you a drink?" he asked my breasts.

"Sure," I said. "Do you think they have Shiner Bock?"

He was so surprised, he actually looked at my face. "Beer?"

"Yeah." I laughed at his expression. "Was I supposed to say chocolate martini?"

"Baby, if you want a beer, I'll get you a beer," another guy said from behind me. This one was even hotter than the first one, with dark skin and a smoothly shaved head. He looked me up and down and licked his lips suggestively.

It was hard not to laugh in his face. "I haven't seen you before," he said, slipping a muscled arm around my waist to steer me closer to the bar.

"I'm new." I let him keep his hand on the small of my back. "What do you do?"

"I'm an actor—can't you tell?" he said with a wink.

"Been in anything lately?" I asked.

"I'm waiting to hear on a pilot," he said.

So he wasn't too far along in his career. Useless to me.

"Who's Billie Holloran?" I asked him while we waited for my beer.

"She's an exec at HBO," he said. "Why?"

"Her assistant's here."

He nodded. "Lots of assistants here tonight. The big fish all went to the Red and Black Ball at the Hilton. I heard Nike was pissed when they picked the same night."

"So this isn't the party to be at?" I asked.

He shrugged. "At least you can actually talk to the assistants," he said. "I'm gonna head out around midnight, though. Friend of mine is having an after-hours party in the Hills. You want to come with?"

"Maybe," I said. "I have to find my brother."

He didn't seem too pleased about that, but he followed me through a throng of people surrounding a fortyish guy with shoulder-length hair. We found Travis in a booth with Amber, Livia, and another couple. Once he saw the girls, my bald friend was happier. He sat right down and tried to hit on Amber. Livia was on Trav's lap, and I could tell by his eyes that I was going to have to drive us home later. If he even came home at all tonight.

*So what if he's drunk? He's celebrating a paycheck,* I thought. But I was annoyed. Not at Trav, really, just at the whole situation. Things were upside down here. This was supposed to be my town, not his.

Amber was texting on her phone while flirting with the

bald guy. I checked out the new couple, who turned out not to be a couple at all. The girl had super-short hair and a permanent scowl. Within two minutes, she let everyone at the table know that she was gay, which made me absolutely certain that she wasn't. But if that was her pose, more power to her. The guy had blond hair, blue eyes, and blond scruff on his face, and his clothes and his stubble were so perfect that he must've spent more time getting ready tonight than I did.

"What's with all the well-manicured men here?" I asked the bald guy.

He laughed, but I hadn't been kidding.

The blond guy was an agent, or so he said. He'd gotten promoted two weeks before to full agent status, and I was obviously supposed to be impressed by that. He bought me a drink and spent all his time staring at my hair. Eventually he made his move, sitting closer to me and whispering something about my luscious lips. By then, I'd discovered that he was a writers' agent and didn't handle actors. So I excused myself and left him at the table to fight with the bald guy over Amber.

The older man with the longish hair was still holding court at his huge booth, surrounded by a bunch of people, so I went over there and hung on the edges of the crowd to see if I could learn anything.

"Drink, sweet thing?" somebody asked me. This time it was a tall, thin guy with a full beard.

"No, thanks," I said. "What do you do?"

"I'm a producer. Name's Alex." He stuck out his hand, but when I went to shake it, he lifted my fingers to his lips. "You're the hottest thing here tonight, you know that?" he murmured.

"And by 'thing' you mean girl?" I said, trying to get my hand back.

Alex pulled me toward the dance floor. "Let's see how you move."

I wasn't in the mood to dance, but whatever. He was a producer. Producers give people acting jobs. I danced, and I let him grind for a little while when the music got heavy. Finally I said, "Do you make movies or TV or what?"

"Movies," he said, nuzzling my neck.

"What kind?"

"Adult," he said.

Adult. I kept moving to the beat, and he kept trying to hump me. *Adult?*

"Wait, you mean porn?" I said, stepping back.

Alex reached out for my hand. "Yeah. Porn. But none of that cheap shit—I've got good production values."

I don't shock easy, but I couldn't believe how unembarrassed he sounded. Like pornos were just the same as regular movies.

"Come on, sweet thing, I like the way you dance." He was trying to reel me in again.

"I'm only sixteen," I said for the second time in a week.

Alex dropped my hand, turned, and walked away without

another word. This party was starting to get boring. So far the only established person I'd met was a porn king. I went back to the fortyish guy. He was old, so maybe he was a real player. Or maybe he was another perv—who knew? I didn't bother staying on the periphery this time. I pushed myself right up to his table.

"Who's going to get me a drink?" I asked.

The old guy's eyes shot straight to me.

"Obnoxious much?" a girl muttered.

But the guy smiled. "Drinks for the table," he called over to the bar. Everybody cheered. I noticed that most of the people here were female, but there were a few guys, too.

The older guy didn't ask my name, but his gaze kept coming back to me. I knew if I stuck around long enough, he'd come over to talk.

"Who is that man?" I asked a well-dressed Asian guy next to me.

"Ron Haynes," he said, as if that meant something.

"Am I supposed to know him?" I said.

"He's a reality producer," the guy said. "He's got three shows on the air right now. I'm his assistant."

"I don't watch reality shows," I said. "I got my own reality to deal with."

The Asian guy laughed. "Don't we all. My reality is Ron. He likes to go clubbing to find cast members for his shows."

As a studious reader of all the finer tabloids, I knew that if you scored on a reality show, your career could skyrocket. Ever seen *American Idol*?

"So if I get your boss's attention, I might get on one of his shows?" I said in the most flirty way possible.

"But you'll have to do him first," a voice said from behind me. This time when I turned around, it wasn't a guy leering at me. It was a pretty African-American girl with a funky mini 'fro. "And if you do, you might get the gig. But then that's who you are."

"Well, that might be who I am," I said. "But believe me, if I'm going to do someone for a part, it will be for something way better than a crappy reality show."

Her eyebrows shot up, and then we both burst out laughing.

"I don't think you're gonna find who you're looking for at this party," she said. "Ron Haynes is the biggest fish here, sadly. It's basically a D-list party."

"I'm only interested in whoring myself out to the A-list," I joked. "What about in the VIP room? I was going to try to sneak in."

The girl shook her head. "There were a couple of minor actors up there at the beginning, but I saw Hayden leave half an hour ago, and she was the biggest name. It might've been a C-minus-list party when she was here, but no more. Now we're just left with reality producers and the idiots who worship them." She nodded toward Ron Haynes. "And porn producers and the idiots who treat them as if they're human."

"Okay, I've met both of those," I said.

"Right. Then you've got your young agents here looking for talent, by which I mean looking for willing starlets to sleep with."

"Met one of those," I said.

"You've got your wannabe actors, also looking for willing starlets to sleep with."

"Check," I said, thinking of the bald guy.

"Last but not—well, actually, last *and* least, you've got your various assistants all here to schmooze."

"And by 'schmooze' you mean look for willing starlets to sleep with," I said.

She nodded. "Pretty much."

"Damn, I guess I've met everyone at this party," I said.

"See? D-list."

I grinned. "So where are you on the list? Actress, right?"

The girl's dark eyes widened, and then she began to laugh. "I wish. I am not pretty enough, thin enough, or thick skinned enough to be an actress. Or, you know, talented enough. But so few people are."

"So then you must be a porn producer," I said.

She nodded. "You got it. When I'm not working under-cover as an agent's assistant, I'm out trolling for innocent girl meat to lure into the lucrative adult-entertainment racket."

"You're an agent?" Maybe this party would help me after all.

"Assistant," she said. "I work at the Hal Turman Agency."

"Should I know them?" I asked.

"Well, you're new here, so probably not," she said. "We're not one of the big names."

"How do you know I'm new?" I said, a little offended. I thought I'd been working this party pretty well, but maybe I stuck out too much.

My new friend looked amused. "For starters, your hair is at least two inches longer than everybody else's."

I couldn't help myself—my hand went up to my blond hair.

"It's incredible, by the way—your hair," she said. "But it looks natural."

"It is."

"And so are your teeth," she said.

"My *teeth*?" I said. "I got to worry about my teeth now?"

"No, your smile is great. But those are actual teeth, not caps. And they're not as white as they should be. Take a look around—smiles here glow in the black light."

It was true. I burst out laughing. This girl noticed everything, just like me. I had no idea who she was, but I knew for a fact that I'd found my second friend in Hollywood.

"I give it a month before you have some chunky highlights in a weird, unnatural white-blond color and a four-hundred-dollar razor-edge cut," she went on. "Plus, you'll have a smile like Matt Dillon's in *There's Something About*

*Mary*, and you'll have to ditch your jeans for a skirt so short it might as well be a belt."

"Damn," I said. "I knew I got the jeans wrong!"

"Wrong? Are you kidding? Have you seen your ass in those jeans?" she said. "But nobody else wears jeans to a club. And nobody else drinks beer."

"I just can't bring myself to order girlie drinks," I said. "I was hoping it would score me some points for originality."

"New girl, it makes you fascinating," she said. "I'm just messing with you—it's refreshing to see somebody who doesn't look like the Hollywood factory churned her out from a Bratz-doll mold. Why do you think every guy in this place is hitting on you?"

"Guys in every place hit on me. That's just guys." I shrugged. "Tell me about the Hal Turman Agency."

She looked a little startled that I remembered the name. I always remember the important things.

"We're the agency that handles all the child actors. You know, the ones who work in kids' TV until we land them a prominent movie role and they make it big." She took a sip of her drink. "And then they instantly fire us and find an agent at CAA or Endeavor instead."

"Do you represent teenagers?"

"Sure," she said.

"So then you can help me get an agent!" I said.

"I don't know about that," she said. "I'm just an assistant."

"Yeah, but you can tell me what to do. My friend says I have to send my head shot all over. Is that true?"

"Yes. Sort of. I mean, you should send your head shot so people will start to remember your name and your face. But it won't really get you an agent. You need a job to get an agent."

My excitement vanished. "I already tried that," I said. "Didn't work."

"Well, no, because you can't get a job unless you have an agent," she said. "See? It's a system designed to make you fail."

"Somebody must take the new people," I said.

She'd finished her drink by now, and she was just chewing on the little straw as she thought about it. "You're charismatic," she said finally. "That sounds stupid, but it's true. Reality Ron over there hasn't taken his eyes off you."

I glanced at the big producer. He was looking back. I wasn't surprised, but I hadn't been paying attention to him. Usually I know when somebody is watching. I guess I'd been enjoying talking to this girl, so I'd forgotten to keep tabs on the other players.

"There is one agent at my office who I'm friends with—he was the first assistant to my boss before he got promoted, so I knew him when. He'd probably take a meeting with you if I asked," she said.

"Oh my God! Ask," I said.

"Pipe down, girl, it won't lead to anything," she said. "He's got a stack of out-of-work actors as it is—he's not about to sign somebody new in the middle of pilot season, no matter how hot you are."

"But he'll meet me?" I said.

"If I tell him no one at this club could stop staring at you, yeah."

"That's all I need. I can convince him," I said.

"Come by tomorrow—we'll get lunch and you can leave your head shot and résumé for him," she said.

"I'm buying lunch," I told her. "I owe you big time. . . . What's your name, anyway?"

"Nika," she said. "Nika Mays."

"Hi, Nika." I shook her hand. "I'm Chloe Gamble."

Nika's jaw went slack. She looked as if I'd just hit her in the face with a cast-iron skillet. "Are you fucking with me?" she said.

"What? No. What's wrong?" I said.

"Chloe Gamble. You're Chloe?"

I nodded.

"Oh my God," Nika said. "Everyone in Hollywood is looking for you. Chloe, you're famous."

# chapter seven

## Internet Sensation

"Do you have a library pass?"

I glanced up at Mr. Scott, St. Paul's school librarian. He was pushing sixty, and I knew he really didn't give a crap if I was allowed to be there or not. He was probably just asking 'cause he was bored.

"Sure I do." I handed over the fake pass that my chem lab partner had made for me in return for the answers to yesterday's homework. I wasn't blowing off anything important this period, just gym. Getting online—on an anonymous computer that could never be traced back to me—was way more important than playing badminton.

Once the librarian had left me alone, I went straight to the

*Hollywood Reporter* website. Kimber Reeve's face stared out at me as I scrolled through the articles. I ignored it. I didn't need a PR piece to tell me what I already knew—Kimber was a hot new face in Hollywood. But according to Nika Mays, so was I.

"There," I whispered. A message board with a thread about pilot gossip. I clicked to join in and found out a membership was going to cost me. But I only needed to get in for this one day, so I joined for a free trial and gave my name as "Ingrid," just because.

"Met this girl at a party. She said there was a big scandal at NBC," Ingrid posted. "Her name was Chloe Gamble. Anyone know what happened?"

I sat back and waited, forcing my eyes to stare out the windows at the tall palms waving in the breeze. It seemed like an eternity, but I managed to wait for three minutes. Then I hit refresh.

Twenty new posts.

I was so dazzled by the number that I didn't even read beyond the titles of the posts—"You found Chloe?" and "Test Crasher Chloe!" and "Where is she?"

By the time Ingrid's post had been up for five minutes, there were sixty-two responses. I didn't bother to read them. I didn't need to.

"Excuse me, Mr. Scott?" I said, going up to the desk. "I just found out I have a meeting, so I'll be out of school for the rest of the day. Do you think you could let the office know? I'm already so late!"

I tilted my head to the side and gave him the innocent-schoolgirl smile. "Cross your fingers for me!"

He nodded happily. He's sixty, not dead.

"Thanks so much!" I said, already heading for the door. I had a set of keys in my purse. Travis would figure it out when he saw that the car was gone.

I didn't have far to go. The Hal Turman Agency was in the Valley, a ten-minute drive from school. It was a bland stucco building right on the main drag, Ventura Boulevard. I pulled onto a side street and parked without even checking the NO PARKING signs.

Within a minute, I was standing in front of Nika Mays at the front desk.

"You were right," I said. "I'm famous."

A slow smile spread across her face. "Trust me now?"

"There's only one person in the world I trust," I said.

"Yourself?"

"My brother."

The phone rang and Nika answered it, quickly sending the call somewhere else. Then she looked me straight in the eye. "Listen, Chloe, I found you. The whole town is searching, but I found you first. Give me a shot. Let me be your agent."

"I'm here, aren't I?" I said.

"Yeah." She was practically vibrating, she was so excited. "But you see how it is—I'm still backup when the receptionist takes a break. I'm not an agent. I can't even sign you."

"But you said—"

"I know what to do—I know exactly how to handle your career," Nika cut me off. "I've been an assistant here for two years, and I should've been promoted ages ago. You're my ticket."

"Shouldn't I find a real agent?" I said. "At a big agency?"

"You could try. But you won't be as important to them as you are to me," Nika said. "Think about it—you win, I win. You lose, I lose. That makes me the most committed agent you'll ever find. And I *get* you. I can sell you." She paused. "I'm being straight with you here."

"You make me, I make you," I said.

Nika nodded.

"Okay. But how are you my agent if you can't sign me?"

"We'll go talk to Hal," Nika said.

Hal Turman's office was the size of our entire apartment in the Oakwood. You'd think that would make it impressive, but the stale smell and the scratchy-looking burgundy carpet ruined the effect. There was an enormous wooden desk in front of the window and a sitting area with a couch and some chairs in the corner. Framed movie posters hung on the walls, and I could tell they weren't the kind you buy on Amazon. One whole wall was devoted to photos of kids and teenagers that I figured were former clients. A lot of the pictures looked as if they'd been up there for decades, but there were a few recent faces I recognized. Two or three had mouse ears on their heads, and several were holding instruments or singing.

Still, the thing I noticed most was how cold it was in there. The office felt like a meat locker, raising goose bumps on my arms the instant I stepped inside.

"This is the girl?" a voice rumbled from the desk. Because the windows were behind him, Hal Turman was nothing more to me than a shadow against the sun that shone right into my eyes.

"I'm Chloe Gamble," I said before Nika could answer.

"Where's Bonnie?" Hal said.

"Here I am." A fortyish woman appeared in the office door and looked me up and down like I was a slab of beef at the butcher's. She had a pointy face like a squirrel's, and I disliked her straight off.

"Chloe, this is Bonnie Uslan. She's a partner here," Nika said.

"Let's sit," Bonnie said, heading for the couch. She walked like her shoes were too tight.

I took a seat in one of the chairs, and Nika perched on the arm. Only after we'd all settled down and waited for a minute did Hal Turman bother to come over. Now that I got a look at him, I pegged him right away. He was maybe sixty-five, with some gray hair cropped short, an expensive-looking sweater, and both a big gold watch and a gold ID bracelet on the same wrist. He reminded me of the guy who had sold us the Ford back at the used-car dealership in Texas. Only Hal probably had buckets more money.

"Okay, why are we here?" Bonnie said in her nasally voice. "Hal said you found this girl on the Internet?"

"No, Chloe and I met at a party," Nika said. "But even before that, I had heard all about her through the assistant network. She crashed a network test at NBC, and afterward everyone wanted to know who she was."

"What the hell kind of stunt was that to pull?" Hal said, looking at me for the very first time. Well, he looked at my nipples, which were poking through my shirt because it was so damn cold in there—and now I understood why he kept it that way.

"I need a job," I said. "If they'd have let me read, I would have gotten that part."

"So what happened—they threw her out?" Bonnie asked Nika.

Nika put her hand on my arm to keep me from answering. I guess she could tell that Bonnie was getting on my nerves. I don't like to be ignored, and that woman hadn't so much as glanced in my direction.

"Yes, but the rumor is that she really wowed Todd Linson and she put on a great show. Everyone is curious. She's a celebrity." Nika turned to Hal. "Get a PR person on this thing right now, and we can take control of that curiosity and turn it into work for Chloe."

"I don't like it. It's a stunt," Bonnie said. "She's just some hick who doesn't know how to behave."

"Hey," I snapped. "I've got more talent in my left butt cheek than you've got in your whole scrawny body."

"How do we know that?" Hal said while Bonnie fumed. "They didn't even let her read, right?"

"No." Nika hesitated, shooting me a concerned look. Apparently it hadn't occurred to her that I might be just a talentless hack who knew how to make a scene.

"I don't need some attention-craving troublemaker on my list," Hal grumbled. "She's pretty enough, but that and a nickel will get me four more minutes on the parking meter."

"Who's your favorite singer, Hal?" I asked.

His eyes shot to me, sizing me up. "Mr. Tony Bennett."

"Someone I know," I told him. "I'm only sixteen."

The tiniest hint of a smile crossed his face, then was gone so quickly that I wondered if I'd imagined it.

"Alicia Keys," Bonnie said, like that proved she was down with the youth of today.

"Who the fuck is Alicia Keys?" Hal demanded.

Hal obviously didn't get out of his overrefrigerated office very much. It wouldn't do me any good to sing Alicia. So I changed plans. I stood up, faced him full-on, and started to sing:

*Your rodeo days are over;*
*All the bull riders' names are new.*
*Now you look for love in the eyes of strangers*

While your family waits at home, prayin' for you.
So come pick up your pickup.
Take your cowboy boots, too.
Don't bother to leave them old Levi's you wore,
And don't hit your ass on the way out the door.

I could care, but I don't.
I could cry, but I won't.
I could run, but where to?
'Cause wherever I'd be,
I'd still remember you.

Now you'll never know me,
Miss chapters of my life.
Never hold my children
When I become a wife.

So listen, Daddy . . .

Near the end of the line
When your days become few,
The Lord won't open up heaven,
But I will say somethin' to you. . . .

I'll kneel at your bedside,
Whisper soft as I can.

*You ain't nothin' but a big ol'*
*Silver belt buckle wearin' a man.*

*I could care, but I don't.*
*I could cry, but I won't.*
*I could run, but where to?*
*'Cause wherever I'd be,*
*I'd still remember you.*

Silence. They all stared at me. Once again, the sick feeling from the room at NBC began to creep up my spine. No reaction, just people staring at me, so quiet, making me think I'd done the unthinkable twice. But I took a deep breath, trying to push down the feeling.

"Was that Alicia Keys?" Hal said, turning to Nika.

"No, that was me," I said. "It's the only song I ever wrote."

Nika was grinning, and Bonnie's face looked even more squirrelly than before. Hal sat silent for a moment, staring at my frozen nipples.

"So if we do this, and I'm not saying we are doing this, you listen to what we say, do what we tell you. No more stunts like at NBC," Hal said.

"Okay," I said, my heart starting to pound.

"We've broken every young actor and actress you've ever heard of. We know what we're doing. You don't."

I nodded, remembering what Nika had said at the party.

Hal broke the young actors, and then they all got better agents someplace else. He didn't mention that part.

"I'll behave," I said.

Hal grunted and pulled himself up from the chair.

"On one condition," I added.

He stopped halfway up and stared at me. "You don't get to have a condition."

"I haven't signed a damn thing, so I can have as many conditions as I want," I said. I pointed at Nika. "*She* represents me."

Bonnie squawked. "She's not even an agent!"

"That's not my problem," I said. "And actually, I have another condition, Hal."

He narrowed his eyes.

I pointed to Bonnie. "*She* stays the hell away from me."

Bonnie was on her feet now, her face red with rage. "Get out of here, you little bitch! How dare you talk to me that way! You're nothing! You'll always be nothing!"

"Shut up, Bonnie," Hal growled. I realized for the first time that he was a big guy, and right now his eyes were blazing. "Don't you ever speak to a client of ours like that again."

Bonnie's face went from red to white, and she clamped her mouth shut.

"We'll get you papers to sign by the end of the day," Hal said. He offered me his hand and I shook it.

"And I'll find her a lawyer to look them over," Nika said.

Hal frowned. "What does she need a lawyer for?"

"Because she doesn't trust you, Hal," Nika said. "And that goes for the rest of the town, too."

"Show some respect, young lady," Hal said. "Remember, you work for me."

"You might pay me," Nika said, "but I work for Chloe."

She turned and walked out before he could respond. I gave him a cheerful smile and followed, swinging my butt a little more than usual to give him a nice show.

I bet he was pissed off. I bet he was going to take it all out on Bonnie. I couldn't have cared less. She was just another dead armadillo on the highway to where I was going.

# Nika Mays's Manuscript Notes: Early Career Section

When you make agent, there's usually some kind of ceremonial "let's take you out to lunch" moment with your boss. Not for me. For me, there was a bitch session.

By the time I was summoned from my cubicle back into Hal Turman's office, he and Bonnie had obviously made their peace. She was leaning her bony ass against his desk, staring me down with her arms folded across her chest, which is her typical position when talking to female staff members. I'd been furious when my friend Michael got promoted to agent over me the month before, but Michael had just shrugged and said Hal was a sexist pig. My own personal theory was that the sexism came from Bonnie. There are successful businesswomen who like to help those a few rungs below them on the ladder. And then there are successful businesswomen who'd prefer to push the younger versions right off the ladder. Bonnie was one of those. I think my obsession with Chloe Gamble started the moment she got Bonnie in trouble with Hal.

"That was quite a show your little friend put on," Bonnie said.

"It was." I decided to act as if she were talking about Chloe's singing instead of Chloe's brassy behavior. "I've already put a call in to a songwriter I know to see about working with Chloe on that single."

"We're letting you take her on, Nika," Hal said from behind his *Titanic*-size desk. "But it's a test case. Probation."

"Meaning?"

"Meaning you're not an agent, and your one smart-ass client doesn't make you an agent," Bonnie snapped. "You're still an assistant, you still relieve the receptionist, and you get no raise."

I looked right past her, focusing on Hal. "Fine. But I get an agent's percentage of what Chloe makes. The same percentage every other agent here gets on their clients."

"You're dreaming if you think that girl is ever going to make any money. She's been blacklisted all over Hollywood," Bonnie said. "I checked. The studios have her on a watch list."

"Then you know how notorious she is," I told her. "No bad publicity, right, Hal?"

"That depends on who's doing the spinning. Let's see what you can do with the girl," Hal said.

"Do I get my percentage?" I asked.

Hal sat there with his fingers steepled, nodding. "Sure, honey, you get it."

"Good." I glanced at Bonnie. "The same lawyer I find for Chloe will put that in writing."

"You just keep that little bitch away from me," Bonnie said as I left the room.

"The way I heard it, you're the one who has to stay away from her," I said. "I believe that's in Chloe's contract."

Outside Hal's office, three other agents and the receptionist were waiting. When I walked out, they surrounded me like I was Paris and they were the paps.

"Did they let you sign her?" Michael asked. "Did they promote you?"

"Chloe Gamble is my new client," I said. "I get the same percentage as Bonnie, and Bonnie can't come near her!"

"I cannot believe you found Chloe Gamble," the receptionist said.

"You lucked out," Michael agreed. "I'll buy you lunch to celebrate. We can kick around some ideas on how to launch Chloe."

*Nice try*, I thought. Michael had always been my friend, but that wouldn't stop him from trying to steal Chloe. They say in Hollywood beauty is skin deep, and that goes for friendships, too.

"Tomorrow, okay?" I told him. "I need to make some phone calls now."

To that lawyer, to our contracts department, to everyone who was going to make it rock-solid official that Chloe Gamble was mine, all mine. I raced back to my desk, snatched up my phone, and got on it. Just like Madonna, I knew that I would not stop. Not until Chloe Gamble was a star.

# Launch

"I'm not feeling it, Chloe," Alan said. "You can do better."

I bit my tongue to keep from giving him some sass, as my daddy would have said. I'd already done the dumb scene twice and I thought it was pretty damn good. But Alan was sitting there like usual, shaking his head a little, narrowing his eyes a little, and sounding infuriatingly reasonable.

"It felt right to me," I said. I didn't want to waste the time of everyone in the acting class by beating it to death. It was a cheesy love scene. Will and I had made cow eyes at each other and said all the goopy lines. Done deal.

"Me too," Will added helpfully. He would have agreed with anything I had said, though—he figured that was the way to get me to like him. Really it just annoyed me. People who don't stick to their guns are irritating as shit.

"Remember what we talked about last time? Simplicity?" Alan said. "That's what we need here. You need to find the simple truth in this character, Chloe. Find a piece of yourself in her and use that as a way in."

I rolled my eyes. I couldn't help it.

"Care to elaborate on that feeling?" Alan asked, his voice amused.

"Okay. I'm frustrated," I said. "I'm saying all the words, I'm telling myself that I believe them, and you keep saying it doesn't work."

"You're saying the words but not making the audience feel them."

"Well, maybe it's the damn scene!" I burst out. "She's willing to let this guy walk all over her just because she thinks she's in love."

There was a tiny moment of silence, and then Alan cleared his throat. "She *thinks* she's in love?"

"She *is* in love," Del piped up from the back of the room.

"Please, there's no such thing," I said before I could think. Alan's eyebrows shot up and I had a bad feeling I'd said too much.

"You ever been in love, Chloe Gamble?" he asked.

"No. Love is for people too dumb to realize the truth," I said. "If someone says they love you, it's only because they want something from you. Like in this scene—he just wants to get in her pants. And she might let him, because she thinks she's in love."

"An interesting take," Alan remarked. "Let's try this: Stop thinking about love, because Chloe Gamble doesn't believe in love. In fact, stop thinking at all. While you do the scene, I want you to concentrate on one thing only—listening to your partner."

"I don't get it," I said.

"Turn off your brain—if that's possible—and focus all your energy on hearing what Will says."

I turned to Will and took a moment to push down the

frustration welling up inside me. Will was staring into my eyes, and somehow he seemed to sense when I was ready. He began the scene.

My mind went to my first lines. I forced myself to stop thinking about them. I stared at Will, who was gazing at me adoringly. I *listened.*

He was telling me about my eyes and how he saw them in his dreams. I felt myself starting to react, wanting to snicker at how lame that sounded. But I pushed the thought away and listened. Now he was on to my hands and how his own hands trembled every time they brushed against mine.

*It's actually sweet,* I thought. *My eyes, my hands—not my ass or my great legs or anything.*

Will reached for me, his eyes boring into mine. My character answered, letting him take her hand, wanting him to hold her in his arms. The words came out of me, but I wasn't really thinking about them. I was just paying attention to Will. He slid his arm around me, his grip tentative as if he was afraid it was still just a dream.

I leaned into the embrace as I spoke, relief flooding through me—well, through her, my character.

Will bent to kiss me. I let him. She wanted him to.

His tongue snaked into my mouth.

"Hey!" I yelled. I jerked away and smacked him across the face—hard.

"What the hell was that?" Will cried.

I just stared at him, breathing hard. I felt violated. I felt furious.

The room erupted in applause. "Nice work, Chloe," Alan said, in the way Alan says things.

I glared at Will. "Ass hat," I hissed.

"Will, if you ever do that again, you're out of my class," Alan said. "Chloe, when he did that, what did you feel?"

"Pissed off," I said.

"Yes, rage. Simple rage," Alan said happily. "There's a lot more of that in you, I think. Though we'll try to find some other emotions, just for variety."

Everybody laughed. I wanted to smack them all just like I'd hit Will. What was so funny? My heart was still slamming against my chest, anger coursing through my veins.

"He slipped me the tongue," I snapped. "His character wouldn't have done that—that was just him."

"And?"

"And . . . I wasn't expecting it," I said. "I was in character and he did that and it pulled me right out."

"You're mad because he pulled you out of the scene?" Alan said. "Kind of shows how deeply you were feeling it, doesn't it?"

"I guess." The anger was draining away now.

"You got out of your own head because you were focusing on Will," Alan said. "Focusing outward allowed you to simply *react*."

"I felt like my character was reacting, not me," I said.

Alan smiled. "That's called acting, Ms. Gamble. Welcome to it."

"She ain't comin', Clo. She was just yanking your chain," my mama said the next day.

"She said she'd be here at six and it's only five after," I said. "Get your feet off the table."

"My nails are drying." Mama left her feet on the coffee table. I hoped she'd have the decency to take them off when Nika arrived. Travis and Jude were huddled in the kitchen, talking about something. Normally I'd be curious, but right now I was too nervous to butt in. Where was Nika? I was never going to believe I had an actual, honest-to-God Hollywood agent until I had a signed paper in my hand saying so.

"Calm down, honey—nobody in LA is ever on time," Amanda said from the balcony, where she was smoking one of those long, skinny girlie cigarettes. "She probably hit traffic, or she's trying to park."

"You mind not blowing that shit in my air?" Mama whined, waving her hand around like she was having a fit, even though Amanda's smoke was blowing out over the parking lot.

"You have your vices, Early; I have mine," Amanda said.

"I got one vice. You got smoking *and* eating," Mama said.

"Being a bitch counts as a vice, Mama," Trav said from the kitchen.

The doorbell rang, saving me from all of them. Mama and Amanda had taken to bickering like two old biddies on a bad sitcom, and Travis had barely taken his eyes off Jude since she got here. I wondered whether his so-called girlfriend, Livia, would have liked that. I pulled open the door. Nika grabbed me and kissed me on the cheek.

"Papers!" she said, handing me a big manila envelope. "I found an associate at Webster and White to look them over for legal issues, so no worries."

"Plus, the associate is cute with a capital *Q*," said the guy with Nika. "And *I'm* the one who found him, so you're welcome."

Nika grinned. "Chloe, this is my friend Marc. He's an assistant at Slade. They do PR for a lot of the Disney Channel kids."

"And we hook people up with hot lawyers on the side," Marc said. "No charge for the pimping service."

"So I have an agent and a lawyer?" I said. "*And* a publicist?"

"You've got a bunch of assistants helping you out this one time," Nika said. "Except me—I'm in it for the long haul. Who's everyone else?"

"Jude, photographer. Amanda, stylist," I said. "That's my mama and Travis."

Nika shook hands all around, stopping to give Trav a once-over. Her friend Marc did the same.

I left them to make small talk while I took the papers into

the bedroom and read all the tiny print from beginning to end. I didn't understand half of it, but at least I could say that I had read every word. When I got back into the living room, Nika was on the beige couch next to Mama.

"Okay, let's talk strategy," Nika said. "We're here to launch Chloe Gamble."

"Let me sign the papers first," I said. "I won't be able to enjoy this unless it's official."

"Great." Nika laid out the papers on the coffee table. There were little sticky banners all over that said "Sign here."

I grabbed the contract, flipped to the back, and picked up a pen. "Hold up," I said, my hand frozen over the last page. "I didn't look over this signature part. Why's my mama's name here?"

"Oh, we'll need a parent's signature since you're a minor," Nika said. She smiled at my mama. "Then we need siggies on a few more forms, too, to set up the Coogan Trust Account."

"What's that, now?" My mama's ears pricked up at the word "account."

"The Coogan Account," Marc said. "There's a law to protect child actors from unscrupulous parents. The employer has to put fifteen percent of the actor's earnings into a trust fund that nobody can touch until the kid is legal or gets emancipated."

"It's named after Jackie Coogan," Nika said. "He was this super-famous child star who made millions of dollars, but his parents spent it all and he ended up broke."

"Wow. What kind of parent would do that?" Travis asked. His voice wasn't snarky or anything, but I knew exactly what he meant. And so did Mama. Her face was taking on its stubborn-two-year-old expression, the one that signals Trav and me to start running. You don't want to be near Mama when she's in that pissy mood.

"We gotta talk about the money part right now?" I said.

Nika shrugged. "I guess not. You have to open the Coogan account within a week of signing an employment contract, but since you're not employed yet, we can wait." She turned to Mama. "Mrs. Gamble, you'll need to get me a copy of Chloe's birth certificate to set up the account, so you might want to dig it out beforehand."

My mama just stared at her blankly.

"We left Texas in kind of a rush. We didn't think to bring stuff like that," I said. "Trav, you think maybe you can get Coop to sneak into the house and find it? Mama, where's the birth certificate?"

If you've ever seen somebody who's just gotten a drink tossed in her face, you'll know what my mama looked like right then—wide-eyed with shock, her mouth hanging stupidly open, her breath all shallow.

"Mama, you do have our birth certificates, don't you?" Trav asked. "We must've needed them for school."

"Nobody ever asked for proof in Spurlock, honey," Mama said. "Those school secretaries known me since I was five. And they sure as shit knew I was knocked up with twins!"

I took a look at Nika and saw that her brow was furrowed. She and Marc exchanged a worried glance. *Well,* that *cat's outta the bag,* I thought. I'd been hoping to pass my mama off with some tiny bit of respectability, but I guess that's a dream for another girl with another mama.

"We'll call the county offices and get the birth certificate sent," I said.

Nika nodded, her gaze on Mama. "You know, if you want to set aside more than fifteen percent, we can ask them to do that," she said.

I felt a rush of affection for my new agent. Set aside more money so Mama couldn't touch it? Seemed like a good idea to me. Except for the part where Trav and I still had to live on what we didn't hold back.

"You crazy? There's no way we're gonna give away even more money to some silly law," my mama said. "We need that money for expenses."

"It's not giving the money away," Marc said, talking really slowly as if Mama were a child. "The money goes into a bank account so that it will still be there when Chloe is an adult. Otherwise it might all get spent and she'd have nothing to live on in the future."

Thing is, my mama isn't a child, and when it comes to money she understands more than anybody gives her credit for. Like right then, she knew what we were all talking about and she knew that we were talking about *her*.

"I'm more interested in what we're gonna live on right now," she snapped. "How'm I supposed to pay the rent and buy food for these children and make sure they got their school uniforms and all? Bad enough the government wants to take away fifteen percent."

"Technically, all of those expenses should come from your own employment, Mrs. Gamble, just as they would if Chloe were a regular nonworking teen," Nika said politely. "The Coogan law states that all the money Chloe makes belongs to her alone, not to the family."

I shot a glance at Travis. He shook his head. That was not going to fly with my mama.

Mama was on her feet. "Forget it, then! I'm not signing those papers! I'm not gonna keep my family in this here expensive city if I gotta be in the poorhouse to do it! You telling me I can't use Clo's money to buy her clothes and shoes and pay for them fancy photos—"

"I did Chloe's head shots for free," Jude said.

"Well, her makeup don't buy itself," Mama practically shrieked. "Her Cheerios don't buy their damn selves!"

"If the money's all mine, can't I decide to give some to my mama for expenses?" I said. My pageant money had been paying for our whole life lately, so what was the difference? I was used to supporting Mama, but Nika didn't need to know that. "Mama don't make much yet as a seamstress."

"Damn straight," Mama said, shooting Amanda a nasty look. Amanda just rolled her eyes.

"Well, the law states that a parent has to be with you on set at all times, Chloe," Nika said. "So if that were to cause some kind of financial hardship because your mother couldn't work . . ."

My mind had got stuck on the part where I was going to be saddled with Mama all the time, but luckily Trav was paying attention.

"So Chloe can decide to pay Mama for going on set with her?" he asked.

Mama clapped her hands. "You mean I'm like her manager? Like that Lohan lady—she manages her kids' careers."

"No!" I said, and Nika was saying it right along with me.

"We could set it up so that a percentage of the money goes to a joint account, and you can use it to pay Chloe's professional expenses," Nika went on, putting a hand on my arm to settle me down. "Her acting classes, her wardrobe, things like that."

"How much? Twenty percent?" Mama said.

"Ten percent, no more," Travis cut in. Bless him for being willing to take on Mama. "Fifteen percent to the Coogan account, ten percent to you."

*And ten percent to Nika as my agent,* I thought. That's what agents make—I'd read it in enough magazines. So if I made a hundred bucks, I was already out thirty-five before it reached my pocket. Still, it was worth it. My mama was never gonna support my career out of the goodness of her heart. But for ready money, she'd be the perfect mother. And as long as I controlled her cash flow, I could hope to control her embarrassing behavior.

"And it goes in my name?" Mama said.

"She said a joint account, Mama—you and Clo both," Trav said.

I could see the wheels turning in my mama's head. Should she argue to get it all in her name, or should she try to wheedle me into that later, in private? I laughed.

"What's so funny?" Mama asked, jolted out of her scheming.

"Us, talking like we got money to spend," I said, still laughing. "Just 'cause I got an agent doesn't mean I got any work. There is no money. I haven't made a dime."

Marc giggled to back me up, and Nika joined in. I watched my mama, hoping she'd go along with the so-called joke and forget about arguing.

"But when there is money, I get my fee," Mama said stubbornly.

"Yeah, Mama," I said. "Plus, we'll have an account saving up money for later."

Nika looked at my mama nervously. So did everyone else in the room.

Mama slowly sat back down and stuck her feet up on the coffee table again. "You children are always acting like I want to take your money!" she said, but now she was just complaining.

Travis was about to make some smart remark—I could see it on his face. I shut him up with a single look. I needed my mama to think this was all okay, because I needed her to sign those agency papers. I'd figure out the money stuff later, when there was a paying job. And at least I'd have fifteen percent of it safe from her.

"Jude, do you have your camera?" I asked. "Take a picture of me signing my agency papers!" I snatched up the pen, pasted on a smile, and tried to make it all seem fun. Jude pulled out her little point-and-shoot and snapped away while I wrote my name about twenty times on all the different copies.

"Now you, Mama," I said. I held out the pen. Jude held up the camera. Everyone in the room held their breath.

"Oh, fine," my mama said. "We're in it together, right, Clo?"

"Always," I said.

Mama grabbed the pen and started signing, and by the end of it all she was grinning and laughing and probably imagining what 10 percent of a million dollars would buy her.

"Okay, let's get down to business," Nika said. "Launching Chloe."

"Head shots," Jude said. She laid out a small stack of photos on the coffee table. "We have saucy Chloe and beauty-queen Chloe, hot off the presses and ready to send out."

Nika grabbed them, and Marc whistled. "These are good," he said.

"Perfect. We'll get them out there," Nika said. "I'll set up some general meetings around town."

"What's that mean?" my mama asked.

"Casting directors are always looking for talent, so they'll do meet and greets with new actors," Marc said. "Chloe will need to get to know them—they're the first stop on the way to getting an audition."

"But what job's it for?" Mama said. "One of them pilots?"

"It's just for them to meet Chloe," Nika said. "There is no specific job. They meet her, they shoot the shit for a while, and hopefully they remember her the next time they have a role to fill."

My cheeks got a little warm. I was supposed to meet the casting people before there was even a job to talk about? No wonder everyone at NBC had thought I was an idiot. I wondered just how many steps in the process I'd tried to skip.

"What about parties?" Amanda asked.

"Definitely. She needs to get to as many openings and events as possible," Marc said.

"I'll dress her," Amanda said. She cut me off just as I opened my mouth. "You listen to Mandy, honey. I know you can make your own choices. All I'm gonna do is help you accessorize a little."

"I've got standing guest-list slots at a lot of the clubs, and the firm always has tickets to movie openings," Marc said. "I'll sacrifice a few for the cause. The more parties she shows up at, the more people will recognize her. Maybe we'll even get her face in the tabloids."

"No, we need to be selective," Nika said. "She's only sixteen—I don't want her showing up to a party at the Playboy Mansion."

"Hang on," Travis said. "She's not going to a bunch of clubs by herself. Besides, how's she gonna get in? She's not even legal."

"Don't worry, sugar. I can go with her," my mama said. "As a chaperone, like when I go on set with her."

"Not a chance in hell, Mama. I don't need you making a drunken fool of yourself when I'm trying to get noticed," I said. She'd signed the contract. I could drop the nice act now. "There's no booze on set, but there's plenty flowing at a club."

Mama's eyes got all teary. "How did I ever raise such a disrespectful child? You have no idea what I've—"

"Save it, Early," Amanda cut her off. "We're talking about Chloe, not you."

Mama shut right up. I had to give Amanda her due—she seemed to have taken my mama in hand after less than a week of working together.

"There's always the fame-whore route," Jude said. "Hook her up with a reality star or a celebutante and she's famous by association."

"No way," Travis said. "Clo's not the friend. She's the main event."

I don't think I've ever loved my brother more than in that moment.

"It's just a way to get you noticed, Clo," Jude said.

"How about music videos?" Marc said. "It's a little old school, but if we find the exact right video for her to star in, she gets noticed."

"I could do that," I said. "Some real actresses have done videos. Katherine Heigl did that one, and Angelina Jolie, too."

"I have a better idea," Nika said suddenly. "Chloe, that song you sang in Hal's office—you said you wrote it, right? Nobody else can claim to own it?"

"No, I wrote it," I said. "I mean, I never wrote it down but it's mine."

"Then here's what we do. We shoot you singing that song. Nothing but you singing. Then at the end we put your name and an e-mail address—my address at the agency. Then we put it on YouTube. And we wait."

"Wait for what?" my mama said.

"For it to happen. For people to get in touch," Nika said.

"I don't get it," Trav said. "How are they supposed to find it? There are five billion homemade videos on YouTube."

"People are out there looking for Chloe right this second," Nika said. "Clo, you saw it yourself—just by posting your name on a message board you got a ton of hits. Think about it—you're in an acting class. You go to school. It's not as if you're hiding. They're going to find you, and *soon*."

"So this has to happen *now*," Marc said. "You're right."

"Jude, can you shoot video?" Nika asked.

"Sure. It's not my forte, but I've done it," Jude said. "Chloe knows me and my camera are here to help."

"And Amanda, you can dress Chloe? For free?" Nika said.

"She can take her fee out of Mama's pay," I said. Mama's mouth dropped open, but Nika didn't give her a chance to protest.

"Travis Gamble, you look like a guy who knows how to post a video," she said.

Trav grinned.

"And Marc, you'll leak word once the video's up, right?" Nika said.

"I have drinks set up every night this week," Marc said. "The whole assistant network will know Chloe's online before I'm done."

"Excellent. When can we shoot?" Nika said.

"Hold on a sec," Jude put in. "I've got a digital video camera. It's not the best, but it'll do for visuals. And I've got lights, obviously. But my dv camera has a crappy little mike. If we're trying to showcase Chloe's voice, it won't work. She'll sound awful."

Nobody spoke. The quiet hurt my ears. Ideas and plans had been flying fast and furious, and I'd gotten all caught up in it. I couldn't stand the idea of this all falling apart. "Doesn't anybody know a guy with a microphone?" I said. "That's all we need, right?"

"Not just a microphone—all the sound-recording equipment," Jude said. "I do know a guy—he does sound for a few cable shows, and he runs the whole sound system for a theater downtown. He might be willing to help us out, but he won't do it for free."

I ran through our funds in my head. We needed three thousand for next month's rent, and we'd already burned through almost a thousand on clothes and food and gas and cabs, not to mention Mama's bar bill. We'd started with ten thousand, but I figured we were down to maybe two that we could live on, and we'd still only be able to pay the Oakwood for one more month....

"I'll pay for it," Travis said.

Mama beat me to it. "What are you on about, Trav?" she said. "How're *you* gonna come up with anything?"

"I got another catalog job," my brother told me. "Jude was just telling me about it."

"Catalog of what?" Mama squawked.

Trav had slipped. Now my mother would be after his cash like a cat stalks a canary. Maybe we should set up a Coogan thing for Travis, too.

"I think I'm going to have a second career as a booker for your twin, Clo," Jude said. "One of my friends has a shoot for novelty underwear coming up—you know, boxers with Santa on them and, like, underwear that says "Eat me"—stuff like that. I showed her Travis's pics from the Sears catalog and she, um, she liked his package."

"The size of the package is very important in novelty underwear," Travis said, trying to keep a straight face.

"Let me see!" Marc cried, jumping up from the couch. "I want to see the crotch shots!"

Jude handed over a portfolio and Marc immediately began flipping through, oohing and aahing at all the photos of my brother's man parts. Travis turned so red that even my mama had to laugh. Poor Trav was having a real initiation into the homosexual life lately. He'd clearly managed to get over Jude's being gay, but he didn't know what to do with a gay man. He should've hung backstage at more of my beauty pageants— fully 90 percent of the pageant coaches were self-described "pageant queens."

"Travis, you sure?" I asked him while Marc whooped it up. "You don't need to do this just for me. I'll find a way to pay the sound guy."

"Don't be stupid," he said. "It's wearing underwear and a goofy smile in return for serious dough. Why wouldn't I do it?"

"So we're set?" Nika said. "Jude, can you call the sound guy right away?"

Jude nodded. "I'm on it."

"Where are we shooting?" Amanda asked.

"Omar lets me use the Studio School room here at the Oakwood to shoot head shots," Jude said. "We can shoot there, as long as it's not being used for tutoring."

"What'd ya do, blow him?" my mama said, all class.

"No, I did his head shots for free." Jude laughed. "Everybody here wants to be an actor, you know."

"Let's aim for tomorrow before school hours, if the sound guy can make it." Nika stood up. "I'm going to take Chloe's papers to work for countersigning right away."

Nika knew exactly what I wanted to hear. "Thanks," I said, walking her to the door. "I'm not gonna relax until it's official."

"Girl, please." She laughed. "You're not going to relax until you're dead. You don't know how."

"True." When we stepped out into the hall, I dropped my voice so the others couldn't hear me. "Are you sure about this?"

Nika's eyebrows drew together. "About what?"

"This whole plan. I know everybody's all excited and willing to help, but . . ." I bit my lip. "I just mean, isn't it a trick? Like a stunt, the way sneaking into NBC was? I don't want to get known as the girl who pulls stupid shit all the time."

Nika shook her head. "It's not a trick, it's *you*," she said. "It will show everyone that you're more than just a stunt. You've got chops. You do it the way you did in Hal's office and everybody in town will come knocking."

"Sorry!" Marc said, barreling through the door. "I just had to bust on your brother a little more, Chloe. He's adorable."

"You leave that boy alone," Nika said. "He's an innocent

kid from Texas—he doesn't need to get hit on by an experienced homosexual his first month in Hollywood."

"I'm not into turning straight men toward the light," Marc said. He winked at me. "Nika knows I go for older men, anyway."

"They can pay the bills," I said.

"You know it." Marc kissed me on the cheek. "I like you already, Chloe Gamble. We're gonna make you an itty-bitty starlet and then a big-girl star!"

His words still had me grinning as I went back inside.

"Just what the hell are you thinking, Mama?" Trav was saying. He looked pissed off.

"Uh-oh, what's she done now?" I said.

"Mama's got a date," Travis said, rolling his eyes. "With some musician."

"I'd hardly call him 'some musician,'" Jude put in. "The man's a star, at least back in Nashville, and that's saying a lot."

"Hold on," I said. "What are you all yammering about?"

"I met this lovely gentleman yesterday and he invited me for a drink," Mama said. "I don't see what all the fuss is about."

"Sorry, honey, it's my bad," Amanda said. "I sent your mama to measure Lester Orcutt for a new pair of leathers— she's got a way with the male clients, you know."

"I'll just bet she does." I shot my mama a look, but she had on her innocent face, the one that suckers men everywhere into wanting to protect her and believe her lies and buy her Bacardi and Cokes.

"I was very professional," my mama said. "Although I might've gotten the measurements a teeny-tiny bit wrong. It's hard to fit pants when the client is *engorged*, so to speak."

Mama looked pleased as punch with herself. I could see why Trav was disgusted.

"You're supposed to be makin' money, Mama, not makin' a fool of yourself," I said.

"And you should've turned him down," Amanda put in. "You don't shit where you eat, Early, especially in Hollywood. You get Lester angry at me, I lose one of my biggest clients."

"How'm I gonna get him angry?" my mama asked. "And why shouldn't I take a night out for myself? I've been working my fingers to the bone tryin' to support you children, and nobody's puttin' fifteen percent of it away for *me*."

"You've been an assistant seamstress and laundress for a couple of days," I said. "It's hardly difficult labor. And besides, you're a married woman."

"That doesn't stop your daddy from steppin' out with all them little sluts!" Mama snapped.

"Isn't Lester married, too?" Jude said. "I thought he was on wife number three?"

"Number four," Amanda said. "Plus he's got a girlfriend out in Venice and a baby with some ex–porn star in Chatsworth. That's in addition to his four legit kids. Trust me, no woman should give this man the time of day."

Mama brushed her fingertips over the bright red polish

on her toes, checking to see if they were dry. "Y'all're acting like a bunch of old hens," she said. "I don't want to marry the man. I just want to see what the Hollywood nightlife is like, have some fun, and it don't hurt if he wants to buy the drinks. More money for Chloe's big music video."

"Don't do me any favors, Mama," I said.

"Trust me on this, Early—steer clear," Amanda said. "I love Lester Orcutt dearly, but he's bad news."

Mama slipped her heels on and stood up. "Lord knows why I should take romance advice from a couple of children and a fatty. And *you're* so unnatural you don't even like men," she added, frowning at Jude. "I'm the only one here that's actually been in love the proper way and given birth and been responsible for two lives. I know how to handle myself better than all y'all, thank you very much."

Travis and I glanced at each other and busted out laughing. "Mama, I've seen stray dogs more responsible than you," I said.

"And with better manners," Trav said, shooting an apologetic look at our friends. But I figured by now everybody understood who Mama was and what she was about.

Mama's eyes teared up. "I don't know how you two can be so darn mean to your own mama! That kind of childish behavior is just exactly why I need a night out to myself with some adult company." Her chin trembled a little, like she was holding back the sobs. "You're not the only one with dreams, Clo!

I sacrificed my youth to you children and now I want to have some fun of my own. I'm only thirty-three years old! I still got time. Don't I deserve to be happy just once in my life?"

"Save it for someone who's buying, Mama," Travis said. "Maybe you oughta be on camera instead of Chloe."

"Bite your tongue," I told him. "She don't need any encouragement to bring on the drama."

"You are ungrateful children." Mama grabbed her purse and stalked off. "Don't bother waiting up."

As the beige door closed behind her, Trav's face grew serious. "That's no good, Clo," he said. "That there will lead to disaster."

"Hang it higher," Jude said early the next morning. "I don't want a reflection from the white wall above it."

I sat back and closed my eyes, blocking out Jude's super-bright lights and the shimmery blue-green fabric Amanda had brought for us to use as a background. It matched my eyes, she said, and she was right, even though my mama always says my eyes are straight-up blue—she doesn't want to admit that I have any of my daddy in me. Travis was busy tacking the fabric to the wall of the Oakwood schoolroom with thumbtacks we'd hijacked from the bulletin board in the local supermarket.

"I'm using liquid eyeliner, so don't open your eyes until it dries," Livia said, just before I felt the cold, wet brush slide over my lash line. I had to admit, I was pretty impressed that she'd shown up at six in the morning to do my makeup. Travis said she worked as an assistant to some makeup artist as her day job, but that only meant Livia considered herself to be an actress, not a makeup person. It had to be hard on her to help another actress, one with an agent and a horde of Hollywood people trolling the Internet for her. Namely, me.

"Done," Livia said.

I opened my eyes, grabbed the hand mirror she'd brought, and checked myself out. Livia had done a heavy-lidded, smoky-eyed thing that would've got me kicked out on my butt if I'd ever showed up to St. Paul's for morning mass looking like that.

"I love it," I said. "I don't think I've ever looked this good in my whole life."

Livia didn't answer, but her permanent sneer got a little deeper.

She couldn't take a compliment—not my problem. If she didn't want to be a makeup artist, she shouldn't agree to do people's makeup. You'd never find me working in this town as anything but an actress, because what would be the point? The trick is knowing what you want. Far as I could see, Livia wanted Travis more than she wanted to be an actress. Letting your boyfriend talk you into underperforming was just begging to be a doormat.

"Coffee! And a tea for Ms. Gamble," Marc said, appearing

in the doorway with a tray from Starbucks. "Also, there's some guy outside named TJ. I get the feeling he's not a morning person."

"That's the sound guy," Jude said, heading out there.

"Chloe Gamble, you're a stunner." Marc came over with my tea and stopped to inspect me.

"Thanks to Livia," I said. It's just like Klink had told me at NBC—you always had to be nice to the crew. Plus, it seemed to annoy Livia more when I was all sweet. "She's a fantastic makeup artist."

"I need coffee," Livia said, and walked off in a huff.

"Who did the outfit?" Marc said. "You or Amanda?"

"You like it?" I asked, smoothing the skirt of my former beaded pageant gown. I'd torn the whole thing apart last night and repurposed it—that's what Amanda called it. The dress had a mysterious, sexy feel now, with every hint of beauty pageant removed. Amanda claimed she was just helping, but she'd done most of the work.

"I like it. It's very J. Lo-ish." Marc took one look at my face and laughed.

"Can I pull it off?" I said.

"Is there anything you can't pull off?" he asked.

*Crashing a network test*, I thought. "Nope," I said out loud. Never admit a weakness.

"Hey, everyone, this is TJ, the sound guy," Jude said, coming back in with a big black case full of equipment. The heavyset man behind her was lugging two more cases. Travis ran over to help.

TJ glanced around the room, frowning. I knew what he was seeing—a bunch of nobodies in an ugly room, making an amateur music video. My happy buzz began to fade.

"I'll need my money upfront," TJ said.

Before I could even react, Nika was moving toward him. "Let's go talk outside. Chloe needs to concentrate on getting ready."

"It's okay," I said. "Trav, can you pay this nice gentleman so we can get moving? I just know he's gonna make me sound like a star." I gave TJ a wink, and his eyes stopped roaming around the room and stayed right on me.

"Thanks," he said as my twin forked over the cash.

"You get the thanks," I said. "Comin' out here to help me at the crack of dawn!"

TJ shrugged. "I have a one-year-old kid. I don't sleep anyway." He pocketed the money and began unpacking his gear.

"Let's see you against the backdrop, Clo. I need to check the lighting," Jude said.

The second I stepped onto the "stage," everything else began to fade into the background. I was alone up there, the fabric like a soft haze behind me, the lights so bright in my eyes that I could barely see. It felt as if I'd stepped into a private little world, one where people dressed me and did my makeup and brought me tea and treated me like a pampered little princess. I laughed out loud.

"What's so funny?" Travis said, and I realized he was standing to the side, just out of the light.

"Nothing. I'm just . . . home," I said with a kind of goofy grin.

"Well, don't get too excited. We're gonna have to go search for Mama when we're done shooting," my brother said. "She never came home last night."

I waved him off. "We find that country singer, we find Mama. She'll come home when he gets bored with her, don't you worry."

Jude stepped up and held some little doodad in front of my face. She pressed a button and a flash went off. I was still blinking back the dizzying dots of light when she announced, "I'm ready. Stay right where you are, Clo."

"My turn." TJ appeared and held up a tiny microphone. "I'm gonna attach this to your dress . . . somewhere." He searched the flimsy fabric for a place to hide it.

"We can stick it in my bra," I said. "Will that work?"

"Works for me." He reached for the bra, then stopped. "Sorry—is that okay?"

I grinned. "You're a professional, right?"

TJ relaxed. "I'm not a professional bra grabber, if that's what you mean." But he worked quickly, hooking me up to the mike.

"Boy or a girl?" I asked. "Your kid?"

He blinked in surprise. "Um, a girl. Daisy."

"I love that name," I said.

"Thanks." He gave me a strange look as he headed back over to his gear. "Can you give me a test, Chloe?"

"Testing," I said. Then I sang, "Testing!"

"We ready?" Jude asked.

"Yeah." TJ disappeared behind the black boxes and Jude stepped into my little circle of light.

"Let's just run through it once, Chloe," Jude said. "So I know what to expect. I'll shoot it straight and then we'll play around for another few takes."

"Okay." I took a deep breath and closed my eyes. Alan's class popped into my mind, and I smiled. Alan's class. I liked it there. I did "nice work" there. When I started to sing, I pretended I *was* there, in front of the black room, acting.

"Hold on." TJ's voice broke my concentration. "Sorry, Chloe, I want to adjust something." I could just make him out past the lights, changing the levels on one of his machines. "Test?"

"One, two, three," I said.

TJ gave a thumbs-up. "Perfect!" he called. "We're good to go. Sorry to interrupt."

But he didn't have to apologize to me. I wanted him to fix the sound; I wanted him to make it as perfect as possible. If I ever found Klink again, I'd have to thank him. *Be nice to the people who make you look good*—he was right. Be nice and maybe it will surprise them, like with TJ, and maybe it would make them do a better job. And when they do a better job, I look even more like a star.

A smile spread across my face. It was coming—I could feel it! My time was finally here. Travis, Jude, TJ, even Livia—they were all here for *me*. It might be nothing but a crappy conference room in a condo park, but I was the star.

"Let's see it, Chloe," Jude called. "Action."

This time I didn't think about acting class. I just thought about how right it felt—that moment, that feeling, the lights on me, only on me, the camera aimed at me, the sound of my voice filling the room. Right then I knew that if I couldn't have this feeling of being in front of the spotlight each day for the rest of my life, well, I'd die.

The song came pouring out of me. I wasn't even thinking about the words or the tune or anything. I was just *feeling*, pure and simple. When I got to the end, I sang the chorus again: "I could care, but I don't. I could cry, but I won't. I could run, but where to? 'Cause wherever I'd be, I'd still remember *you*." Then I simply stood there, gazing into the lights, my breath coming fast. I'd sung that song about a million times before, but it had never sounded like that. There was the briefest moment of silence, until Nika whispered from the shadows, "Say your name, girl."

"Oh, I'm Chloe," I said. "Chloe Gamble."

"And cut," Jude said.

That's when they all applauded. Even TJ was whistling

from the back of the room. I laughed, soaking it in. "You can edit that last part out, right?" I called to Nika.

"Over my dead body," she said. "That was the most important part!"

When the lights were off and the magic feeling had faded a little, I went over to say thanks to TJ and shake his hand. You've got to be nice all the way through, I figured. After all, who knew when I might need him to do me a favor?

"Hey, did you really write that song?" he asked me as he closed up his last case.

"Sure did," I said.

"You should write some more, like maybe seven or eight more," he said. "My cousin has a little recording studio up in Van Nuys, and I'll be your sound engineer."

"Hang on—you mean I should record an album?" I said.

"You can sing, but it's also a damn good song," TJ said. "Not many pop stars write their own stuff. It'd set you apart."

"I'll think about it," I said. "See if inspiration strikes me."

TJ laughed. "It'll strike when you're not expecting it. Good luck with the video."

After he left, Travis came over with Livia. "I have to swing by Jude's so we can upload all this," he said. "You coming, Clo?"

"I was thinking of heading to school," I said. "My history teacher is getting on my case for missing too much. You don't need me for the tech stuff, do you?"

"It's *your* stupid video," Livia said. "Why should Travis have to deal with it for you?"

"I don't mind," Trav said. "I'll just tell the attendance office I was working all day. I have my novelty underwear shoot this afternoon anyway, so it's kind of true."

"Thanks, Trav," I said. "I'll pay you back one day."

My brother might've answered me if his girlfriend hadn't chosen that moment to stick her tongue in his ear. Travis didn't seem tired of her bizarre behavior, but I can tell you I was just about done with it.

"I'll go to Jude's and oversee the uploading," Nika said, turning me away from them. "You just worry about school."

"Here's my card, Chloe," Marc added, tucking it into my bra strap. "If this all works, I hope you'll consider letting me handle you."

"Handle me?" I asked.

"Yeah, do your PR. I won't charge you," he said. "I'll hip-pocket you, do publicity for you, in return for you pulling me up with you when you reach the heights."

"Like with Nika?" I asked. "You help make me, then I help make you?"

He nodded.

"So I do have a publicist after all," I said, excitement building up inside me. If this was all it took to get people on board, I'd have an entire entourage before long! A little voice inside was whispering that it could all go away just as easily. One more NBC-level disaster and these people would vanish like a puff of Amanda's cigarette smoke.

But so what? I wasn't going to fail. Now that I knew what my life could be like, I would never let myself fail again.

## E-mail from Travis Gamble

I've got some crushing news for you, Coop—and for the rest of the locker room, too! I think I'm done with Livia. Or she's done with me. Whatevs. I asked her to do my sister's makeup for this video thing (check YouTube for Chloe Gamble tomorrow, BTW). Because Livia does makeup—that's how she makes money. And she's my girlfriend and Clo's my sister, so she should want to help out, right? Made sense to me. Anyway, afterward Livia fucking FLIPPED OUT—she was all, "you have no respect for me as an actress" and "you should be helping me, not your stupid sister." I don't know what her damage is—Clo was totally nice to her. So I say, you know, chill—I'm always gonna help my twin sister, and then Livia takes it to a whole other level. I mean, fucked-up shit, like why is Chloe so important and maybe I'm in love with Chloe and maybe I should be dating Chloe instead—I'm telling you, man, messed up. So I go to leave, 'cause I'm not gonna listen to that. And then she's all, "I never want to see you again" and "you'll never find anybody like me again!" Yeah, I hope not, 'cause she's batshit crazy!

So that's it for my fling with the hot older actress. I still never saw her apartment—she only ever wanted to make-out in public. I did see a lot of strange places that way, though.

I don't know, Coop—I think I'm losing control of the Gamble women. You know I only came here to keep them safe, but right now my mama is off doing God knows what and Chloe's causing trouble even when she don't mean to. She didn't do a thing to Livia, but Livia HATES her. That's how it seems to be for Chloe—people either hate her or love her. Jude says Chloe inspires strong feelings. But if that's true, it might not be such a hot idea for her to get all famous like she wants to. Who knows what kinds of psychos will come after her one way or the other?

I guess it doesn't matter, 'cause there's no stopping Chloe. All I can do now is wait and see if this YouTube video works. Spread the word, my man—we need this thing to go viral or else Chloe's career is going nowhere.

# chapter eight

## Payoff

"Let's all turn to page two thirty-eight," my history teacher said while I was working the keyboard.

It was hard to type with my BlackBerry held underneath my desk, but I just couldn't wait one more second. Ms. Klonsky was droning on about the Treaty of Versailles, and how was I supposed to concentrate on that?

There was a rustling of paper as everybody in the classroom turned to the correct page in the textbook. I quickly flipped the pages and tried to see the BlackBerry at the same time. Using a cell phone in class was a serious don't and could get me sent straight to the principal.

The screen changed, and I caught my breath.

Screw history. I pulled the BlackBerry out from under my desk and lifted it up to see better.

"Yeeeeah!" I cried.

Everyone in class turned to stare at me.

"Go, Allies!" I cheered, gesturing to the textbook. "Germany sucks."

Ms. Klonsky looked confused, and the kids sitting nearby all laughed. "Ms. Klonsky, can I have a pass to the girls' room?" I asked. "Now that the war is over, I'm so excited I have to pee!"

Everybody laughed again. Ms. Klonsky's nose wrinkled a little and she hesitated, trying to figure out if I was being smart with her. I just kept my big, goofy Texas smile plastered on my face and fidgeted in my seat a little.

"Okay, don't be long," she said with a sigh.

I leaped up, grabbed the bathroom pass, and took off. Third period—Travis would be in Spanish class. I went straight past the girls' room, up the stairs, and down the hall to my twin's classroom. I knocked on the door, then went right in.

"Señor Garrido, I'm so sorry to interrupt," I said, "but I need my brother right this second. It's a family emergency."

The teacher frowned. "The office didn't call."

"They said your classroom phone wasn't working and they're sending the maintenance guy to fix it," I lied. "They told me to come get Trav myself."

Señor Garrido looked at the phone on the wall, surprised.

Trav grabbed his stuff and hustled me out of the room before the teacher could stop us. "We leaving?" he said when we were halfway down the hall.

"Yup."

"This door's closest to the student parking lot." Trav pushed open a metal door and led the way across a little alley and into the parking lot on the other side. Our Ford looked pathetic among all the Mercedeses and Land Rovers. Travis peeled out the second our butts hit the seats. Once we were beyond school grounds, stopped at a light on Ventura Boulevard, he glanced over at me. "You want to tell me what this is all about?"

"Look!" I handed him my BlackBerry, the Google search-results page still up.

"Holy crap," Trav said.

We sat quietly for a minute. And then Travis started to laugh. He pulled over to the side of the road, turned off the car, and just howled.

The Studio School was letting out for lunch when we got back to the Oakwood. Those little red-haired twins darted straight for the pool, and a couple of the actors headed next door into the Oakwood fitness room. I looked around for Kimber Reeve, but the closest thing I got was her boyfriend—or ex-boyfriend—Max.

"Chloe! Hey, girl," he said, kissing me on both cheeks like we were French or something. "I saw your video."

*So that's why we're kissing now,* I thought.

"I can see why Kimber hates you so much," he added.

I laughed out loud. "I don't think you're supposed to be that truthful," I said. "Kimber wouldn't like it."

"Kimber can kiss my ass," he said.

So he was the ex-boyfriend for sure. "You guys ended badly, huh?" I asked.

"Who knows? We had a fight and the next day she and her mom were gone, moved out without even telling me they were leaving."

"Kimber moved?" I said. It made sense—her show had been picked up. "Where to?"

"Hell if I know," Max said. "But listen, I have the perfect guitar riff for the beginning of your song."

"Mm-hmm," I said, but I wasn't really listening anymore. My eye was on Trav, because his eye was on the fitness room and he'd gotten weirdly quiet. I looked through the window in the door and spotted Livia on one of the treadmills, flirting with some guy.

"I'll see you upstairs, Clo," my twin said, taking off. Looked like Travis was an ex-boyfriend now, too.

"That song got stuck in my head and I ended up staying awake half the night working on it. . . ." Max was saying.

I checked out the dude Livia was talking to—a tall, thin guy who looked familiar somehow.

"Oh my God, it's the porn guy!" I burst out.

"What?" Max tilted his head—and his dreads—to the side, confused.

"Alex—he makes pornos; I met him at a party," I said. I pointed to the fitness room. "I guess Livia must've met him there, too."

Max peered in the window. Alex was on his cell phone now, and Livia was done with her jog. "Oh, that dude. I see him around here a lot," Max said. "Didn't know he was a perv. Anyway, think about it. The song. It would make Kimber mad if we did it together."

It certainly would. "I like the way you think," I said. "But I have to see Livia."

I pushed open the door to the gym and went inside. Livia was tossing her towel and her iPod into a gym bag.

"Livia," I said. "You know who—"

"Get outta my way," she snapped, pushing past me. "I'm done being nice to you."

Wow. Today must be the day for honesty, what with Max busting on Kimber and Livia busting on me.

"Okay, so I'm guessing you and Trav are on the outs," I said. "But I'm just trying to warn you—"

But Livia was gone, out of the fitness room, letting the door swing shut in my face. I turned around to look at Alex. He'd obviously been staring at my ass.

"Think I should tell the landlord that you're trolling for talent here?" I asked him.

His eyes moved up to my face, and he shrugged. "Omar's an old friend of mine. I've been renting a studio here for years."

Figured. I left without even looking at him again. If Livia was dumb enough to give that dude the time of day, it was her own fault.

"I've got the bubbly," Marc said when I opened the apartment door half an hour later. "Let the YouTube premiere party start!"

I felt as if my entire body was vibrating already, but I lunged for the champagne. Champagne to celebrate *me*! I'd never had that before.

"Down, girl," Marc said. "For you little ones, I have some sparkling cider. Don't wave your fake IDs at me," he added, taking one look at Trav's face. "I know you're severely underage."

He handed the bottle to Nika, who was set up at the kitchen table, booting up her laptop.

"Can we get down to business, please?" Jude called from the couch. Her computer was already open on her lap. "I've been dying to look at YouTube all day, but I wanted to wait."

Nika nodded. "Me too."

"Well, I couldn't wait. I searched myself on Google and came up with five pages worth of me!" I said. "Search!"

Marc did a little drumroll on the kitchen counter while Nika and Jude typed into their laptops. "Twelve thousand views on YouTube," Jude said.

"How long's it been up?" Marc asked.

"I posted it around five last night," Travis said. "So less than a day."

Nika let out a low whistle. "I'm searching MySpace. . . . God, there must be fifty different pages. All these people put your video on their MySpace page."

"It's the same on Facebook," Jude said.

My pulse was pounding in my ears and my skin seemed electrified. People I didn't even know were looking at me, right this instant, watching me sing and loving me so much that they had to stick my video onto their own sites. That was weird. It was incredible.

"Okay, *now* we break out the champagne big-time," Nika said. "You're on Perez Hilton."

"Shut up, she is not." Marc ran to look over my agent's shoulder.

"What's that?" Travis asked.

"A big gossip blog. Like the online version of *Us Weekly*," I said, sinking down next to Jude on the couch. She grinned at me, and I think I smiled back. Who knows? I was practically having an out-of-body experience. Perez Hilton talks about Britney Spears and Selena Gomez and Lindsay Lohan. Not about me.

"I think it's time to check my e-mail, Chloe," Nika said.

I nodded.

"Sweet Jesus, that's a lot of messages," Marc said. I ran

over to look as Nika scrolled through e-mail after e-mail titled "Chloe Gamble."

"Check your voice mail," Marc said. "The ones who really want her will call first."

"Okay, I'll do it on speaker." Nika dialed her cell, then set it on the table so we could all hear. As soon as she entered her password, the message came on: "Your voice mailbox is full."

"It worked," Nika said wonderingly. "It really worked."

*Pop!* The cork on the champagne bottle flew through the air and Marc started filling glasses, ignoring the bottle of sparkling cider on the counter. He handed the first glass to me.

"Here's the *Variety* headline," he said. " 'The Gamble pays off!' "

## Nika Mays's Manuscript Notes: The Don't-Do

It's a tricky thing to launch a new career. So tricky that a lot of agents won't even do it. They get big, they have a nice list of clients who bring in the commissions, and they just concentrate on keeping the jobs coming. Someone else can break in the newcomers—someone like Hal Turman—and once the work is pouring in and all the career land mines have been avoided, then these agents will step in and steal the clients. It's obnoxious, it's vaguely unethical, and it's much, much easier than navigating those career land mines yourself.

Hal wasn't much for teaching, but that didn't stop me from picking up a few pointers over the two years I'd worked for him. Back at Stanford, the career-counseling office had said that my liberal-arts degree meant that I had "learned how to learn." It had sounded like complete bullshit, but maybe they had been right. Because Hal Turman had made himself a legend by launching careers. He was over the hill—his last huge star was maybe a decade ago—but I had to give him this: Hal knew how to start people off in Hollywood. And after watching him in action, so did I.

For starters, I knew that the sheer number of people who wanted to meet Chloe was a blessing and a curse. I couldn't send her out to five hundred meetings and still hope to keep the mystique that had surrounded her ever since NBC. Everybody in town wanted a meeting, and most of them were probably just curious. Curiosity wasn't going to get Chloe a job. So the first thing I had to do was figure out where to send her. Who was serious? Who was looking to hire her? And who did we want her working with?

That was the topic of discussion in Hal Turman's office the morning after the YouTube celebration. My boss wouldn't have known what YouTube was if it had walked up and kissed him on the lips. But he knew what a full voice mailbox was: It was a gold mine.

"She's a kid. She's gotta play a kid," Hal said as soon as Chloe arrived. "I don't want to hear any of this sixteen-playing-twenty-five bullcrap."

"But I can—" Chloe started.

"You can play twenty-five when you're forty," Hal cut her off. "For now, we'll send you to Disney, Nickelodeon—what's that new one, Nika?"

"It's called Snap," I said.

"Right. And we'll meet with all the casting directors who work with kids." Hal was simply going through his usual checklist of how to start a career. But I knew already that Chloe Gamble wasn't going to follow any checklist.

"I'm not a kid," Chloe said.

"Sorry—you prefer 'child'?" Hal asked. "Because those are the only two options."

"I don't want to be a child star; I want to be a star," Chloe said. "I'm already too old to even watch those channels."

"And Olivia Newton-John was twenty-nine when she played a teenager in *Grease*," Hal said. "This town loves youth, young lady. Don't be too eager to grow up."

Chloe looked like she was about to let him have it—I could already read her well enough to know when she was ready to blow. I had to step in. "He's not wrong, Chloe," I said. "You can't start out as a superstar, not if you want a long career. You have to work your way up. There's no need to rush into a high-profile job when you haven't even learned the game yet. Cut your teeth on a teen-oriented show, learn how it all works and then when you get the really big job you'll be ready."

"Fine," Chloe said. "Get me a job on some teen show."

"'Some teen show.' Listen to her," Hal said, throwing his hands into the air. "What you need to learn, sweetheart, is the art of the Don't-Do."

*Here it comes*, I thought. Hal never got through a meeting without describing the Don't-Do. He wasn't aware of it, but there was a tiny bit of graffiti in the women's office bathroom, right above the toilet paper in the left-hand stall. It said "Don't Do Hal."

"You're new in town. The world's your oyster," Hal said. "That's what you think. But if you go grabbing at the first thing that comes along, you're going to look cheap. So you don't do it."

"Don't do what?" Chloe asked.

"The job. You say no to the first offer. Then you say no to the second offer. Then when the third offer comes, what do you do?"

"You say no," Chloe said.

"That's right. You Don't. Do. It." Hal sat back in his gigantic chair, nodding and beaming as if he'd just taught her a valuable life lesson. He hadn't even noticed the sarcasm in Chloe's voice.

"So that's your plan. I don't do any jobs," Chloe said.

I stood up quickly. "I'll set up those meetings, then. Thanks for your help, Hal." I practically shoved Chloe out the door. Bonnie was loitering nearby. One look from Chloe was all it took to get her moving back to her own office.

"We can use the conference room," I said. "I want to get you scheduled for all of next week, and we'll spend the rest of this week prepping."

"What's to prep for? I just say no," Chloe said. "Course, if I keep saying no to paying jobs, my brother and I are gonna get kicked out on our butts and have nothing to eat. But at least I won't look cheap."

"Don't worry about Hal. I can handle him," I said.

"I don't need an agent to teach me how to play hard to get," Chloe said. "I thought an agent was supposed to find me a damn job!"

"I will. But Hal has a point, Chloe. You have to be choosy—you can't just take the first gig that offers you money."

"Watch me," Chloe said.

There was a fire in her eyes that made me take a step back. Ambition, fury, need—some combination of all those things, blocking out everything else. I'd seen it before, when she had sung her song for Hal and Bonnie. That day, Chloe's drive had been on my side. But today, it was standing in my way.

"Be reasonable, Clo," I said.

The fire blazed up, and for one brief, crazy moment I thought she might hit me. "Reasonable" was not in Chloe's vocabulary when it came to her career.

Looking back, I should have realized at that moment that Chloe's ambition was a double-edged sword. Had I known then what I know now—it would have saved me a lot of heartache.

"I'm going to get you a job," I went on, talking fast. "But I want you to be Natalie Portman. Not Tara Reid."

Chloe blinked, surprised.

"You read the tabloids—I saw a stack of them

in your apartment," I said. "When's the last time you saw Tara Reid's name in print?"

"They make fun of her online sometimes," Chloe said.

"Right. Because she hasn't worked in years. Know why?" I said. "She took every job that came her way, no matter what level of crap it was. And while she did that, she went out partying instead of getting an education. So people got bored of seeing her face in the gossip rags, and they got bored of seeing her in the same bimbo role time and time again, and she got a tiny bit too old to play that role, and that was it for her career. But Natalie Portman, she chose her roles carefully. She took only quality films, and she took time off when she needed to, to go to college. She knew it wasn't all about getting the quick money."

"She didn't need quick money—she had rich parents," Chloe shot back.

"Well, then, be Anne Hathaway," I said. "She started out in teen roles, and look at her now! It's because she waited until she actually was a grown-up before she took grown-up parts. People liked her because they thought she was sweet and classy, like her teen roles. She wanted to keep those people on her side, so she didn't insult them by playing a stripper in a horror movie."

"I do read those magazines, so here's what I know," Chloe said. "Anne Hathaway's father was a lawyer. She went to an expensive college, just like Natalie Portman. Just like Jodie Foster a long time ago. Just like that bitch Kimber Reeve probably will in a few years. Well, I hate to tell you this, Nika, but I ain't no rich girl from a nice family. You got stuck with a poor girl from Spurlock, Texas, who can't afford to go Ivy League. My parents suck and my life was one big pile of shit up until the day I arrived here. I need things to happen now. I can't afford to wait. If you want a good girl who's willing to follow the rules, go get Kimber to be your client."

"Are you kidding? A rich girl from a nice family would never take a chance on an agent's assistant," I said.

Chloe laughed, and the fire in her eyes went out. But just for a little while.

## E-mail from Travis Gamble

Hey, Coop. Chloe says to tell you thanks for talking up her video online. It was pretty tight, huh? It totally worked, BTW—Clo's got all kinds of big Hollywood meetings set up because of it. I thought it was a stupid idea at first, but I guess her agent really knows what she's doing! Anyway, she's gonna be out of school all next week, and then if she gets a job she might have to stay out for good. Nika—that's the agent—is some big brainiac from Stanford, and she's talking to the school about doing homeschooling for Chloe, where Nika will oversee Clo's education and Clo will send things in to St. Paul's for grading and stuff. It sounds like a pain in the butt to me. You know how smart Chloe is—why does she even need school? She aces all her classes without even studying. Whatever—the point is that St. Paul's might not let Chloe do it because she doesn't have a parent to sign the homeschooling papers. Know why? 'Cause Mama's still MIA.

Remember I told you she went out with that country singer? Well, she must've taken off with him. We haven't seen her in a week. Keep it quiet, though—it's embarrassing. Me and Clo are okay, don't worry. We still have some cash from Chloe's beauty pageant and the money I made from modeling. I did get another underwear gig (shut up)—this booker called me and she wanted me to do magazine ads for Jockey. Jude says it's a big step up because it's not just catalog work—it's actual advertising for a huge company. But the shoot was for tonight and my team's got a huge match against this team from Brentwood. I was willing to skip the match but Chloe said no way. The only reason we have a scholarship to St. Paul's is my soccer, and she doesn't want to ruin that. She got that stylist Mama worked for to give her some sewing to do, just so we could earn some food money. Chloe says the beauty-pageant money can't be touched for anything but rent.

I feel guilty, man. Why should my sister have to stay up all night sewing just so I can play soccer? Clo's got school and she works at an acting studio and she has all this Hollywood stress. All I gotta do to earn money is smile and stick my ass out in some Jockeys. But you know Chloe—she calls the shots.

I hope all those meetings get her a job soon.

## Meet and Greet

Monday Morning. Burbank.
Kathy Boutry, VP of Development, the Disney Channel.

"Is my hair okay?" I asked Nika as we waited in the lobby of the Disney Channel offices.

"Well, you still didn't get your expensive razor cut," she said. "But I guess it looks okay."

I stuck my tongue out at her.

"Can I get you guys anything?" the girl at the desk called over. "Water? Diet Coke?"

"No, thanks," I said. Diet Coke for a meeting? Seemed weird. Though I wasn't really sure what a "meeting" was. Not an audition—Nika had been clear as a bell on that. Nobody expected me to whip out a monologue and start acting. Far as I could tell, all I had to do was look pretty—but in a flirty little dress and loose, flowy hair kind of way, nothing beauty pageant-y—that's what Amanda had said.

And then I had to "tell my story"—that's what Nika had said.

How any of that was going to land me a job, I had no idea. But they were the pros. And I'd promised Hal that I would do as told.

"Chloe Gamble!" the Disney Channel executive said, appearing from a door on the other side of the room. She was probably twenty-five and had on a hip power wardrobe from Banana Republic. I liked her right away.

Nika stood up. "Chloe, this is Kathy," she said.

Kathy gave me a nice, firm handshake that any pageant coach would approve of. "I saw your video—it's amazing. Am I your first meeting?" she asked.

"Unless you count crashing a network test at NBC," I said.

Nika froze. Kathy Boutry froze. They both looked a tiny bit panicky.

"Which I don't," I said. And we all laughed. *So the NBC fiasco still makes people uncomfortable,* I thought. Noted. No joking about that again, ever.

**Monday Afternoon. Santa Monica.**
**Emily Griffith, Development Executive, the Cartoon**
**Network.**

"You guys need anything? Water? Diet Coke?" the development executive asked. Her name was Emily. Or Emmy. After three meetings, I had started to lose track of the names. On the pageant circuit, I had made sure to memorize everybody's name. But here I had Nika, and she knew them all and kept track of their names and titles. It must be what having a coach was like for all those pageant princesses. For the first time ever, I didn't have to do all the work myself.

"No, thanks," I said. Nika and I squeezed ourselves onto the love seat stuffed into the small office—Emily/Emmy called it a couch, but if that was a couch then I was Kimber Reeve. The small talk started up, same as in the other meetings. The weather here was incredible. Not humid like in Texas. Did I know how to find my way around town yet? How did I like the Oakwood?

I didn't even have to listen to myself answer the questions. I looked around. The office had framed posters on the wall, most of them for animated movies I'd never heard of.

"So what made you decide to do the big move to Hollywood?" Emily/Emmy asked.

My attention snapped back to the meeting. "You know, it's the funniest thing," I said. "I honestly didn't even give a thought to myself. My mama and daddy decided to split up, and my poor mama was so sad. . . ."

I paused, letting her nod sympathetically. I'd learned to put the pause there after meeting number two, when this particular bit of info had seemed to draw a good response.

"And I said, 'Mama, you need a fresh start!' and we just hopped into the car and took off for Hollywood!"

"Wow," said Emily/Emmy.

"Yeah." I smiled my best brave-daughter smile. "So . . . you do animated movies?" I asked.

"That's our bread and butter," Emily/Emmy said. "But we've got a new mandate to do live action. We're shopping around for the perfect script right now. . . ."

She kept talking and I kept nodding, but I wasn't listening. They didn't even have a movie to make yet.

It didn't matter how nice this woman was—she was not going to be offering me a job before the rent was due.

## Tuesday Afternoon. Hollywood.
## Robert Zimmer, VP of Current Programming, Nickelodeon.

"I think you're an incredible fit for Nickelodeon," said the Nick executive. He was the first straight guy I'd met with and his name was Rob. The junior executives in the room—two more Banana Republic–wearing twentysomething chicks—nodded like bobblehead dolls, their almost identical brunette layer cuts swinging.

"Really," Rob went on, playing with his shiny new wedding ring and pretending not to stare at my legs. "It's a no-brainer."

"We'd absolutely love to work with you, wouldn't we, Chloe?" Nika said.

"Sure," I said. "Did you have anything specific in mind?"

All three Nickelodeon execs stared at me, baffled. "Of

course, yeah," the guy said. "We'll get you in to meet with a couple of our producers."

"When?" I asked.

"As soon as possible," Rob said. "We'll talk later, Nika?"

"Absolutely." My agent stood up. Another meeting over, and still no job.

"You mind telling me what we're doing?" I said to Nika as we climbed back into her Mini Cooper to drive to the next meeting.

"Hmm?" She tucked her Bluetooth headset behind her ear in case anybody called.

"I've been chatting like a cheerleader on speed for two days now and nobody has even mentioned an actual role in a movie," I said. "Or a TV show. Or anything."

Nika shrugged. "These are general meetings."

"What's that mean? Generally useless?" I asked.

"Everybody likes to work with people they know, so the first step is getting them to know you," Nika said. "It might seem useless, but now that these execs have a feel for who you are and what your energy is, they'll have a better idea of what parts you'd be good for."

"So I'm supposed to just sit around and wait while they think about me?" I said. "How's that going to get me a job?"

"It's a process, Clo," Nika said. "You can't just show up and land a starring role in a movie. Hollywood doesn't work like that."

I felt a rush of annoyance, but I forced it back down. Alan was always saying that you had to be aware of your emotions in order to access them for a role. Well, I was aware of how frustrated these meetings were making me—that was for sure. But Nika had a point. I'd tried to skip over the process at NBC and it had gotten me nowhere.

"Okay," I said. "I'll be good."

**Wednesday Morning. Hollywood.**
**Kieran Sumner,**
**President of Development at Collins/Grey, Paramount.**

"And that over there is the famous water tower," Kieran Sumner said, gesturing out the window at the studio. It looked just like NBC, except for the apparently famous water tower.

"Wow!" I cried, all enthusiasm.

He nodded, picking a speck of lint off his Armani pants. "Hey, can I get you two something to drink? Water? Diet Coke?"

"Do you have root beer?" I asked, just to see.

Kieran's perfectly groomed eyebrows drew together in confusion, but then he smiled. "I'll check."

After he'd sent his assistant on a root-beer hunt, Kieran turned back to us. Nika and I had more room on this guy's couch, and his office was big enough to have four different framed movie posters on the wall. Clearly Kieran was a step up from the execs I'd met before.

"Are you familiar with any of our stuff?" he asked.

"Doubt it," I said. Under the coffee table, Nika stabbed me with the heel of her shoe. "I mean, I'm so new in town," I went on, quickly putting the perkiness back into my voice. "I just can't even keep track of all the different studios and production companies and networks and all."

He smiled sympathetically. "It can be overwhelming."

"So what do y'all do?" I asked.

"We've found a nice little niche in young-adult entertainment," he said. "You know, teen soaps. Family series. But we're branching out. This year I found a show to take us a bit more adult—*Virgin*."

I sat up straight. "You're the people who produce *Virgin*?" How on earth had Nika gotten them to agree to meet me? I'd figured anyone involved with that show would avoid me for the rest of my life.

"Well, it originated with us. Since then another studio has got involved, and of course the network." He sounded a little pissy about it. "We're not really hands-on anymore, but my boss still has an executive-producer credit. It would never have got made without us."

Nika was nodding, so I nodded, too.

"It must be frustrating, to lose control of your own show," I said.

Kieran shrugged. "It's still good to have the credit, especially now that it got an early pickup. We get buzz from it, same as everyone else."

My mind felt numb. I'd been to enough meetings now to know what an early pickup meant. It meant Kimber's show didn't even have to wait until NBC announced their fall schedule. *Virgin* was already a go.

I sat through the rest of the meeting with a smile frozen on my face. Kimber's show was going on the air. She'd be a TV star. She'd have photo shoots and interviews in magazines in order to promote the show.

No wonder she'd moved out of the Oakwood.

She was a success. Right that second, Kimber Reeve was a working actress.

And I wasn't.

## Thursday Afternoon. Century City.
## Michael Duval, Casting Director.

"Can I get you anything?" the casting director asked. "Water? Diet Coke?"

"I'd love a water," I said. By now I knew that having a bottle to swig from gave me time to think of good answers to all the stupid small-talk questions.

He handed over a bottle of Evian. "Where's Nika?" he said.

"She was on a call. She'll be here in a few minutes," I said. I'd left Nika in the car, trying to settle on a date for my meeting at ABC Family.

The casting director—Michael, not Mike—nodded. "Well, thanks for coming in. We're at the last stages of casting, but I just had to meet the notorious Chloe Gamble." His eyes roamed all over my body. He hadn't looked me in the eye even once, which was weird because he was obviously gay.

But I didn't care. All the meeting boredom had fled from my brain the second I heard the word "casting."

"What are you casting?" I asked.

"Um, *Ritual.* I thought you knew that." He began scrolling through his BlackBerry, looking confused.

"No. I thought it was just a general meeting," I said. "But I'd rather talk about an actual project. I'm so sick of talking about myself."

He laughed. "That's hard to believe. Most actresses love to talk about themselves."

"Well, I'm completely fascinating, that's true," I joked. "But tell me about *Ritual.* It sounds like a vampire flick or something, but Nika said you do mostly comedies."

"Yeah. Sorry." He tapped at his BlackBerry. "I was supposed to be talking to you about a high school romance we've got coming up. It's not even greenlit yet—Nika's just getting you into the mix."

"But what's *Ritual?*" I said.

"Oh, it's a slasher film. You know, psycho loose in the woods, performing some ancient druid ritual on a bunch of campers." He shrugged. "We've got Casey Armistead and Ben Wilson as the two leads."

I nodded. I'd only ever seen them on TV, but as far as I could tell from the magazines, a lot of TV people do horror movies during the summer hiatus.

"Can I read for that movie?" I asked. "If you're almost done casting, you must be shooting soon, right?"

"Next week," he said. "But it'll be an R-rated film."

"Can I read for it?" I said again.

Michael shrugged. "Sure. Let's see what you've got." He rummaged around on his desk, then handed me the sides. "I'm looking for the first group of girls that get slaughtered," he said. "Let's see . . . why don't you read Camper Number Five? You don't mind if I put you on video, do you?"

By the time Nika arrived, I was on my second read-through. The scene was only one page long, and Camper Number Five said exactly fifteen words.

My agent did not look happy to see me reading sides from a horror film.

"Michael, I thought we were here to talk about *Soul Mates*," she said.

"Chloe wanted to read for *Ritual*," he told her. "She's fantastic. I'm still filling in the camper girls—I need two more."

Nika glanced at her watch. "You know what, we've got to get going. Chloe's got a meeting at Lifetime."

"Do I have to meet anyone else to get that part?" I asked Michael.

"Well . . . usually you'd read for the director," he said.

"Chloe, this isn't what we're here for," Nika put in.

"You can't just hire me yourself?" I said, focusing on Michael. "You liked my audition, didn't you? And you know I'm pretty enough."

"I do have some wiggle room." Michael shot Nika a look. "It's a small part and she's got buzz. I think the director will take my word for it."

"We're not interested in an R-rated film," Nika said.

"Yes, we are," I said, ignoring the death stare she was giving me. "If it's shooting soon and I can get paid soon."

"Let me put a call in to the director," Michael said. "Nika, we'll talk later."

In this case, "later" meant "in two minutes." We hadn't even pulled out of the parking garage when Nika's BlackBerry rang. She hit speaker and Michael's voice filled the Mini Cooper.

"We're in," he said. "The director saw Chloe's video online and he's willing to take a chance. It'll be about fourteen days of shooting."

Nika was frowning. But she said what I wanted to hear: "What's the offer?"

"Twenty-five," Michael said.

"Let me talk to Chloe and I'll get back to you in a bit." Nika hung up and glanced over at me.

"Twenty-five hundred will pay almost the whole rent for a month," I said.

"It's not twenty-five hundred, Chloe," Nika said. "It's twenty-five *thousand*. Welcome to Hollywood."

*chapter nine*

## Nika Mays's Manuscript Notes: Career Don'ts

I hate horror movies. A lot of people do. Ask anyone with a college degree, and they'll probably
tell you they don't like horror flicks. Oh, sure,
they can rattle off a list of all the psychopathic
killers from Freddy Krueger to Jigsaw. But they'll
say they hate that garbage.

They're lying.

They must be, because horror movies make more
money than any other kind of film. Other genres
come and go, but horror is a perennial. There
are lots of different kinds—stalker films, psycho

films, sci-fi horror, torture porn, and vampires, werewolves, and zombies, oh my!

People like to be scared. Make a movie that scares them, and they'll go see it. All you need are blades and blood and a willingness to be disgusting. What you don't need are movie stars. (If you put a movie star in a horror film, you get *The Silence of the Lambs*, which nobody will admit is a horror flick.) When you're making a horror film, you need one or two B-list names—TV actors or has-been movie actors. And the only reason you need them is to get the movie greenlit. Most of the parts can be played by unknowns. People aren't going to see your movie for the acting, anyway. And here's the secret: When you don't have to pay for big-name stars, you can keep your budget low.

Horror films are cheap to make, and people will go see even the crappiest horror film. That's an arrangement designed to turn a profit. And that's why so many of them get made.

But think about that for a moment. So many slasher movies. So many actors getting stabbed, shot, beaten, hacked up, devoured, or clawed to death. And so few of them showing up in any other movies, ever.

It's easy to get cast in a horror movie. It's

hard to get cast in anything else. There are a few big stars who started out in crappy slasher flicks, but odds are their publicists won't even put those films on the credit sheet. Movie stars don't want to be associated with the horror genre, period.

Which is why doing a horror movie is an awful way to begin an acting career. It gets the actor typecast as a Bad Horror-Movie Actor. If the actor is female, it generally gets her typecast as both a Bad Horror-Movie Actor *and* a bimbo, because let's face it, most female characters in horror movies are bimbos. Once the actress has that reputation, it's hard to convince casting directors to see her as anything else.

That's the argument I used with Chloe Gamble. She might have gotten this one job without even auditioning for the director. But she wouldn't get the next job, or the next. She wouldn't get better jobs, because she'd be a Bad Horror-Movie Actor.

I should've known better than to argue with Chloe. The girl had been mainlining tabloids since she had learned how to read. When she surfed the Web, it was to find info on Hollywood. She knew plenty about the industry, including all the huge stars with horror movies in their pasts: Renée Zellwegger, Johnny Depp, Jennifer Aniston, Leonardo

DiCaprio. And on and on and on. They'd managed to get past the stereotype and get better work. As far as Chloe was concerned, she would too.

Kimber Reeve had already done two low-budget horror flicks. And now she had a show on NBC.

There was no way I'd ever convince Chloe using that argument. So I dragged her back in to see Hal Turman.

"No way, no how, not on my watch," Hal bellowed, waving his hands around like he was having a fit. "Young lady, you are not even old enough to watch this piece-of-garbage movie in a theater!"

Chloe just folded her arms and stared him down. I held my breath, hoping that Hal's tactic would work better than mine.

"Child actors do not do films with an R rating!" Hal said. "R means nudity, profanity, gore—things you shouldn't even know about."

"I'm sixteen," Chloe said. "And I knew about that stuff when I was six."

"That's not the point," Hal said. "The point is, we want to sell you as a young girl, somebody for other young girls to look up to. And the parents of those girls are not going to take it kindly if they see you running bare-assed through the woods!"

"I'm not doing nudity," Chloe said.

"Just because you're not nude doesn't mean they'll put you in real clothes," Hal said. "Believe you me, they will have you dressed like a two-bit hooker."

"I don't care," Chloe said. "It's twenty-five thousand dollars."

"Chloe, think about the Internet," I said. "Miley Cyrus. Vanessa Hudgens. They take some really tame photos, and those pictures end up online and wreak havoc on their careers. Their fans are young and impressionable. Parents flip out about stuff like that."

"I'm not stupid enough to take naked pictures of myself," Chloe said.

"No, but when you get to be a big star, this horror movie will be online," I said. "Trust me, the second you're famous, the scenes you film will be right there for anybody to find. Parents aren't going to like that, either."

"It's the wrong image and that's final," Hal said. "We're selling you as a kid; you ought to act like a kid."

I wondered, later on, whether Hal had ever had this problem before. He'd broken a million young stars, just like he had said. Lots of them had gone on to be train wrecks, developing drug problems, marrying the wrong people, a few of them ending up dead before their time. He must've come up against Chloe Gamble-level stubbornness before, right?

I should have asked him how to deal with it. Because when Chloe signed the contract to play Camper #5 in *Ritual*, all I could do was throw up my hands and hope for the best.

## Taking Care of Business

"Thank God for small-town clerks," I said while Travis got ready for school. "You remember Joe Pepperidge—used to babysit us while Mama went out drinking? He works at the Spurlock Hall of Records now."

Trav was drinking OJ straight from the carton, so he didn't even answer.

"I managed to talk him into sending my birth certificate next-day mail. I got yours, too, just in case," I said. "Now that I got that contract signed for *Ritual*, I only have a week to set up the Coogan account. The birth certificate will be here in time, but I'm willing to bet Mama won't."

I paused, giving Travis time to chew on that.

"Don't even think about it, Clo," my twin said. "You ain't forging bank papers."

"You know nobody can ever tell my signature from Mama's," I said. I'd been forging my mama's name on report cards and permission slips and pageant applications for so many years, I knew her signature as well as I knew my own. "I forged the papers for all that homeschooling stuff and even Nika didn't know."

Travis looked me straight in the eye. "I'm not playing, Chloe. This isn't about school or some stupid beauty pageant. You're talking about bank accounts and legal documents. You can't forge them. It's against the law."

"Who's gonna know?"

"I am." He kept staring at me. "And if you do it, I'll tell Nika."

"You will not."

"I will."

My brother's expression was so serious that I took a step back. He'd never ratted on me before, not to anyone. I couldn't really believe he'd do it now, either. But he was dead serious, and I had to respect that.

"Fine. Then what'm I gonna do?" I said.

"We have to find Mama." Trav sighed and ran his hand through his sandy hair. "You think Amanda will give us the number for that country star?"

"Mr. Lester Orcutt?" I said. "It so happens that I have his number right here in my BlackBerry."

"What?" Trav's mouth fell open in shock.

"I was at Amanda's sewing those skirts for her the other day, and I got the number from her client files," I said. "I was afraid we might need it."

"You snooped around Amanda's files?" Travis sounded appalled.

"I didn't want to put her on the spot," I said, and I meant it. "Lester's her client. She's not supposed to give out his number to anyone. She has to sign nondisclosure papers and all for her famous clients. That's why I'd rather forge Mama's name."

Travis rolled his eyes and reached for the phone. "I'm calling him."

"No, let me," I said, pulling up the number on my Black-Berry. "He likes girls."

Lester Orcutt himself answered the phone.

"Hi, Mr. Orcutt. I am just so sorry to bother you," I said in my best Texas twang. "My name is Chloe Gamble, and I believe you're acquainted with my mama, Earlene?"

"Sure, I know Early," he said, his gravelly voice friendly. "I didn't know she had a kid."

"Yessir, me and my twin brother, Travis," I told him. "Thing is, we haven't seen our mama in a few days and we . . . well, we were hoping maybe you'd be able to help us find her? We're gettin' a bit worried."

"I'm sorry, honey—wish I could help you out," he said. "I haven't seen Early in two days. We had a little misunderstanding. . . ."

"I see," I said.

"Yeah, she just stormed out and that's the last I seen of her," Lester went on. "She drinks a lot, you know."

"I know," I said. I didn't bother to point out that it was the understatement of the year.

"Tell you what—if you find her, you tell her to call me," Lester added. "She's a fire cat, your mama. I bring her all the way to Branson, and she pays me back by taking off on me!" He chuckled, as if Mama were some kind of amusing, badly behaved pet.

"Branson?" I said. "Where's that?"

"Branson, Missouri, honey," he said. "That's the last place I saw your mama."

"You think we'll get there before dawn?" I asked Deborah, my set teacher. My chaperone, really, it's not like she'd be teaching me anything I didn't already know.

Deborah smiled at me from behind the wheel of her CR-V. "I hope so. Your call time's five thirty."

I leaned my head back against the seat and stared out the window at the freeway. It was four in the morning, pitch black, and we were in the middle of what looked like a bunch of barren, rocky hills with no buildings . . . and traffic hadn't moved in five minutes.

"How can there be a traffic jam now?" I asked.

"Construction, maybe." Deborah yawned.

So far, I didn't have much of an impression of her. She was maybe thirty, sort of pretty, kind of smart, and mostly just vague. Nika had managed to talk St. Paul's into accepting Deborah as my tutor, and she'd talked the studio into approving Deborah as my on-set guardian, seeing as how Mama was nowhere to be found. Turned out that Nika was pretty impressive to school types, and she'd basically agreed to act as my parent until Mama showed up again. The St. Paul's people had no problem with that—they'd seen Mama up close and personal and they probably thought Nika would do a better job.

Still, I wished Nika could've come to the set herself. Deborah was boring.

"You ever been to this place before?" I asked a while later. We'd left the freeway and were on some little road heading into the mountains. "The location?"

"The Angeles Forest? Sure. Lots of things shoot up here," Deborah said. "When the scene calls for woods, they come here. When they need desert or fake alien planets, they go out to Vasquez Rocks."

"Oh." She had a way of making everything sound boring—maybe that's why I thought she was dull. Here she was talking about movie sets, and she could barely stay awake! "So you go to a lot of sets, huh? Did you ever want to be an actor?" I asked.

"Sure. That's why I came to LA. But that life is a little too insecure for me, you know?" Deborah shot me a look, then laughed. "I guess you don't know yet. Anyway, I started tutoring to pay the bills and now it's just what I do. I'm a set teacher for lots of kids."

*You're a failure, you mean,* I thought. *A failed actor.*

Deborah pulled up next to a scruffy guy with a headset on. He was lounging against a tree on the side of the one-lane road, half asleep.

She rolled down the window. "I've got Chloe Gamble."

The guy pulled a rolled-up stack of paper from the back pocket of his jeans, unfurled it, and ran his finger down the first page. He flipped to the next page and nodded. "Here she is. Trailer nine. Base camp is about a mile up, then take a left. It's the Sycamore Flats campground."

"What's base camp?" I asked as she drove us on.

"That's where all the trailers are set up," Deborah said. "Cast trailers, makeup, wardrobe, craft services, everything. When you're not actually filming, you'll be at base camp."

When we got to the campground, I saw what she meant. It might be a regular park campground on a normal day, but today it was a huge movie set. Gleaming white RVs were parked all over the place. About five of them clustered around the picnic area, surrounding the old picnic tables and grills. Other trailers dotted the grounds. Deborah parked in the field with a bunch of other cars, and we made our way to trailer nine. On the way, I spotted signs on the doors of the RVs— little stars like you see on dressing-room doors, with names on them. The first one I saw had two doors with two stars, though I didn't recognize either of the names. As Deborah led the way toward a huge trailer at the end of the campground, I squinted at the stars on other doors. There was an RV parked by itself, as far as possible from the rest of the group. It had only one door, and the name on the star was Ben Wilson.

My pulse sped up. Ben Wilson was no Brad Pitt, but hell, he was on a hospital show that twenty million people a week watched. I could hardly believe I was about to make a movie with him.

"Here it is," Deborah said.

The trailer was big, but it had no names on the door. Just a piece of masking tape with words scrawled in marker— "Camper Girls Group B." Inside, it was a big room with some couches and tables and one small easy chair for each of the five girls who had to share the trailer. Three other girls were sitting around inside. One of them glanced over and pulled the earpiece from her ear.

"Hey. They said to send everyone straight to wardrobe," she said, immediately turning back to her iPod.

I dumped my bag on an open chair and turned to Deborah. "Are you allowed to wait here? I want to try to figure things out by myself, finding the different trailers and all."

She hesitated, chewing on her cheek and thinking it over. You should never let people have time to think.

"I always learn better that way," I rushed on. "Once I figure it out, I know it forever. My acting teacher says it's learning by experiencing."

"Technically, I'm supposed to be within sight of you at all times," Deborah said. I opened my mouth to argue, but she just grinned. "I think I can see the wardrobe trailer from here. Just be careful and text me if you need me."

"Okay," I said, relieved. I hadn't expected her to turn out to be cool.

I practically skipped back to the main group of trailers. All around me, people with headsets and clipboards were hurrying around. Over in the trees I could see a bunch of lights, and a cherry picker—twice the size of the one the Spurlock Fire Department has—was rising above the tree line. Inside it was a guy with a gigantic movie camera.

The wardrobe trailer looked just the same as all the others, but there was music drifting out the open door. I wasn't sure if I should knock or not, so I kind of rapped on the wall.

A fortyish woman with her hair in a do-rag appeared in the doorway.

"I'm Chloe Gamble," I said. "They told me to come right here."

"Chloe Gamble?" She grabbed some papers and began looking for my name, just like the guy on the road had.

"I'm on page two of that thing," I said.

"Just use your character's name—it's easier," a guy's voice called from inside the trailer.

"Oh. Camper Number Five," I said.

The wardrobe lady nodded. "Can you wait for a few? I've got to finish with Ben." She nodded toward the picnic tables twenty feet away, her eyes wide, and I got the feeling I was doing something wrong by being there. It must've been Ben Wilson's voice from inside. Maybe I wasn't supposed to bother the star when he was in wardrobe.

I turned toward the picnic tables.

"Hold up!" Ben Wilson called from the trailer door. He was wearing a cop uniform, and I smiled. On TV he's always in scrubs. It just looked wrong to see him in anything else. He waved me back over.

"I didn't mean to interrupt," I said.

"No worries. Did you say you're Chloe Gamble?" he asked.

"Yeah." I offered him my hand. "I love your show."

He shook it. "You do?"

"Well, my mama does," I admitted.

Ben chuckled. "That's more my demographic. So are you *the* Chloe Gamble? YouTube?"

"Yeah," I said, surprised.

"My daughter has been playing that video about five hundred times a day for the past week," Ben said. "She's completely obsessed."

I made a face. "Sorry. Even I wouldn't want to watch myself that much!"

"You're the last person I expected to see here," he said. "What are you, fifteen?"

"Sixteen."

"In a slasher film?" He sounded like a concerned dad. Or at least what I imagined a concerned dad would sound like. I wouldn't know.

"My agent just about burst an artery when I said I was gonna do it," I admitted. "Is it really that bad?"

His face softened and he shook his head. "Everybody does these movies. Look at me."

"I know it's a crap film, but I really need the money," I said.

"I remember what that's like. Don't you worry about your agent's arteries. All those people flocking around you, giving you advice—they don't necessarily know what's best. You listen to your instinct. That's *my* advice."

"Thank you," I said, acting all calmly even though my heart was going a mile a minute. I couldn't believe it. Ben Wilson, famous TV star, was chatting with me like . . . well, like it was normal.

"Just do good work, Chloe Gamble—that's the secret," he said. "Good work will get you more good work."

"How am I supposed to find the good work when I'm just looking for *any* work?" I said.

"Aha! That's the hardest part about show business."

"You're done, Ben," the wardrobe lady said. He gave me

a wink and headed off in the direction of the two big trailers. "Remember, do good work!"

The wardrobe lady waved me in. "Sorry about that," she said as she flipped through a rack of clothes inside the trailer. "He wasn't supposed to be here this early, but when the star wants to get dressed, he gets dressed. But now we're in a hurry."

She handed me a tiny pair of cutoff jean shorts and an even tinier T-shirt.

"This thing is as thin as tissue paper," I said, pulling it over my head.

"No bra," she said, studying my chest.

"Okay." I undid my bra and slipped it out the arm of the T-shirt. "Is that it?"

"That's it," she said. "Now you get over to makeup, next trailer." She pulled out the sheets of paper again and crossed off my name.

When I stepped outside, it felt like stepping into a freezer. I was dressed for August, but it wasn't even May yet and we were high up and it was barely light out. All in all, it was damn cold.

One of the headset guys walking past glanced at me and did a double take.

"It's cold," I said as he gazed at my chest. It was the same as in Hal Turman's office. What was it with men and nipples?

This dude had the decency to blush. "Yeah. You need to bring a robe or something from now on, something warm to wear between takes." He pulled off his hoodie and held it out to me.

"Really?" I said.

"Yeah. I have more clothes on."

"Thanks," I said, pulling his sweatshirt on. I snuggled into the warmth. "I'm Chloe. Camper Number Five."

"Cam. Production assistant," he said with a cute smile. "You should get some coffee—it'll keep you warm."

"I only drink tea," I said.

"Oh. I don't think there is any. It's pretty much just a Thermos of coffee and some doughnut holes," he said. "It's a low-budget flick."

"Never mind. I don't need anything right now," I told him. "Can I ask you something, though?"

He lit up like I'd just propositioned him. I had to hand it to the guy—he hadn't looked at my chest once since the first time I had caught him staring. "Anything," he said.

"Everyone has those papers." I nodded to the sheets on his clipboard. "What are they?"

"It's the call sheet," Cam said. "Didn't they leave one in your trailer?"

"I haven't spent much time there," I said. "I'd rather soak in the atmosphere out here."

"You can have mine—I'll grab another one." Cam handed it to me. "It's like the Bible—it'll tell you everything you need to know."

"Thanks," I said. "I better get to makeup 'fore I get myself fired!" I gave him a little wave and took off. *Be nice to the crew and they'll help you out,* I thought, pulling Cam's sweatshirt tighter around me. *Totally true.*

In the makeup trailer, a girl with jet black hair was chugging a Red Bull as she leaned on the sink in front of a mirror.

"I'm Chloe Gamble," I said. "Camper Number Five."

She waved me in, still drinking. "I'm Grace. That's Keiko," she said, nodding toward the other makeup girl.

I looked around. Three huge mirrors lined the wall, all lit with those little round lights just the way you see in the movies. Each mirror had its own chair, a giant swively thing that looked like a cross between a dentist's chair and a La-Z-Boy.

The redhead at the third mirror swung around with a squeal. "Chloe!"

It was Cristina from my acting class, only she looked even more gorgeous than usual. Keiko was just finishing up her makeup.

"Hey, Cristina," I said. "I didn't know you were doing this movie." I noticed she was wearing the same tiny T and short shorts as I was.

"I didn't know *you* were! Good for you," she said with a big smile. I felt myself smiling back. Usually I'd get my hackles up if I spotted some competition. Hell, usually my competition would too. But she seemed genuinely happy to see me.

"It's nice to see a familiar face," I said, sinking into a

makeup chair. "This is my first film shoot," I told Grace.

She nodded, already wiping my face with a cotton ball.

"Maybe we're in the same trailer," I said to Cristina. "Number nine?"

"No, I'm in a two-banger this time," she said. "That means it's just me and one other girl. If you're the star, you get a trailer all to yourself. This is my fifth horror flick, so I guess I'm moving up!"

"Oh." I was surprised to find myself feeling disappointed. It would've been nice to have had somebody to hang with. "So you're not playing a camper?"

"Yeah, I am. I'm Hot Camper," she said.

I stared at her for a second.

"That's her character's name," Grace explained.

"How come you get to be Hot Camper and I'm only Camper Number Five?" I said, only half joking.

Cristina shrugged. "Because I'm showing my tits and you're not."

I must've looked like a shocked little schoolgirl or something, because Cristina and the two makeup women laughed.

"You really get a better trailer because you're showing your tits?" I asked. "Do you get more money, too?"

"Sure," Cristina said, examining her makeup in the big mirror. "I'm making ten thousand more for the breasts. It would be higher if I did full frontal, but they're not going that far in this movie."

I couldn't help myself—I looked at her breasts. They were definitely nice and definitely fake. I wondered if the ten thousand was enough to pay back the doctor who had created that money-making rack.

"Seriously?" I said. "I'd do that for five thousand!"

Grace snorted. "If you're gonna prostitute yourself, at least get a good price." She began sponging base makeup onto my face.

"Did you just call me a whore?" Cristina joked.

"I think it's just good business. Who cares about showing your knockers in some stupid slasher flick?" I said.

"Well, I'll never get a role on the Disney Channel," Cristina said. "BFD. I've gotten plenty of work in horror movies!"

"I should totally do that," I said, closing my eyes so the makeup girl could paint on some eye shadow. "I could use the money."

"You can't—you're too young," Cristina said. "Thanks, Keiko—I look great."

I opened my eyes to see Cristina starting to get up from the chair.

"Wait, why am I too young?" I said. "I know what I'm doing."

"Of course you do, but you're underage," Cristina said. "Underage girls doing nudity is a big no-no."

"Lawsuits, jail time, yada yada yada," Grace said.

Cristina came over to stand behind me, watching my face

in the mirror. She seemed amused. "Even in Hollywood, there are laws, Chloe. Besides, you don't really think your mom would let you be naked in a movie, do you?"

"She wouldn't care," I said. She wouldn't even know, but that was none of their business.

"Oh. Then in that case, you should get yourself emancipated and do all the nudity you want," she said.

Both makeup women frowned at her.

"What?" Cristina said. "She'd get more work that way. You gotta use it while you're young."

"Hang on—what do you mean?" I said. "I thought it was illegal."

"You get emancipated—like, divorced from your parents," Cristina said. "So legally you're an adult and you can make your own decisions and access your own money and stuff like that."

"Plus you can work longer hours and be naked for all of them," Grace said drily. Keiko actually laughed.

"That's why casting directors like it if you're emancipated," Cristina said, ignoring them. "It lets you compete with adult actors—then the studio doesn't need to worry about paying for your tutor, making sure you don't work too long, all that garbage."

"Close your eyes again," Grace said.

"Think about it," Cristina said. I waved over my shoulder as I heard her leave the trailer.

I would think about it. I definitely would.

# E-mail from Travis Gamble

Coop! Prom with Betsy Richmond? Sweet! Good for you.

Things are good here, too. You won't believe this—remember I told you about that Jockey ad that I couldn't do? The booker must really like me, 'cause she called again wanting to know if I'm free to work the night after tomorrow. So I'm about to tell her I've got another soccer scrimmage, but then she says it's not an underwear shoot. Get this: They're looking for a model to do a walk-on part in SHALLOW PEOPLE! Dude, you know I love that show—it's freakin' hilarious. I mean, I'm not a real model, but if they want me to go on my favorite show, am I really gonna say no?

So I told the attendance office I had an audition and I left. Chloe does that all the time, even when it's not true. (Well, she used to. She does that on-set tutor thing now.) And the audition is weird as hell, man—a bunch of pretty boys with gym bodies all sitting around, and they call us in one by one, and when it's finally my turn I go in this little room and this lady hands me a script and I say one line: "Is it okay if I leave my surfboard here, brah?"

I'm serious.

And then they're all, "Thanks, we'll call you." And that was the whole thing. So here's the really fucked-up part: I got the job!

Actually, no, HERE'S the really fucked-up part: They're gonna pay me $7500.

I keep telling you, Coop, Hollywood is insane.

So now I have to come up with an excuse for Coach about the

soccer scrimmage. I'm thinking maybe I'll tell him about Mama being gone and call it a family emergency that I gotta go look for her. It's got to be something big because otherwise he'd never forgive me for bailing on the scrimmage. If he knew it was to do a TV show, he'd kick me off the team and then bye-bye, scholarship. Chloe would kick my ass if I got us booted from school. (Guess I can't tell her about the soccer scrimmage, either.)

Whatever. It's only this one time.

## Rising Star

"Don't you ever just want to take a nap?" I asked Deborah at one o'clock in the afternoon on my third day of shooting. She'd picked me up at the Oakwood around four-thirty that morning. She had to be tired, but she was busy grading my calc homework anyway.

"I have to turn in your work to St. Paul's every day," she said. "Otherwise I won't get paid."

"Well, I know what that's like," I said. In three days of being chaperoned by Deborah, I still hadn't found a single interesting thing about her. Didn't matter, though—as long as she stayed out of my way, I was fine with her.

I wandered over to the trailer door and peered out. Over by the next trailer, the first assistant director was talking to Cristina. I thought about going over there to get some face time with him. I'd discovered yesterday that Jake—everyone called him the first AD instead of "assistant director"—was actually kind of important even though his title sounded lame. He seemed to be running everything, and the actual director only turned up when the cameras started rolling.

But Cristina probably needed to get in good with him, too. If it had been any other actress, I would've knocked her out of the way. But I was feeling generous this morning. I'd find a way to flirt with Jake later.

There would be plenty of time. For the past two days, we'd filmed one scene over and over and over again. But mostly, we sat around and did nothing. For hours. It was just like a beauty pageant—tons of sitting around followed by maybe an hour of work. Except at the beauty pageants, my mama had been my chaperone and she never made me do homework while I was waiting. Deborah did.

"I'm gonna take a walk," I announced, letting the trailer door slam shut behind me. Two of the other campers were asleep inside, but I didn't care. They weren't friendly to me, so I wasn't friendly to them.

"Hey, Cam!" I called to my friend the PA. He seemed to be guarding the entrance to base camp today, and he jumped when he saw me.

"Hi," he said in a nervous voice, as if we hadn't been flirting for two days.

"What's up?" I asked. "We've never had somebody here before."

"There are fans in the park," Cam said. "I got a radio from down below that a group of kids was trying to sneak on set."

"Armistead Heads?" I asked. The second lead actor in the movie was Casey Armistead, from a TV show about skateboarders. I'd never seen it, but I knew about him from the gossip magazines. He was playing the hot young journalist who partners up with Ben Wilson's older, wiser cop to catch the mass murderer. I'd only read the scenes I was in, but it was pretty damn obvious that Ben was the one who ended up being the murderer.

"Actually, they're here for you," Cam said.

"Sorry?" I said.

"The fans—they were looking for you. That's what Jo said—she's the one on the road today."

My brain was still trying to process that when a Mini Cooper pulled up to us. "I'm here to visit the famous Chloe Gamble," Nika said from the driver's seat.

"Nika!" I practically yelled. "There are people trying to sneak in just to see me!"

"I know. TMZ posted a rumor that you were doing this movie, and then Perez Hilton posted where it was filming." Nika grinned. "Girl, you've got the gossips following your moves now!"

"I'm sorry, but we can't let Miss Gamble's fans on set," Cam said, all polite and weird.

"This is Miss Gamble's agent," I told him. "She's allowed to visit, isn't she?"

"Of course! I just meant—" Cam seemed flustered.

"Back in a sec!" Nika cut him off, pulling away to park in the dusty lot.

"Campers in ten!" Jake the AD yelled from the trailers. He spotted me and waved. "Chloe, ten minutes."

I waved back, then turned to Cam. "I wasn't even sure he knew my name yet."

"You're famous now," Cam said.

"That why you're acting so weird?" I asked.

He blushed and laughed. I headed over to where Nika was climbing out of the car. She frowned at my shorts and T-shirt. This morning the wardrobe lady had given me a robe to wear over my clothes to keep me warm. I'd wondered why she had suddenly got so concerned about me, but now I had a feeling I knew why.

"Everyone's acting different today," I said to Nika. "You think they know about TMZ?"

"Are they kissing your ass?" Nika asked.

"A little bit."

"Then they know," Nika said. "Hal was right about your wardrobe. You look like a Hooters waitress."

I pulled the robe closed and tied it. Nika didn't approve of my doing this movie, and I still felt a little worried about it. I'd never given a crap if Mama or Daddy didn't approve of me, but with Nika it was different. I didn't want her to be mad at me.

"I'm supposed to be on set in ten minutes," I said.

"I'll walk with you." She slipped her arm through mine and I relaxed. She couldn't be too mad if she was here to visit, right? We headed for the tree line, where my scene was shooting.

"It's kind of a hike," I said. "They have little ATV things to drive the big stars up there, but the rest of us have to hoof it."

"It's good to be the star," Nika said.

"Seriously. The rest of us have cold pizza for lunch, but Ben Wilson and Casey Armistead get custom-cooked meals."

"Don't be surprised if you at least get hot pizza today," Nika said. "And this movie of yours is helping us out in more important ways, too."

"Like what?"

"Marc leaked word that you were doing a film—we didn't say what, although obviously the gossips found out—and I started getting calls yesterday. All of a sudden people wanted to offer you actual roles. I heard from three different indie producers and a TV show that wanted you to guest."

"Oh my God!" I said.

"Yeah, but you can't because you're shooting *Ritual* for the next two weeks," Nika said.

My heart sank. Maybe Hal had been right; maybe I should've said no to this movie and then I could've gotten those other jobs. "I thought you said the movie was helping us."

"It is, Clo—people are all pissed off because you're unavailable. I had a casting director yell at me for not giving her the first shot at you. What does that sound like?"

"A bitch?"

"It's the Don't-Do!" Nika shook her head. "I hate when Hal's right. But now that I have to keep saying no to work, people want to hire you even more. If only we could get you to film another week on this movie, I bet I'd have five jobs lined up when you're done!"

"Nika! Are you serious? I was afraid I messed up by taking this job."

"So was I," she said. "But since you got hired on one film so fast, everybody figures you must be good. Hal always says, *Work breeds work.*"

"*Good* work," I said, thinking of Ben Wilson. "Good work breeds good work."

We'd reached the set by now, a pretty little hollow in the trees with a pond and a waterfall. The waterfall was really just a trickle, but there were a bunch of guys up there with a pump. Whenever we started shooting, they pumped water from a big tank and ran it over the lip of the waterfall to make it look more impressive.

The other four camper girls were there in their shorts and T-shirts, shivering. Cristina stood to the side, waiting as a wardrobe assistant fastened the back of her T-shirt closed with Velcro. Today we were filming the scene where her shirt came off.

I pulled off my robe and handed it to Nika. "Can you hold this for me?"

"Yeah, but listen, I have really good news. I wanted to tell you in person," Nika said. "So I'm getting all these calls about you, and last night—"

"Campers on set," Jake the AD called. He came over and gave Nika a smile. "Sorry to interrupt, but we need Chloe now. And one of the producers is here—he's asking if he can talk to you for a few?"

"Sure. I'll catch up with you after, Clo." Nika walked off with Jake while I headed over to the edge of the pond. I was dying to know what Nika's news was, but I had to focus on doing good work, like Ben said.

I closed my eyes for a moment and tried to center myself, focusing on my breathing and letting the "camper" settle into my body. Alan would be proud when I got back to class. I could tell him I'd used all his techniques in a real movie.

When I opened my eyes, Jake was back. He lined us all up the way we'd rehearsed yesterday. "Okay, girls, we're shooting the run through the water. Everybody scream—you're being chased by a vicious killer," he said, sounding bored.

He stepped out of the shot and a camera assistant held up a computerized slate with the scene number on it. From somewhere behind all the cameras, the director yelled, "Action!"

I screamed and ran, following Camper Number Four into the frigid water. It got up to about my knees, so I had to move slowly to get through, which made my braless boobs swing around like crazy. My nipples sprang out the second I hit the water, and so did everyone else's. *They should call this movie* Headlights, *not* Ritual, I thought as I followed the girl in front of me to the edge of the waterfall.

"Cut!" yelled the director.

The continuity PA appeared, looking us over and fixing anything that had changed during the scene. Luckily the water wasn't deep enough to reach our shorts or we would've had to change between every take.

We did three more takes of that scene, and I didn't even glance over to see if Nika was back during that whole time. This movie might be getting me more work, but I had to admit that it was kind of embarrassing. Maybe if I had a real role, like Cristina, I would feel less like an idiot. But instead all I had to do was blend in with the other girls, like we were all interchangeable.

"Great job, girls—we've got what we need on that scene," Jake said. "Let's try to shoot the death before dinner break. We need only two campers for this, in addition to Hot Camper. Chloe, why don't you stay. And Camper Number Three."

Cristina grabbed my hand. "You get to be in my big scene!" she said, excited.

"Yeah." I tried to sound enthusiastic, but really I just wanted to get back to Nika and hear the news.

"Okay, we're setting up fast," Jake called. "Let's get it done and maybe we'll get home before midnight!"

There were some laughs and cheers, and Jake led us closer

to the waterfall. "Listen up, girls—it's just a quick shot. You're going through the waterfall. Just go right underneath so the water falls on your hair, then head straight for the camera. Hot Camper, you go last and the killer will grab you once the others are off screen."

"Am I doing the whole death now?" Cristina asked.

"Just the tits and the scream," Jake said. "We'll do the close-ups after dinner with the F/X people."

Cristina nodded.

We sloshed back through the pond and over to one side of the waterfall while a guy with a handheld camera set up right on the other side of it. The shot would look as if the whole line of campers had waded through the pond and climbed up past the fall, with Camper Number Three, me, and Cristina bringing up the rear.

"Action pump!" yelled the AD.

The pump whirred to life up above us, and water began pouring over the edge.

"Action girls!" The director barked.

Camper Number Three plunged under the waterfall and I watched it drench her hair, then her shirt—which became almost see-through as soon as it got wet. I had one brief second to think about that before it was my turn.

*Who cares if it's a wet T-shirt contest on film?* I thought as I stepped under the cold water. The thin material of my shirt plastered itself against my chest and I remembered what Nika had said. This was the scene that would be on the Internet when I got famous. Nearly nude Chloe Gamble. Well, so what? The only thing wrong with that was that I should've been paid more to do it.

I walked past the camera, still breathing heavily and keeping my eyes wide with fear. I was running from a killer, after all.

Behind me, I heard a splash.

I turned to see Cristina in the waterfall. A stuntman stood behind the pouring water, but from where the camera was, all you could see was his hand sticking through the waterfall. The hand grabbed Cristina's T-shirt and yanked. It popped open right on cue, as if he'd torn it. Cristina's perfect breasts spilled out while she screamed. Then another hand came through the waterfall, this one holding a ridiculously big hunting knife.

"And cut!" the director yelled. "Sweetheart, can you wiggle around a little next time?"

Cristina nodded. The wardrobe assistant went over and put her shirt back together, and they lined us up under the waterfall again.

This time, when I got off screen, Cristina was bouncing and jiggling her breasts around. It made no sense. Why would you do that when somebody was grabbing you and trying to stab you? Obviously they weren't going for "real" here.

"Great, honey—twist to the left a bit," the director yelled, and Cristina did.

*That's the best she's ever going to get*, I realized. Later on, they would come in there with some fake blood or something and they'd shoot a close-up of Cristina getting stabbed. Which meant a close-up of her breasts looking all luscious while coated in blood. She'd done five movies like this, she'd said.

It was so clear at that moment—no one would ever cast Cristina as anything else. Nika had told me that people got typecast from doing these movies, and she was right. Cristina wasn't doing good work here; it wasn't going to lead to anything better. All it was going to lead to was another horror movie and another naked death scene.

*That's not going to be me,* I promised myself. It didn't matter how much money they paid me—I had to make sure I wasn't doing humiliating work. I had to avoid falling into the trap that Cristina was caught in even if she didn't know it.

But how?

"Can I have my client back now?" Nika said, appearing at my side. She wrapped the robe around my shoulders and shoved me a little behind her, as if she knew Jake and the cameraman had just been staring at my body for the past twenty minutes.

Jake nodded, and Nika hustled me back down the path toward base camp. "What did the producer want?" I said. "Am I in trouble?"

Nika laughed. "God, no. They want you in two more scenes. The writer is working on them already to get you more lines. Oh, and they're putting you in Cristina's two-banger after she's done shooting."

"Really? Just because of TMZ?" I asked.

"The producers see a way to get the movie noticed," Nika said. "It's a win for them, and it's more money for us. Now maybe Bonnie won't go complaining to Hal because I took half the day off to come here."

"Am I powerful enough to get her fired yet?" I asked.

"I wish." Nika laughed. "So listen, remember I mentioned that new network, Snap?"

"Kinda," I said.

"They're launching this summer. Teen-based programming, to compete with Disney and Nick," Nika said, her voice brimming with excitement.

"And . . ."

"And this morning they called me for a meeting!" Nika cried.

"Is that your big news?" I asked. "I don't mean to sound ungrateful, but I've had just about all the meetings I can stand. Didn't you say you got job offers?"

"Chloe, relax. You can live off this stupid movie for a while. We have to think long-term now," Nika said.

I opened my mouth to argue with her. Then I shut it again, picturing Cristina with her jiggling boobs. That was the road to nowhere. Nika was trying to find me a road to somewhere.

"It's not just another meeting," she went on. "They want to talk to us about one of their shows, called *Cover Band*. And Leslie Scott is going to be there."

"Who's Leslie Scott?"

"The network chairman, or rather, chairwoman," Nika said. "She's incredibly hot right now. She came from Showtime and she started at MTV, so the feeling is she's going to bring a little edge to the teen market."

"And I'm meeting with her? The big boss?"

"Yeah, that's why I'm so psyched!" Nika said. "Leslie's based in New York, and she's only in town tomorrow—and she wants to see you. Do you have any idea how huge that is?"

"Tomorrow when?" I said.

"Eleven."

"But, Nika, my call time is ten o'clock tomorrow," I said. "I can't go."

"Shit," Nika said. She thought about it for a minute. "Shit!"

"Maybe I can flirt with the first AD and get him to move my scene to later in the day," I said.

Nika shook her head. "Clo, they're happy with you, but not happy enough to change the whole shooting schedule. You don't have that kind of firepower yet."

"Just set the meeting," I said. "I'll handle the rest."


"So let me get this straight," Ben Wilson said. "You're getting a bigger role in this movie, a bigger trailer, and more money. But you still don't want to work tomorrow."

"I know that sounds ungrateful," I said from my perch on the couch in his trailer. The place was big enough to have a living room, a dining area, and a separate bedroom. It sure beat the one lumpy easy chair I got. "It's just that my agent says this meeting is a once-in-a-lifetime chance. It's a TV show, and it's for a new network just for kids. Some big important person is gonna be there, and I just hate to let my agent down."

"Your agent will survive," Ben said.

"I know, but . . ." I bit my lip, trying to look contrite. "She told me not to do this movie because it was an R-rated film— she knew the wardrobe would be awful and all, and she said it wasn't appropriate for me. And I insisted. I took it anyway."

Ben opened his fridge, pulled out a bottle of water, and handed it to me. "And now you regret it."

If I couldn't go to the meeting tomorrow, I'd definitely regret it. I sighed. "I look like a Hooters waitress in that wardrobe," I said sadly. I'd never been to a Hooters, but Nika had said so.

"Well, it's certainly not what I'd want my kid to wear," Ben agreed.

"You told me I should do good work and I'm trying my best, but how good am I ever gonna look while I'm screaming my head off and bouncing all over the place?" I gave him my best sweet-little-girl smile. "I'd sure love to get a role on a kids' network. I thought I was ready for this kind of movie, but I'm just not."

He sat down at the table and studied me for a few seconds. "What makes you think I can help?"

"Well, you were so nice to me the other day," I said. "And I noticed that your name is number one on that call sheet thing. I figured that means you're the most important person here."

"I don't know about that." He laughed.

"You're more important than me. I'm number twenty-six," I said. "I'm not even on the first page."

"Don't be sad about that," Ben said. "On a movie like this, you *want* to be number twenty-six."

"Can you give me any advice? How bad would it be if I just didn't show up here tomorrow? You know, if I went to the meeting instead?"

"It would be breach-of-contract bad," Ben said. "It's not like a normal job where you can just call in sick or something. Not at your level, anyway."

"What about at your level?" I asked. "You're in the scene with us tomorrow. It's the one where all us camper girls run out of the woods and you're there with your cop car. So if *you* can't shoot, well, *we* can't shoot."

"So you want *me* to call in sick?"

"No, I didn't mean that! Gosh, you must think I'm terrible. I didn't mean to put you on the spot or anything." I let my chin tremble a little, as if I might cry. "I just thought you might know a way to get the schedule changed, since you're number one. They won't change the shooting schedule for me."

"Drink your water," he said, getting up. "Let me call a friend of mine."

I sat there and obediently drank my water while Ben went

into the other room and talked on his cell for a few minutes. I couldn't hear what he was saying, even though I tried. But I could tell he was happy with the outcome by the way he walked when he came back out.

"Problem solved," he said.

"What?" I gasped.

"I called a friend of mine who knows Ellen's booker. She managed to get me on for tomorrow."

"Wait, *The Ellen DeGeneres Show*?" I said. "How could you get on there so fast?"

"They bumped someone." Ben shrugged.

"But what about the movie? Won't they be mad?" I asked.

"Maybe. But it's in my contract that I get time off for promotional duties related to my TV show. And Ellen loves the show, so there's plenty to talk about."

"If you're off taping *Ellen*, you won't be here, so they won't be shooting my scene." I jumped up and threw my arms around him. "Thank you so much! You got me my meeting!"

"You're welcome." He grinned. "But I do want something in return."

I swear my heart skipped a beat. Here I'd been acting all sweet so he'd think of me like his daughter, but he thought we were bartering. When a guy says he wants something, it usually means something nasty. *Oh God, will I have to let him feel me up now?* I thought.

The smile was still frozen on my face. "What do you want?"

"A picture," Ben said. "You and me, and if you'd autograph it for my little girl, it would make her month."

"Oh." I sank back down onto the couch, so relieved I felt dizzy. "Of course I'd love to do that! I've never signed an autograph before."

"It won't be your last," Ben said.

"Count on that," I told him.

## On Stage

"You want to tell me what we're doing here?" I said to Nika a few hours later as we settled into two theater seats inside a giant soundstage at CBS Television City.

"Believe it or not, we're here to see my *second* client," she said. "You want to tell me how you got out of filming tomorrow?"

"All I needed to know was the guy who's number one on the call sheet," I said.

"You got Ben Wilson to help? Jeez, you learn fast."

"So do you, if you've figured out how to get another client already," I said. "Should I feel threatened?"

Nika laughed, but she didn't answer. She was being weird. She'd said she was going to drive me home from the set, but instead she'd taken me here, to CBS. The studio was right in the middle of Los Angeles, but once we got inside the walls, it felt like we were in a whole different world. It was where they made a bunch of really famous television shows—like *American Idol*—and it really amped me up to think that maybe someday I'd be a real part of it all.

It hadn't been easy for me to get in—the guards at the gate still had me on their watch list from my NBC fiasco. Nika had argued with security for a full ten minutes before she wore them down.

"Hello, guys and gals—welcome to the show!" A guy on the stage was talking now, his mike a little too loud and his voice a little too cheerful. "My name's Sam and I'm here to give the lay of the land. First things first, no cell phones ringing during the taping. Please silence them. Second—"

"I hate this part," Nika said, pulling out her BlackBerry to check e-mail.

Sam was annoying, sure, but I didn't see why she was so bored. The place itself was cool enough to keep me interested— part theater, part high school auditorium, part film set. The seats were on bleachers like they had back at Spurlock High, except back there it was benches that gave your butt splinters. Here it was actual seats with cushions, but you still got the feeling that the wooden bleachers holding you up might collapse at any second. The room was gigantic, if you could call it a room. It was more like a warehouse, but Nika called it a soundstage, and it was divided into a bunch of different sections. In front of us was a living room set. It looked kind of familiar, but at the same time totally bizarre, because what was a living-room doing here?

Then there were a bunch of offices and other rooms off to one side. Whole rooms, only their ceilings stopped at eight feet while the ceiling of the whole place was probably fifty feet high. It looked as if people had come into this huge sound-stage with some drywall and just built rooms wherever they felt like it.

Looking up and around, all I could see were lights. Lights everywhere, and four big cameras up front, all trained on the living-room set.

"Is this that show about the two guys who run a motel on the beach?" I asked. "They have a bet to see who can sleep with more guests?"

Nika nodded.

"My brother loves that show," I said. "So if you have an in here, can you get me an audition?"

"Just be patient," Nika said. "If you're even familiar with that concept."

I grinned and sat forward in my seat to watch the crew buzzing around the set, checking props and setting up cameras and stuff. It was much more interesting than Sam's emcee-ing, which seemed to be a mix of bad stand-up comedy and instructions about how to act during the show. Right now he was talking about how the scenes might be filmed several times and it was important to laugh just like we did during the first take. It made total sense when you thought about it, but I heard gasps of surprise from the rest of the audience.

Then there was a burst of applause, and the two stars of the show came out to wave to the crowd. I'd only seen a handful of episodes, but I still felt a chill run down my spine when I saw those guys standing ten feet away from me. I happened to know that one of them was the highest-paid actor on television. Right now, he was probably making about ten thousand dollars a second. I wanted to get where he was, and tomorrow wouldn't be soon enough.

The lights went down on the audience, and the white-hot stage lights went up on the living-room set. They filmed a short scene about the two guys and their two latest dates, played by Victoria's Secret models. Those girls could not act. It was okay, though, because the stars of the show were actually pretty funny.

"You need to get me a part as one of their dates for an episode," I whispered to Nika while they got ready for the next scene.

"Patience," she whispered back.

I watched while they moved all the cameras over to another little stage that I hadn't even noticed before. This one was set up to look like the boardwalk outside the guys' motel, and the lighting had changed so that it looked like sunlight instead of lamplight. I was amazed at how much faster they shot these television scenes than the ones I had been doing in the movie. It seemed a lot more fun, and there was the energy of the live audience that made it seem a lot more like theater—or a pageant.

The Victoria's Secret girls came onto the set, this time in even slinkier outfits, and took their positions on lounge chairs. Then the lead actors found their marks standing behind the girls. The director yelled, "Action," and then a surfer dude came strolling down the fake boardwalk, carrying a surfboard and wearing a Speedo. He tossed his blond hair out of his eyes, grinned at the girls, and propped his board against the side of the patio.

"Is it okay if I leave my surfboard here, brah?" my twin brother asked the highest-paid actor on TV.

The Victoria's Secret models checked him out. The women in the audience behind me gasped and murmured their approval.

But nobody on the face of God's green earth was more astonished than I was.

"Oh, hey, there's my new client," Nika said casually. "Isn't he cute?"

I wanted to holler at her. Hell, I wanted to holler at Travis! What was he doing here, shooting a TV show? He wasn't an actor! He'd never wanted to be an actor! I was supposed to be the star in our family, and I was busy shooting a crap movie about some wannabe druid killer while Travis was on a famous sitcom!

It wasn't fair.

But Travis looked damn good. And pretty damn happy. I felt the anger drain out of me as I watched my twin saunter off stage with the models gazing after him.

"I think he's gonna go far," Nika said.

"Of course he is," I said. "He's a Gamble."

"Why didn't you tell me?" I asked Travis as he drove us home. I was beyond exhausted by now—it was nearly midnight and I'd been awake since the crack of dawn.

"You've been on set sixteen hours a day all week," Trav said. "Besides, I wanted to surprise you. And I thought I could get the money fast, like from my modeling shoots, and then we could just pay next month's rent right away and stop worrying."

"But you can't get the money until you set up a Coogan account," I said. "Right?"

"Yeah, that's what Nika said." Trav sighed. "Sorry."

"Travis, you just made seventy-five hundred bucks working for a major network," I said. "You hung out with famous actors and you got about fifty tourist women all hot and bothered. Just what on earth are you apologizing for?"

"Plus, I flirted with one of those Victoria's Secret girls." Trav wiggled his eyebrows at me. "Us underwear models, we understand each other."

"So that's what you are now, a model?" I said. "Or are you an actor?"

"Chill, Clo, I'm just me," Travis said. "This is all a goof. Am I supposed to say no when folks want to give me money for nothing?"

"I guess not. Just don't let it mess up your real life—soccer and school and all that." He didn't answer so I swatted him on the arm. "Promise me."

"I promise I won't let it mess up my real life," Travis said. He didn't mean it, whether he knew that or not. I remembered that high from standing in the lights while I filmed my YouTube video. He had to be feeling the same thing from filming an honest-to-God CBS TV show.

"I'm not being a nag; I'm watching your back, Trav," I said. "Just like always. You want to be an actor—good for you. But it's all or nothing. Unless you're willing to go at it a thousand percent, you won't make it big. You'll end up just another twenty-year-old dropout doing tiny parts in crappy horror movies."

"Someone you know?" Trav asked.

"A girl from my acting class," I said. "My point is, I don't want to be responsible for that happening to you. You could've stayed in Spurlock and been hot shit."

"I'm fine here; I like it here," Trav said. "You don't have to take care of everyone all the time, you know. I'm doing pretty well on my own."

"Damn straight," I said. "You made more money than I did today! And you're all respectable while I'm just a horror-movie chick who dies halfway through the movie."

Trav pulled up to a red light a block from the on-ramp to the freeway. "Hey! Turn here," I said, spotting the street sign. "Turn right."

He did, and then he pulled over to the side of the road while I flipped through our Thomas Brothers map book. "What are we doing?" Trav asked.

"I think this road leads up into the hills," I said, studying the map by the dim light of the moon. The inside light in the Ford had been dead for ages. "It does—go up here and turn left, and then we hit a twisty street that should take us to the top."

Travis was already driving. "What's at the top?"

"Lester Orcutt," I said.

Trav looked at me sideways. "You memorized his address?"

"I remember everything, you know that. Besides, I figured we might have to pay him a visit one day. If we want him to help us find Mama, he's gonna need some persuading."

"He told you Mama bailed on him way the hell back in Missouri."

"Yeah, but he must have some idea where she went. I don't know Branson, Missouri, for shit. If we can get him to help us, maybe he can call in some favors and get somebody there to look for her."

"You're asking a lot," Trav said.

"That's why I need that horn-dog to get an eyeful of me," I told him. "Slow down—it's one of these places."

Travis peered into the darkness. We were on a narrow, winding road with no lights at all. Every so often the trees cleared and we got a view out over the city that showed how high up we were. On both sides of the road were walls and gates. You couldn't even see the houses.

Travis parked as far to the side as possible, and then we got out and walked up to Lester's gate. It was locked, but there was a little keypad and a camera pointed at us. I pressed call on the keypad. The light on the camera lit up.

And the gate clicked open.

"Guess he got his eyeful," Trav said sarcastically.

"Don't be such a big brother about it," I said, pushing open the gate.

"I *am* eight minutes older," Trav said.

We followed a stone walkway lit by little blue lanterns up to the house, a huge Spanish-style place with vines growing all over it and one of those fountains with a statue near the front door. I rang the bell and we could hear it inside, like a huge set of church bells.

"What if his wife is home?" Travis asked. "Or his kids? For all we know, he's still in Branson."

"I'm an actress—I'll think of something if I need to," I said.

Mama opened the door.

Travis and I just stared at her in shock. Well, I stared at her *and* her low-cut silk blouse. That thing was Versace, at least.

"Well, hey there, sugar!" My mama tottered forward on a set of Jimmy Choos I'd never seen and threw her arms around my neck. Then she reached for Travis. "C'mere and give me a kiss, darlin' boy."

"Mama, what the hell?" Trav said instead. "What are you doing here?"

"She's drinking," I said. "Look at her—she can barely stand."

"Don't get your panties in a twist, Clo—I just had a little," Mama said, staggering back inside.

"Where'd you get those clothes?" I asked, following her.

"From Lester. He is exceedingly generous." Mama giggled.

"Where is he?" Trav said. "Where's his wife and family?"

Mama waved her hand in the air as if she could just swat away silly little questions like those. But I took a look at my brother's face, and I'd never seen him so mad.

"Is Lester here, Mama? He told us you ran off on him," I said.

"Well, we had a little lovers' quarrel, honey—you know how it is. But we made up." Mama had reached the living room, where she had a bottle of Cristal set up on the humongous coffee table. "Anyhoo, he's off visiting that girl down in Venice so I thought I'd have myself a consolation drink."

She reached for the bottle. Travis got there first. He just snatched it up and upended it on the expensive-looking rug. That shut Mama right up. Me too.

"We're going home, Mama," he said.

She didn't argue. I guess she knew better, or else she was even drunker than I'd thought. We stuck her in the backseat of the Ford and she was asleep before we got back down the hill to the freeway entrance.

Travis didn't say a word on the ten-minute drive back to the Oakwood, and neither did I. There was no way to make it okay that his big night had been ruined by finding his mama acting like a kept woman to some horny musician.

We woke her up and helped her inside like we'd done a hundred times before. But once we were in the apartment and Travis was heading for the bedroom with Mama's arm around his neck, I said, "Hang on a sec. Sit her down at the table."

"C'mon, Clo, I wanna lie down," my mama slurred.

"Did Nika give you the papers for your Coogan account?" I asked Trav. He nodded, going for his school backpack.

I grabbed my own papers off the kitchen counter and slapped them down in front of Mama. I handed her a pen.

"What's this?" she mumbled.

"It's time to be a mama, Mama," I said. "Sign these."

Mama glanced up at me, bleary-eyed. Then she signed her name. I put Trav's papers in front of her and she signed those, too. Then Trav and I dragged her into the bedroom, pulled off the expensive new shoes, and dumped her onto the bed. She'd already passed out again, and she lay there snoring.

"Think she'll remember in the morning?" my brother asked.

"It's about money—she'll remember," I said.

"Hard to believe we're stuck with her," Travis said. "That Coogan thing is supposed to protect us, but all it means is we have to keep Mama around to sign papers and spend our cash."

"We don't have to be stuck with her," I said, looking down at my drunken sot of a mama. "We can get ourselves emancipated, Travis. We can divorce Mama."

# chapter ten

## Snap

"Now, you remember to smile, young lady," Hal Turman said from the driver's seat of the biggest Mercedes I'd ever seen. I never knew Mercedes made boats like this until Hal and Nika had pulled up to the Oakwood gates to get me for my big meeting. "Nobody wants a sourpuss like all those pouty fashion girls. People like a little positivity!"

"So all I do is smile?" I said from the backseat.

"And be perky," Hal said.

"Jesus, Hal, you make it sound like a second-grade ballet recital," Nika said.

"Or a beauty pageant," I added. I glanced at Nika, who sat beside me in the huge backseat. "Why's he here?"

I whispered. Hal was so far away he'd never hear us.

"He says this meeting is too big for me," Nika whispered back.

"I can hear you, girls," Hal said. "Leslie Scott will be there. If the network chair is there, the big agent's gotta be there, too. Big fish school together."

I settled back against the soft leather seat and tried to relax, which wasn't that easy when Hal was weaving in and out of lanes without so much as a glance in the rearview. I'd knocked on Amanda's door this morning to make her approve my meeting outfit. She'd replaced my platform sandals with a pair of low-heeled cowboy boots, tossed a necklace over my head, and pronounced me ready to go.

*It's just another meeting,* I tried to convince myself, as Hal pulled into some random building right near the freeway in Burbank. *No reason to be nervous.*

But the way Nika had been talking about this one yesterday, the way I'd had to scam my way out of shooting, just the undeniable fact of Hal's going along with me, well, it all made me think this was a damn sight bigger deal than all those meet and greets I'd done before.

Hal blew past the security desk inside like he didn't even notice it. Nika ran over to tell them where we were headed, and by the time the elevator arrived she had visitor name tags for all of us. I stuck mine onto my purse—who wants to mess up a perfectly cute top with a giant name tag? Hal stuffed his into the pocket of his pants.

"Okay, so Leslie Scott is the major player here, Clo," Nika said as the elevator whooshed upward. "Everyone's going to defer to her. But you'll also meet Bo McNamara—he's in charge of development. He's the main West Coast guy, so be sure to focus on him a little, too."

"Leslie and Bo," I said. "Got it."

"Then there'll be the show runners—they're the ones who created *Cover Band*," Nika said. "That's a husband and wife team, Golden and Golden."

"Seriously?" I asked.

"You'll call them Josh and Diane when you talk to them, but call them Golden and Golden when you talk *about* them," Hal said. "They're important, too."

"So I've got four people to impress," I said.

"No, you've got one person; Leslie," Hal said.

"You just can't forget about the other ones," Nika added. "They're all big players."

"Well, I'm glad it'll be so easy," I said, going for a joke, but nobody laughed.

"Then there will be about five other people in the room," Nika said.

I didn't even have time to respond before the elevator doors slid open and a giant red SNAP logo stared us in the face. Underneath it was a circular desk manned by a girl wearing pigtails and black-rimmed glasses.

"Hi! Welcome!" she chirped. "You're going to go right into the conference room—everybody's already set up. Can I get you guys anything? There's water and coffee and Diet Coke inside."

"Bring me a Perrier, sweetheart," Hal said, striding off down the hall like he knew where he was going. The pigtail girl scurried after him, quickly pointing him in the right direction.

"Don't worry," Nika said to me. "Hal's a fixture—nobody will mind him."

My heart was pounding when I stepped into the conference room. About ten people were seated around the big table, their eyes all on me. *Positivity,* I thought. It was a network for tweens, so they'd be looking for wholesome, youthful energy.

"Wow, look at that view!" I cried, staring over their heads. A row of windows ran the entire length of the room, and the view was of hills and sky. "I'm sorry, it's just . . . wow. Y'all are so lucky to look at that while you're working."

A slim, hip-looking guy stood up and put his arm out, ushering me over to the windows. This had to be Bo McNamara, the main West Coast guy. No one else would've had the nerve to talk first. "As long as you're sitting, it's great," he said. "But when you get close enough to look down . . ."

I looked out the window and down—at a gigantic cement trough that ran as far as I could see in both directions. "What's that?" I asked.

"The LA River," Bo said.

"It's nothing but concrete. There's no water."

He nodded.

I glanced up at him, still standing close, and gave him the virginal smile that pageant judges loved—a smile that says I'm eager, but not experienced. Men eat it up. "I guess that's why you never look down in Hollywood," I said.

Bo grinned, and he didn't move away from me. That's how I knew I had him.

"You can also see the golf course across the river," Hal bellowed. "Lakeside. Best course in the city. I play there all the time."

Bo turned away, our moment past. "Come sit, Chloe," he said, pointing me to a seat between Hal and Nika at the head of the table. "I'm Bo, and this is Diane and Josh Golden."

I gave an enthusiastic smile to an overweight woman and a guy who teased his hair to distract you from the bald spot.

"And here's Leslie," Bo added.

The power suit at the other end of the table actually got up and came over to me. I gave her the firm pageant handshake and looked her right in the eye. "It's so great to meet you. I'm a big fan," I said.

Leslie's smooth forehead didn't move, but her eyes took on a calculating expression. "Usually I'd be the one saying that to you."

"I Googled you," I told her. "I couldn't help myself—I was

so excited for the meeting. You're the youngest network chair, like, ever. Strong women are my heroes." I smiled enough to make even Hal proud.

Leslie couldn't have been more than thirty-five. Google hadn't led me anywhere that would tell me her actual age, but I'd found enough pages to convince me that she was a hotshot. People like that usually appreciate a little hero worship.

"You do your homework." Leslie sounded amused. "Good." She turned and headed back toward her seat, nodding to one of the other women at the table. This one jumped up and began handing out glossy folders with the Snap logo on the front and a bunch of papers inside, all of them labeled "Cover Band" in funky lettering across the top. While she passed them out, Bo introduced the rest of the people. He didn't bother giving their job titles—I guess maybe I was supposed to know who they were, or Nika was. Or else they just didn't matter very much.

All of them kept staring at me. They'd look down when I caught them, or they'd just smile like they were being friendly, but I knew when I was being watched. Pageant judges used to pull that stuff sometimes—pretend they weren't looking when they were. Only there, they were trying to see how you'd act when you didn't know you were being judged. Here, it felt less like judging than like . . . well, like it had felt in front of the lights doing my YouTube video. It felt like I was performing and they were my fans.

"We're launching the network with three shows," Bo said. "One's a contest-based reality show, and the second one is about a girl from a family of genies trying to fit in at middle school."

"Genies? What is that, like gypsies?" Hal said. Nobody bothered to answer.

"And then there's *Cover Band*. That's our high-profile entry, the one we'll be promoting in print ads—we've got billboards, bus kiosks, the whole deal." Bo glanced at Hal sometimes, but mostly he was talking to me.

"Our sister network, NBC, will give us spots for free during the family hour," Leslie added. "We really think it's a home run for the network. Josh, why don't you tell them a little about the show?"

Josh Golden leaned across the table, smiling at me. "Well, we've been working with the development team here—" He gestured around the table. They all grinned and nodded at me, like maybe I was going to toss them a treat or something. "The basic premise is very simple. There's a group of friends—"

"They're not *all* friends," Diane cut in.

"Right. Some of them don't get along," Josh said.

"That's called *drama*," Bo said with a wink to me.

I laughed. "Y'all are so in synch—I love it! You must be a great team to work with. You remind me of me and my twin brother. We finish each other's sentences, too."

"You've got a twin?" one of the development execs cried. "That's so cool! Does he act?"

"He does, just a little," I said. "I'm the drama queen in the family, though! My daddy used to say I was born for the camera."

They all smiled, buying into my cute-Texas-family act. They didn't need to know that Daddy had only ever said that sarcastically or that Mama had still been passed out when I had left this morning. All they needed to see was sweet, bouncy Chloe. Positivity.

"So these friends are all in a band," Josh Golden went on. "But really the band is just a cover for their actual job—they're spies."

"That's ridiculous," Hal cried. "Who's gonna believe a bunch of kids are spies?"

There was a moment of appalled silence, and then Leslie Scott laughed. "Still bitter that you didn't rep those actors in *Spy Kids*, huh, Hal?"

Hal winked at her, and Josh Golden kept talking, though he looked a little rattled now. "The point is, they have the perfect cover and they can infiltrate all kinds of different places because nobody suspects kids."

"And they're a successful band, so they tour a lot," Diane said. "It gives us an organic way in to a lot of different story lines."

"We're not thinking of it as a four-camera show," Bo put in. "We've already got the perfect opening sequence—we'll shoot it outside the studio and bring in sort of a mix of location and stage stuff."

"And will there be actual musical numbers?" Nika asked.

"Absolutely. The band is a real band—we need actors who can sing," Leslie Scott said. "We're planning at least one musical number per episode, with a sound track to be released at the end of the first season."

"Then, during hiatus, you plan to do a live stage tour? Maybe at malls, community centers?" Hal said.

Leslie smiled. "We were thinking amusement parks."

"Well, that's no problem. I can sing," I said.

"And she can dance," Hal said, with no clue whether it was true or not. "She's a triple threat."

But they knew that already. They knew all about me—I could tell by the way they were acting. None of these people expected me to prove myself. They were too busy trying to make a good impression on *me*.

"This just sounds like so much fun," I said, all excited like they'd just given me the lead in their high school musical. "Do you have a script for me to read?"

Everybody looked at Leslie Scott. She nodded to one of the development people, and he handed a bound script to Nika.

"Of course, we're talking to a lot of actresses," Leslie said. "But we'd love to hear what you think of the script, Chloe."

I nodded and smiled. "I just know I'm gonna love it!"

## Nika Mays's Manuscript Notes: Show Meetings

A typical show meeting is a fairly high-stress event. The creators are there, usually writer-producers who have been toiling away on this idea for a year or more. They think of the show as their baby. The development executives are there, too, the ones from the studio that's producing the show and also the ones from the network that's airing it. They've given so many notes and had so many meetings in order to put their fingerprints on this show that they also think of it as their baby. Then there are the heads—head of development, head of the studio, head of the network. These people are the ones who can pull the plug on the show at any moment. Hence the high stress in the room.

If it's a particularly important show—like one that's going to be the flagship for a whole new network—everyone is paying attention. As in, not only everyone up to the network chair, but also her bosses. The people who own the network. The giant corporation that funds it. Everyone wants to be sure that that particular show is the best it can possibly be and that the actress starring in it is the absolute best choice for the role. Better than all the other girls in Hollywood, better than the Kimbers and the Selenas and the Mileys.

For all of those reasons, Chloe's meeting for *Cover Band* should have been super stress-ful. It should have been a room full of defensive writers, frightened executives, and one impe-rious, judgmental network chair. I was expecting questions about Chloe's background, her lack of any real experience. I think Hal was expecting that they might want her to do a song and dance number or something. God only knows what Chloe was expecting, but it didn't matter because she went in there flinging her Texas charm around and they were putty in her hands.

Chloe had a way with people. Men were dazzled by her, and women—well, they were dazzled, too. But it was more than that, more than Chloe's defusing the stress of a big meeting.

It was that the meeting was backward. We should've been the ones on the spot, Chloe and I. We should've been trying to prove to them that Chloe was good enough for their show. But instead, they were trying to prove it to us, trying to con-vince Chloe that the show was good enough for her. We owned the meeting—not them.

They had graphics. They had a mock-up of the show's poster tacked to the wall. Before the meet-ing was over, they had trotted out a PowerPoint presentation of the sets they planned to use for the first episode. They all but did a song and dance number for us.

We said the usual polite good-byes and thank-yous, and Chloe shook hands with everyone and called them all by name—her beauty-pageant training; she always knew how to make everyone feel special. We said we'd be reading the script and they said they'd be meeting with other girls. We rode the elevator back downstairs, walked out to the parking garage, and climbed into Hal's whale of a Mercedes.

Then Hal turned around and looked at me. "This one's a Do. You've caught a tiger by the tail here, honey. Nice find."

"What's he talking about?" Chloe asked.

"That meeting was completely backward," I told her. "They were selling you instead of you selling them."

"I know," Chloe said. "So?"

"When they said they were meeting with other actresses? They were lying," I told Chloe. "I don't think they have any intention of even showing the script around. They were selling it to you, Clo. They want you."

They wanted her so much, in fact, that they called to make the offer before we'd even dropped her off at the Oakwood. Twenty-two episodes of *Cover Band* at sixty-five hundred dollars per, ours for the

taking. Chloe was squeezing my hand so tightly that
I couldn't even feel my fingers. She was bouncing
up and down in her seat just like a regular teenager, thrilled that she'd been offered an actual
TV series. That's when I caught Hal's eye in the
rearview mirror and did what I knew I had to do.

I said no.

# E-mail from Travis Gamble

Coop, tell the team to watch next Tuesday's SHALLOW PEOPLE if
they want to see some real talent. (Can you believe I play a surfer?
I've never even been in the ocean.) It was cool to be on set and all,
and those models were smokin' hot. It's all good as long as Coach
doesn't figure out what day it taped! But here's the best part: I cashed
my check after school today, except for the percentage that has to
get put away for later. (Did I tell you Mama came back? She was so
wasted when she signed my bank paperwork that she didn't even
know it was for me, not Chloe. So we're not telling her that I have a
Coogan account, too. The less she knows, the better, Clo says.)

ANYWAY, I had thousands of dollars in cash, so what was I
gonna do with it, right? Me and some of the guys from soccer went
to this used-car dealership nearby and I traded in the Ford—for
a freakin' ESCALADE! Am I Hollywood or what? It's got some
mileage on it (a hundred thou', to be exact), but whatevs—I'm only
gonna drive it around town. And the passenger side has a few dings,

there's a mystery leak, and the air conditioner's busted. So I figure a couple hundred bucks for some parts and I'll have it good as new. My friends were all, "You have to take it to the Caddy dealer to get it fixed." These rich kids are clueless. Wait'll they see how I pimp my own ride—they'll all be coming to me with their cars, too.

When school's out for summer, get your butt to LA and I'll drive you around in style!

## Fan Favorite

"Oh my God, look!" I said, scrolling down the ChloeGamble.com site dedicated to me. "Somebody did one of those Marilyn Monroe things with my face—you know, with all the different colors over my picture!"

Jude peered over my shoulder and squinted at her laptop, which I had commandeered so that I could surf poolside. "It's Andy Warhol," she said. "He did a series of silk-screened prints of Marilyn Monroe—"

"And look at this one!" I cut her off. "This guy re-created my whole video starring himself." I turned up the volume, then turned it right back down. "Too bad he can't sing for shit."

"Keep it quiet," Amanda said from the next lounge chair over. "I'm trying to enjoy my new toy." She played with the dial on her new iPod, courtesy of my first paycheck from *Ritual*, which I'd cashed right after I got home from my meeting at Snap. Amanda wouldn't take any money for being my unofficial stylist, just like Jude wouldn't let me pay for the head shots she'd done for free. But they were willing to take my gifts. They'd even come to the mall with my mama and me.

Retail therapy, Jude called it. Something to take my mind off the fact that Nika had turned down the offer from *Cover Band*. Well, I'd bought three bikinis, five new outfits, and two pairs of shoes. Plus the iPod for Amanda and a new zoom lens for Jude. I let Mama pay for her own stuff, since she'd already insisted on being paid her percentage of my money.

But I didn't feel much better.

When my BlackBerry buzzed, I practically leaped on it. "Nika?"

"Good news," my agent's voice came back. "I just talked to Marc, and he talked to a friend of his who works for MTV back in New York, and she went to college with Leslie Scott's assistant."

"And?" I said.

"And it turns out that Leslie Scott has a ten-year-old daughter and a twelve-year-old stepdaughter and they started the Chloe Fan Club on Facebook about an hour after the video went up."

"So her kids are fans. How does that matter, when we're doing the Don't-Do?"

"Clo, we have so much more power than I even thought!" Nika said. "Just hang tight. I'm coming over there."

I hung up and looked at Jude and Amanda. Neither of them said anything, but I knew what they were wondering.

"No job yet," I said. "Nika told them we were fielding other offers—those were her exact words. But it wasn't true. Why is she listening to stupid Hal Turman?"

"Honey, Hal's even older than me," Amanda said. "It's possible he just might know what he's doing."

"Well, it's stressing me out. I'm going to look for more fan sites," I said, turning back to the computer.

"Maybe I should stop you before you find the inevitable Photoshopped picture of you naked," Jude said.

"No! You think?" I started to type "Chloe" and "naked," but that's when Trav showed up. He took off his shades—new, I noticed—and looked around at me and Jude, at Mama relaxing in the hot tub, at Amanda with her tunes.

"What's going on?" he said.

"Nika turned down an offer for me to do a TV show," I said. "They were about to pay me a hundred and forty-three thousand dollars for the season!"

"Minus the Coogan percentage, and Nika's percentage, and Mama's percentage," Trav said.

"It's still a hell of a lot of money," I said. "But Nika says we can do better."

"And Chloe's head is about to explode," Jude told him. "Even though she's totally famous online and we're all going to be rich, thanks to her. I got two new jobs today just by dropping the Chloe G. bomb."

"And I got a new iPod!" Amanda said.

I closed my eyes and let the afternoon sun soak into my skin. It felt good to relax, even though I had to get up at three in the morning tomorrow and go back to being Camper Number Five. The flimsy shirt and the embarrassing script didn't seem so bad now that I had money in my pocket. It was nice to pay back my friends for helping me out. It was nice not to worry about Travis's having to support us with underwear money.

But it would be a hell of a lot nicer if I had a steady TV gig. Everybody was counting on me to become some big star, and so far all I'd managed to do was get my shirt wet in a slasher film.

I sat up quickly, my mellow gone. Maybe I could just call Leslie Scott myself and take the job. Nika would kill me, but I'd have a regular paycheck, at least for a little while.

Trav had taken the lounge chair next to mine, and he was checking e-mail on my BlackBerry. "Think I should get one of these?" he said.

"Yeah. And I should get a new one," I said. "I changed the mailing address on my account, but Daddy still knows the phone number."

"Does not," Trav said. "I doubt he ever called it even once."

"You may be right," I said. "Who cares, though? We got a real sweet mama these days. Now that I've got money, she's the most supportive person in Hollywood. My biggest fan."

"Who's the loser with her?" Trav said. "I don't want to have to carry her home again."

I glanced over at the hot tub. When we got to the pool, my

mama had gone straight there to loosen up her "aching back," as she called it. What it really meant was that she didn't want me to smell the liquid in her water bottle, which was probably vodka, and she thought the hot tub would get her buzzed faster. I didn't care, I had bigger fish to fry today. Only now Mama wasn't alone in the hot tub.

Alex the porn king was with her.

"Oh, for God's sake," I muttered. "She's worse than a cat in heat."

I was halfway to the hot tub when the pool gate opened and Kimber Reeve walked in. Our eyes met instantly, but I managed to get the fake smile onto my face faster.

"Well, hey, Kimmy!" I said. "And Mrs. Reeve—how are y'all?"

"It's Mrs. Williams," her mother said stiffly.

"Right, sorry," I lied. "Y'know, that cute boyfriend of yours told me y'all had moved out. Is that true?"

"We took a condo on Wilshire, in one of those high-rise buildings," Kimber's mom said. "It's not much. A thousand times better than the Oakwood, of course, but—"

"When *Virgin* gets picked up for a second season, we'll buy a house," Kimber said. "But for now we're being prudent."

"Y'all are smart," I said. "Why, my agent told me that ninety percent of new shows on those big networks don't make it past the first season."

Kimber rolled her eyes. "We should go. We just came by to drop off the last check for my acting coach. I fired him."

"Yeah, I guess you know everything about acting now that you got a job," I said, dropping my Texas goober act. It was only fun when Kimber was annoyed by it. "Congrats on the *Virgin* pickup, by the way. Your career is going great."

"Thanks," she said. "I didn't even have to crash any auditions to get it!"

I laughed. She laughed. We totally hated each other.

"But I heard you're doing a horror film," Kimber said snidely. "Good for you."

"Why, Kimmy, it is just so sweet of you to follow my little ol' career," I said. "I guess you must really care about me."

Kimber's eyes flashed with annoyance. "Let's go, Mom," she snapped. They headed for the main office without saying another word.

I headed for the hot tub. "Mama! Get outta there—that man is a world of trouble," I said.

My mama's eyebrows shot up, but she didn't move away from Alex. For all I could see underneath the bubbles, she might have been sitting on his lap. Or worse.

"Mama, so help me, I will empty out that joint account if you don't get your ass outta that hot tub," I said.

"Just calm down, Clo—I'm comin'," Mama said, hauling herself up out of there. "No need to shriek at me."

I looked at Alex like he was the slimiest piece of algae in the pond. "You keep away from her and I won't tell my brother what you do for a living," I said, jerking my head toward Trav, who was glaring at him.

Alex held up his hands in surrender. "I was just enjoying the Jacuzzi," he said.

I left him there and followed Mama over to our friends, wondering how much one of those high-rise apartments on Wilshire would set me back.

"Chloe!" Nika came barreling into the pool area, waving her cell around. "I just got off a conference call with Hal and Bo McNamara!"

Every single thought of my mama vanished. "What'd they say?" I cried.

"Oh, lots of crap about how you're new and green and nobody knows if you can act. And then Hal talked about how he's seen every starlet since Patty Duke and you're the hottest, blah blah blah," Nika said.

I just stared at her. I couldn't even process what she was saying. Who was Patty Duke?

"Don't torture the girl, Nika," Jude said. "Did you make the deal or what?"

Nika handed me a notepad that said HAL TURMAN AGENCY at the top. Scrawled on the page was a number: $11,500.

I raised my eyes to Nika's. "Per episode?"

She nodded. "For twenty-two episodes. You get top billing and at least two solo songs on the first sound-track recording."

People say that when you're hit by a car or something, you

can have an out-of-body experience and your life flashes before your eyes. Well, my life flashed before me right that second and it was filled with things I was never going to have to live with ever again—my mama and daddy fighting, Trav and I walking ourselves to our first day of grade school, beauty-pageant princesses laughing at my banged-up pageant suitcase, Daddy kissing that little slut in Abilene, Mama passed out drunk in the back of the Ford. All of it passed and gone and forgotten forever, because now my real life was going to start. I now lived in the land of forgetting.

"You did it," I said. "Nika, you did it!"

"No, you did," she told me. "Here's how much they wanted you, Clo—they're putting up a billboard on Sunset right now, and they already had it ready to go with your name printed on it!"

"I'm on a billboard?"

"Let's go!" Trav jumped up from his lounge chair. "Let's all go watch them put it up!"

My head was still buzzing from the news, but I had enough sense to stop him. "We can't all fit in the car," I said. "I'll go with Nika."

Travis puffed himself up like a peacock. "Actually, we *can* all fit. I got us a new car, Clo, big enough for the whole posse."

"What? Lemme see, sugar!" Mama squealed and ran off toward the parking lot, Jude on her heels and Amanda following more slowly.

"Chloe?" Nika said.

I looked at her, still dazed.

"You *can* act, can't you?" she said.

And we both burst out laughing.

When we got to the parking lot, Travis was showing off a shiny black Escalade. Mama had already climbed into the front, and Jude had her camera out to document our first Hollywood ride. Next to me, Nika shook her head.

"The next member of our team will obviously have to be a business manager," she said.

"You kidding? I'll be making more than two hundred fifty thousand dollars this year. We can afford a damn Caddy," I said with a grin.

"White trash, much?" Kimber Reeve said, looking at the banged-up Escalade. She jingled her keys in my face as if that proved anything.

"Trash is cash, Kimmy," I said. "We're going to see the billboard for my new show! I'm at the top of the call sheet."

Kimber's mouth dropped open.

"Hey, maybe it will be right next to the *Virgin* billboard. Isn't there one on Sunset?" I asked Nika. "Of course, your name's not on that one, though, is it, Kimber? Only top-of-the-call-sheet stars get in the print ads."

"What are you talking about?" Kimber's mom asked, since Kimber was too furious to talk.

"Chloe just closed on *Cover Band*," Nika said. "It's the launch show for the Snap network. But I'm sure you're very proud to have a role on *Virgin* . . . Kimber, is it?"

"Kimber Reeve," Kimber said with a tight smile.

"Nika Mays. I'm Chloe's agent." She handed Kimber a business card. "You give me a call if you ever want something bigger than fifth billing."

Nika looped her arm through mine and pulled me toward the Escalade. "What was that?" I asked. "Gimme one of those cards."

She handed one over, a small ivory card that said NIKA MAYS, TALENT AGENT in sharp black lettering.

"Hal promoted me as soon as we got back from your meeting at Snap," Nika said, her voice full of laughter. "No raise yet, but I got the title! And the receptionist ran to the printer at lunch to get my cards made. She's actually sucking up to me."

"Isn't that just the best feeling in the entire world?" I said.

"Actually, I thought that not having to cover the front desk at work was the best feeling in the world, until I heard Bo McNamara say that we had a deal." Nika squeezed my arm. "It was a total high."

I looked over my shoulder as I climbed into the back of the Escalade. "Maybe so," I said. "But for me the biggest high of the day has got to be seeing the look on Kimber Reeve's face!"

## Day One

It wasn't NBC. It wasn't even a famous studio. It was a medium-size lot crammed into the middle of Los Angeles, filled with a bunch of smallish production companies that all rented space there.

But when Nika pulled the Mini up to the gates and said

## CALL SHEET

SHOOTING DAY NO. __1 of 5__ CALL TIME __7:30 A__ DAY/DATE __Mon., March 9, 2009__
PRODUCER __Diane Golden & Josh Golden__ DIRECTOR __Patrick Harrison__ PREPARED_____

| SCENE | LOCATION | CAST* | PAGES |
|---|---|---|---|
| | | 1,2 | 1-2a |
| 2,3 | ext. Stage 2 | 1,7 | 3-5 |
| 5 | Stage 8 | 1,8,9 | 20-21 |
| 9b | Stage 8 | | |
| | | | |
| | | | |

| CAST # | CHARACTER | ACTOR | MAKEUP | SET | REMARKS |
|---|---|---|---|---|---|
| 1 | Lucie Blayne | Chloe Gamble | 7:30A | 8:00A | secret identity |
| 2 | Sam Edison | Jonas Beck | 7:45A | 8:15A | |
| 3 | "D" | Jim Frank | | | rehearsal only |
| 4 | Marsha Quentin | Alexis Ben-Thompson | | | rehearsal only |
| 5 | Kaylee Gray | Lizette Pelicia | | | rehearsal only |
| 6 | Johnnie Rice | Ayala Carson | | | |
| 7 | Olivia Blayne | Madison Wills | 9:00A | 9:30A | |
| 8 | Mrs. Blayne | Lynn McNamara | 1:00P | 1:30P | work suit |
| 9 | Mr. Blayne | Brian Robbins | 1:00P | 1:30P | pajamas |

| BITS AND EXTRAS | REPORT TO: |
|---|---|
| 5 background; middle school students | 2nd A.D., stage 8 (CALL TIME 8:00A) |
| 1 teacher | |
| | |
| | |
| | |

SPECIAL INSTRUCTIONS – EQUIPMENT – REMARKS:

Ms. Gamble's guitar case with telescope inside

ADVANCED SCHEDULE:

COVER SET:

my name, the guards handed over a big laminated parking pass. They had a scan of my face and an ID badge already printed out. And it wasn't the mug shot NBC had e-mailed them when the network had put me on the blacklist. It was my close-up from the *Cover Band* publicity shoot I'd done a few days before.

But most important, it said CHLOE GAMBLE. Chloe Gamble worked here, Chloe Gamble was the star of a TV show that was shot here, Chloe Gamble was no longer a Hollywood outcast.

Chloe Gamble is Somebody.

"We're going to need to get you a car of your own now," Nika said as she drove through the lot. She pulled up next to a big soundstage with a billboard on the side of it.

*SNAP.* The network's bright red logo popped against the blue background of the billboard. "Cover Band" was printed in psychedelic type, the letters all wavy and multicolored.

And my face peered out from underneath them, ten feet tall.

"Here we are," Nika said, pointing to a much, much smaller sign tacked to the wall of the stage right in front of the Mini's bumper. It had my name on it.

"I get my own parking spot?" I said.

"Of course. You're the star." She grinned.

I climbed out of the Mini. "Hmm, what kind of ride would look good in this spot?" I joked.

"You can buy mine. I'm thinking of upgrading," Nika said, "now that I represent the star of *Cover Band.*"

"Thanks but no thanks, babe. I can't be seen in a used car," I said. "A TV star needs—"

"Oh my God, it's Chloe Gamble!" a shrill voice cut me off. I turned around and saw a small group of people following a guy in a cap that said STUDIO TOUR on it. Or at least, they *had* been following him. Now they were standing still, gazing at me.

"Yes, folks, that is Chloe Gamble. She's the star of one of the new shows filming here, *Cover Band*," the tour guide said.

One girl—she was maybe thirteen—came running over to me. "You're Chloe from YouTube?" She started singing. "'I could care, but I don't. I could cry, but I won't.'"

I laughed. "That was pretty good."

"I can't believe it's really you! Can I take your picture?" she asked.

I glanced at Nika. She shrugged. "Get used to it. Do you want to be in the picture with Chloe?" she asked the girl.

The kid just gasped, too excited to answer. "C'mere," I said. The girl actually trembled when I put my arm around her shoulder.

"Let's get your billboard in the background." Nika walked about ten feet away and aimed the camera. I didn't need to see the shot to know what it looked like. A Hollywood billboard on a Hollywood soundstage, with my name and my face on it, larger than life.

And in front, with one of my fans, stood me, with my

natural hair and my natural smile and the light of the flash reflecting like crazy in my eyes.

Me. The star. The one.

## Nika Mays's Manuscript Notes: End of Part One

Chloe Gamble was a star. I was an agent with my own clients. Life was absolutely perfect—at least until Chloe's father showed up.

But that should be a whole book of its own.

\*\*Note to self: Detective Lopez of the LAPD called again today asking about this manuscript. I don't think I ever told anybody I was writing a book, did I? Hard to remember with everything that's happened. (I'm about the best script reader I know, but there are some plot twists even I didn't see coming.) Either way, I can't turn my manuscript over to the cops. Chloe's story would've been valuable enough on its own. But after the murder, it became priceless.

Want more Chloe?
Here's a peek at the next book . . .

# VIP LOUNGE

## Nika Mays's Manuscript Notes:
## Overnight Success

Hurricane Chloe. That's what I called Chloe Gamble in the weeks after she landed her first starring role. The girl wasn't even on the airwaves yet, but Hollywood knew her. And Hollywood wanted her. That's a heady thing for a sixteen-year-old girl. Hell, it was a heady thing for me, and I'd been out of Stanford for three years already.

Here's the thing about Hollywood: It can change your life in a single second. One day an actress is a waitress who owes two months on her rent. The next day she's a star, with four magazine covers scheduled and a shiny new BMW. One day a writer is an office drone answering phones in some cubicle at a nameless corporation and the next day he's got a studio deal and a blurb on the front of Variety. One day a high school dropout is renting out pornos at a video store and the next day he's Quentin Tarantino.

It doesn't happen all the time. It doesn't even

happen very often. But it happens. Maybe an actress has had four hundred awful meetings—meetings where she's told that she's too fat, too old, too green, too talentless, too washed-up, or just "not right." Four hundred meetings that led nowhere. And then, for no reason other than luck, the four hundred and first meeting goes well. The actor meets the right casting director with the right project at the right time, and that's it. Before the actress gets to her car, her agents have been contacted. Negotiations begin. Other projects come pouring in, just because the formerly available actress is now completely unavailable. The gossip columns and the paparazzi hear about it and start making up stories. Boom! The actor is famous. Life changed.

All of my classmates from Palo Alto thought I was crazy for putting up with the sexist, low-paying, and old-school atmosphere at the Hal Turman Agency. But every time one of them asked me why I didn't leave Hollywood and get a normal job, I would tell them: Normal is the last thing I want. I want to wake up wondering if this could be the day. That's what keeps us all in show business.

It happened for me the day Chloe Gamble got cast on Cover Band. That morning, I was still a nobody, an assistant at a Ventura Boulevard child talent agency with one sixteen-year-old unproven client on my roster. Then I closed the deal: Chloe to star in the flagship show for the new Snap Network. One deal—a few phone calls back and forth, a little hardball negotiation, and done. Life changed.

By the time I arrived at the office the next day, my world was transformed. The assistants at the agency had started answering my phone for me, even though I'd been one of them just a day before. Life changed.

And it wasn't just me.

Travis Gamble had a new life, too. About twenty minutes after Chloe landed Cover Band, word leaked that Travis was her twin brother. Video grabs of his guest shot on the sitcom Shallow People, shirtless and hot, were up on YouTube almost instantly. Before, he was just a cute male model. Now, he was part of a hot acting family—a young, hot acting family. The tabloids love that. Look at Britney and Jamie Lynn, or Lindsay and Ali. Hell, even Paris and Nicky.

Travis wasn't even officially my client when Hurricane Chloe hit. But right away the calls started. I had serious bookers calling me about modeling jobs in New York, and they weren't just for underwear catalog shoots. I had casting directors calling about TV and film auditions. Travis had always struck me as a kid with his feet on the ground, but when McG's company wants you to read for a role, even the most sensible teenager in the world is going to jump at the chance. I rushed agency papers over right away. My client list had just doubled!

The next thing I had to do was find a reputable modeling agent for Travis, so that I could focus on his acting career. That's Hollywood—one week you're just a high school soccer star. The next week, you've got two agents and a dual career. Like I said, life changed.

Then there was Chloe Gamble herself. She'd morphed from the biggest screwup the town had ever seen to the star of a shiny new TV show in record time. Chloe's life went from zero to sixty over-night. No more school, no more general meet-and-greets, no more lurid horror movies—she was past all that in the blink of an eye. As soon as she closed on Cover Band, Chloe's life became a whirlwind of photo shoots, magazine interviews, wardrobe and makeup tests, music rehearsals, and must-be-seen-at par-ties. The struggling girl who'd clawed her way out of Spurlock, Texas, was now Chloe Gamble, the star.

Chloe was enjoying every moment of it. But she still kept a very keen eye on the bottom line.

"How much do I get paid?" Chloe asked me three days after she'd started work on the pre-production of Cover Band. "For all the extra stuff, I mean."

"What 'extra stuff'?" I asked.

"The photo shoots and the network promos and all those interviews with websites! I mean, it's a lot of fun, but how much do they pay me for that?"

I had to laugh. In some ways Chloe was the shrewdest person I'd ever met and in many ways she was still a sixteen-year-old kid.

"They don't pay you anything extra," I said. Chloe's eyes went wide with surprise.

"The Snap Network isn't paying you all that money just to act in the show. They're also paying you to sell the show. Your job—your only job—is to sell the product known as Cover Band. That means acting, but it also means promoting. We have to get your face on every single blog, gossip site, magazine, and TV show that will have you, because that gives the show a chance to be successful. People will want to see more of you, so they'll watch the show, and the show will stay on the air. Good ratings equal survival in TV. Think of it as investing in yourself."

Chloe understood, but her mind was focused on only one thing. "But I need to pay the rent and the bills. If I wanted to invest, I'd do it with somebody else's money."

"Well, I can help with the clothes," I said.

"Head over to wardrobe at the studio and get them to lend you an outfit whenever you need one."

"My agent rocks!"

"Remember that when the really big agencies come after you!" I said as Chloe breezed out of my office (my own office—with a door and everything!). I knew I'd avoided a potential storm. When it came to money, Chloe was fierce. She saw each dollar she made as an insurance policy against ever having to go back to Spurlock, Texas. That's why I'd been avoiding telling her that she didn't even have a real contract yet. And without a contract, Chloe would have no paycheck. I was hoping to solve this problem before Hurricane Chloe turned into Category 5 Tornado Chloe.

Chloe's Cover Band papers were on my desk, waiting for signatures. Hal thought I'd taken care of the whole thing already, but I was holding the contract back, waiting for my insanely handsome new lawyer friend to look it over. I had questions, and Eric Piper would have the answers. I hoped.

Eric was an associate at a huge entertainment law firm. He was doing me a favor by looking over the contracts and I hoped to return the favor by delivering him a new client who was the star of her own hit TV show. Maybe signing a hot new actress would give Eric an edge, bring him to the attention of the partners of his firm. Maybe it would change his life. And maybe that would change mine. . . .

# Testing

"I love playin' dress-up and all, but how come we have to go through all this?" I asked. For the last three hours I had been in and out of makeup and wardrobe trailers and had tried on about a dozen outfits (lots of short skirts and skinny jeans) and an equal number of hair styles and makeup choices.

"You the star, girl. If you look good, we all look good! Then we can all have us a nice long run and make us some money!" Keesha laughed as she applied coal-black liner to my eyes.

"Amen to that," I said, and laughed along with her.

Keesha, who was listed as the head of the makeup department on the call sheet, was from Baton Rouge. Maybe that's why we got along so well, we were two Southern girls who said whatever the hell we were thinking.

It was a real luxury not having to do my own makeup. Back on the pageant circuit in Texas, I always had to do it by myself. I suppose my mother could have helped, but help is not something my mother gives; she only receives. But now I had the head of the makeup department to do my face, the head of the hair department to do my hair, and the head of the wardrobe department to do my costumes.

I noticed the rest of the actors who had been cast on the show had *assistants* do their hair, makeup, and wardrobe. I had all the department heads. I also noticed everyone—the producers, the writers, the network executives, and the crew—treated me just a little bit better than they treated everyone else. When I was around they smiled more, laughed harder at my jokes, and ran to find me Fiji water. Sure, it felt great to be treated like royalty, but it felt kind of odd, like everyone was acting kind of phony.

Even my friend Amanda, who was working on the show, had changed. Amanda had been kind enough (or desperate enough) to hire my mama to sew when we really needed the money. So I owed her big-time. But on her first day of work she arrived with a box of T-shirts that had TEAM CHLOE printed on the front, pink for women, blue for men. Everyone on the crew put one on. I know I should have enjoyed it more, but I felt sort of *pressured*, like everyone was depending on me to pay their bills or something.

"Do you like them, Clo?" Amanda had asked.

"They rock. That was so sweet of you!" I said.

"Thank you for the job!" Amanda said, giving me a big hug.

How did this happen? How did I go from the NBC security "watch list" to someone who helped people get actual jobs? I really had no idea, but I did know that I never wanted it to change. I had to make myself a success. Too many people were depending on me now.

"You seem a million miles away, girl," Keesha said. "Homesick?"

I laughed. "You've never been to Spurlock."

"But I been to Baton Rouge and I'm here to tell you, bigger ain't better."

"That's not what I've been told," a guy's voice said from the doorway of the makeup trailer. I swung the chair around to get a good look. He was thin, but broad-shouldered and ripped. His hair was thick and dark, his eyes were big and blue, and suddenly, I totally knew who he was.

"Junior Junior!" I said. For years he'd played the oldest boy on *The More the Merrier*, a show about a family with five children and a dad named Junior.

He shrugged, "I'm *praying* this show makes people stop calling me that," he said. "I've been Junior Junior from the time I was three. They had to keep telling me my real name was Jonas."

"Huh," I said. "Am I supposed to feel sorry for you now, Mr. TV Star? Because I totally don't."

His eyes widened in surprise, and then he laughed.

"Chloe Gamble," I said.

"How you doing, Miss YouTube Star? Jonas Beck." He came over to shake hands. Up close, I could see that his skin was as perfect. And he had the straightest, whitest teeth I had ever seen. I wondered if he used those Crest Whitestrips like they advertised on TV. Hell, the guy had been on TV his whole life. Even though he was only a year or two older than me, he probably could have afforded the kind of teeth whitening you get at the dentist's office.

I couldn't believe I was sitting around in a makeup trailer shooting the shit with Jonas Beck! He was totally cool and really relaxed, I guess because he had so much experience and everything. All of a sudden a weird thought popped into my head: Why was Jonas Beck in the *Cover Band* makeup trailer?

"You visiting someone on the lot?" I asked Jonas.

He looked stunned. "Didn't anyone tell you?"

"Tell me what?"

"I'm joining the cast of the show."

## VIP LOUNGE
### Available December 2009
*Because there's always more Chloe . . .*

## About the Authors

ED DECTER is a producer, director, and writer. Along with his writing partner, John J. Strauss, Ed wrote *There's Something About Mary*, *The Lizzie McGuire Movie*, *The Santa Clause 2*, and *The Santa Clause 3*, as well as many other screenplays. During his years in show business Ed has auditioned, hired, and fired thousands of actors and actresses just like Chloe Gamble. Ed lives in Los Angeles with his family.

LAURA J. BURNS is a television and book writer who once dreamed of being an actress, so she's thrilled to live vicariously through Chloe Gamble. She lives in California with her husband and children.

# Check Your Pulse

Simon & Schuster's **Check Your Pulse** e-newsletter offers current updates on the hottest titles, exciting sweepstakes, and exclusive content from your favorite authors.

Visit **SimonSaysTEEN.com** to sign up, post your thoughts, and find out what every avid reader is talking about!